Coming Home

Coming Home

Ava Rose Johnson

SAMHAIN
PUBLISHING

Samhain Publishing, Ltd.
577 Mulberry Street, Suite 1520
Macon, GA 31201
www.samhainpublishing.com

Coming Home
Copyright © 2010 by Ava Rose Johnson
Print ISBN: 978-1-60504-924-3
Digital ISBN: 978-1-60504-895-6

Editing by Heidi Moore
Cover by Kanaxa

First Samhain Publishing, Ltd. electronic publication: February 2010
First Samhain Publishing, Ltd. print publication: December 2010

Dedication

To my lovely dog who kept me company on the late nights I spent writing this.

Chapter One

Brett Miller could remember the last thing his father had said to him before he died. *Things sure do change fast in Texas, kid.* He'd been talking about development in agricultural methods as Brett had walked him to the truck. Neither man had realized just how fast things were about to change. They hadn't realized that less than an hour after Henry Miller steered his truck down the winding drive of Steeplecrest Ranch, he'd be dead.

The last words between father and son echoed in Brett's mind as he watched the coffin being lowered into an open grave, the last in a row of four coffins that had been buried on this sweltering Monday morning. Brett glanced to the left where the minister was throwing earth over his mother's coffin. It was a tradition he'd never understood and one he wanted to put a stop to right then and there. Clara Miller deserved better than to have dirt thrown all over her. So did Brett's father. And Ken and June Armstrong who'd been their companions on the jet when they'd all met their fiery end.

He tried to swallow and found he couldn't. His throat was dry as sawdust. *Damn sun.* He tugged on the tie that held his collar tightly together. This wasn't the weather for a frickin' monkey suit. Beneath the heavy material of the jacket, his shirt clung to his skin, damp with sweat. He could take it all off right now. He knew his parents wouldn't give a damn. Hell, his father would have keeled over laughing if he'd seen his son dressed like this, like a goddamn *lawyer* or something.

Brett's gaze flickered away from the pinewood coffins to Cade Armstrong, Ken and June's twenty-five-year-old son. Now there was a guy who probably wore his suit to bed. He wasn't a lawyer. Come to think of it, Brett wasn't exactly sure what Cade did. Property or something like that. It paid good, he knew that much. Ranching didn't make the same kind of money, but a hefty inheritance handed down through the Miller family since the plantations and his father's eye for good horses had always kept Brett and his family in good financial shape. A good thing if he wanted to buy Cade out of his half of the ranch.

Taking in the guy's somber expression, Brett wished for the first time the merger had never happened. Fifteen years back, Henry Miller and Ken Armstrong had decided to pool their resources and bring together their neighboring ranches that sat at the hills of the Glass Mountains. The merge had widened the pastures, increased the efficiency of their processes and tripled each man's income. An all-round success, but neither Henry nor Ken had factored in what would happen after their death, because Brett didn't want to work with the younger Armstrong and he had a sinking feeling the guy wouldn't sell easily.

Cade's blue eyes found his and Brett looked away, just in time to watch the minister back away from the graves, closed prayer book in hand. The service was over.

Now came the hard part.

Reluctantly, Brett turned to face the mourners who'd come out in their Sunday best for the funeral of four of their people. Steeplecrest was by no means a large town, a thousand people at most, but when they came together like this, a sea of sad, sorry faces, Brett couldn't see an end to the crowd.

"Just shake their hands as you walk through. They don't expect more than that."

The assured male voice in his ear had Brett's hackles rising. He didn't need to turn around to know Cade was standing beside him. Arrogant jerk. Like he needed the advice of a New York yuppie. Ignoring the younger man, he stepped forward and forced a somber smile as he accepted the condolences of family friends. At all times he was aware of Cade at his side, doing the same. Deep down he knew he should feel some sort of bond with the guy, they were facing the same shit, but all he wanted to do was tell the kid to fuck off.

A perfectly manicured hand grabbed his forearm as he made it past the bulk of the crowd. "Brett..."

He forced a smile again and tried not to wince at the sickening pity brimming in the young woman's wide eyes. "Hey, Mary Ellen."

The petite blonde moved closer and wrapped her arms around his neck, pressing her generous breasts against his chest. "I'm so sorry, Brett," she cooed in honeyed tones. Pulling back, she stared up at him. He fought the urge to grimace. He'd gone through high school with this girl, even screwed her a couple of times after too many beers at the local bar, but today it was like looking at a stranger. Hell, he'd felt surrounded by strangers all through the service. With his folks in the ground something was shifting inside him, turning him into someone else. Not the man who'd grown up with these people and could joke and banter with them easily. He didn't know how long it would be before he'd be able to strike up a conversation with any of them again. It was a weird feeling, but a very real one.

"Thanks," he muttered to Mary Ellen, trying to be as subtle as possible as he disentangled himself from her smothering embrace.

He started to walk toward his truck and she was right on his heels. He had to admire her determination. Those stilettos had to be killer to walk in, especially on the uneven surface of a cemetery.

"Do you want me to come over tonight?" she asked, slightly out of breath as she tried to keep up with his long strides.

This time he did grimace. "Not sure that's such a great idea, Mary Ellen. Got family staying at the house."

"Oh." Instead of accepting the brush-off and saying goodbye, she kept staring at him, mouth slightly open.

He was having a hard time keeping his frustration from bubbling to the surface. How had he never noticed how empty her eyes were, as if nothing was going on behind them? He guessed she'd never needed brains, not with those tits.

Quit being an asshole, Brett. Forcing his way past his frustration with Mary Ellen and himself, he started to move again. "Listen," he said, appreciation finally making its way to the fore. "Thanks for coming out."

Once again, that annoying pity veiled her eyes and his appreciation dissipated.

"Maybe I could bring you by some food," she suggested eagerly. "You gotta eat sometime."

"We got it covered." He quickened his steps and gave her a quick wave as he put some distance between them. "I'll see you around."

He didn't look back until he'd reached his blue Chevrolet and when he did she was gone. He released a long breath and ran his hand over his jaw. He probably wouldn't have her knocking on his door anytime soon, a good thing as far as he was concerned. She'd soon find a guy who'd appreciate her for what she had to give.

Ready to escape the mourning nightmare, he moved around the truck to the driver's side, then stopped in his tracks. The rush of freedom he'd been experiencing slowed and then diminished at the sight in front of him. Leaning back against the shiny cab, a cigarette dangling from his mouth, stood Cade. He pulled the cigarette from his lips and held it up sheepishly.

"I quit this shit two years ago." He shook his head, smirking, and then took another drag. "Didn't think I'd fall so fast."

Another surge of frustration rose within Brett and this time he didn't try to hide it. "What are you doing behind my truck?"

If Cade was fazed by his sharp tone, he didn't show it. "Hiding," he replied, throwing the cigarette on the ground and grinding it into the pavement. He jerked his head back toward the crowd. "Saw you with Mary Ellen Sanders."

Brett narrowed his eyes. "So what?"

He shrugged. "Chicks sure do dig this death stuff, don't they?"

What the fuck is this guy's deal? His irritated confusion must have been written plain across his face because Cade straightened and elaborated.

"They go in for all the drama, they like their men to be down and fucked up. Then they can take care of them, fix the boo-boo." Cade grinned, a sudden flash of straight white teeth that caught Brett off-guard. "You're going to get laid real good tonight."

Brett didn't bother contradicting him. Instead, he pulled open the truck's door and swung up onto the seat, needing to get away as fast as the pickup could accelerate. Without saying anything, he shut the door and started the engine. Five seconds later, he left Cade Armstrong behind in a billowing cloud of dust.

"So what are you going to do, Armstrong?"

Cade was standing in the kitchen of the house he'd grown up in. A week had passed since he'd buried his parents, but it seemed longer. The days had dragged, the nights had been worse. He'd considered paying a visit to Billy's Bar and checking out what the town had to offer these days, but he knew if he went anywhere in Steeplecrest he'd be met with somber silence and pitiful stares. He wasn't ready to face that yet.

"Cade, you still there?"

Mike, one of the partners at the firm he worked for, was on the line. Cade held his cell to his ear and tried to form an answer. For the first time in a long while his bullshitting skills were failing him. He hadn't a clue what he wanted to say and he didn't know how to hide that fact from his boss. "It's going to be another couple of weeks, Mike," he finally said. "There's a lot to sort out down here. I'll give you a call when I know more."

"Sure, sure, no problem."

Cade smiled. Despite Mike's assurances, he knew it was a problem. He'd been working for Sullivan & Robson Properties for three years now and had moved to the top at lightning speed, a direct result of confidence, instinct and working his butt off. The longest vacation he'd taken in those three years had been a week. Any more than that and he'd break out in cold sweats. Seemed pretty damn stupid now. Why the hell would he want to go back when he had acres of rolling ranchland at his feet?

He ended the call and dropped the phone on the table. As silence swooped down over him, the pain he'd spent the past week ignoring started to throb inside him. *Christ.* Left with his own company for less than a minute and it kicked off. Grief stabbed at his chest, working its way from the inside out. When alone it hurt him worse than hell and it was all he could do not to shove his hands into his chest and pull out the source of the pain.

Closing his eyes, he waited for the ache to recede but it only deepened. His mother's freckled face flashed in his mind's eye and he slammed his palms down on the kitchen counter. He'd never see her again. She'd never laugh with him on the phone. Never scold him for not visiting at the holidays.

He gave his head a quick shake. Only a week had passed since he'd buried her, so of course he still felt the grief. He just wished it would hurry the hell up and work its way out of his system.

The soft pad of footsteps on the kitchen tiles drew his attention, distracting him from the pain. He turned and couldn't help but grin at the sight of Jessica Lawson, his best friend and occasional fuck-buddy who'd flown in from New York to be with him. When the accident had happened she'd been overseas at a conference and hadn't made it back in time for the funeral. The following day she'd arrived on his doorstep wearing a sundress—fabric so light it may as well have been sheer. And she hadn't been wearing any panties underneath. As a top executive at NY Cosmetics and self-proclaimed man-eater, she didn't do emotion too well.

"Nothing I can say to make you feel better," she'd told him as she'd slipped past him into the house. "So I'll just have to ride the pain out of you."

She'd remained true to her promise and they'd been in bed since she'd arrived. When he was with her, whether laughing at the way she ate a muffin with a knife and fork or driving his cock inside her wet pussy, the pain dulled. He didn't know what he was going to do with himself when she left. Just the idea left him with a sick stomach.

"You okay?" she asked, her eyes soft as she moved farther into the kitchen. "You were tossing and turning all night."

"All night?" He watched her cat-like approach and tried to ignore the fact that soon she wouldn't be here to distract him and he'd be suffering alone. "I was screwing you all night," he reminded her, keeping his tone light as she stopped beside the kitchen table. "Didn't have time for any tossing or turning."

Hesitation flickered in her eyes before she thankfully decided to go along with him. "Oh, that's right," she murmured, drumming her fingers on the table edge. "Now how did I forget a thing like that?"

"I don't know, darlin'," he replied, running his eyes over her sweet figure. Standing in front of him, wrapped in one of his shirts, she looked good enough to eat. He licked his lips and her eyes sparked a come-on.

"Hungry?"

He growled, then closed the distance between them in two quick strides and gathered her up in his arms. "Starving," he muttered before placing her on the edge of the table and hooking her long, golden legs over his shoulders. He stared down at the junction of her thighs, savoring the view. Damn, her cunt was gorgeous. Pink and smooth as silk. He drew his finger along her slit and his cock stirred. Wet too.

She ran her hand along his arm. "You didn't have any breakfast?"

He shook his head. "Nothing in the fridge is as good as this." Lowering his head to her pussy, he darted out his tongue and licked her from the bottom of her seam to the tight bud of her clit. She gasped. Shuddered. He grinned and dug in,

14

slipping his tongue inside her sheath. Always hot for him, always ready. He lapped up her juices, sucked lightly on her swollen flesh. He caught her clit between his thumb and forefinger and squeezed. Her hips lifted off the table.

"Come on, Cade." Her heel dug into his shoulder blade. "I have to hit the road in an hour."

The reminder of her departure stung. So little time for what he wanted to do to her, what he'd been doing to her for the past few days. He didn't know what he'd have done if she hadn't been here this week. Without her company, he was sure the reality of his parents' death would have struck him like a thunderbolt. Having her here had eased the pain, kept the sharp edge of grief on a level. This new way of living—life without family—was seeping into his consciousness, but at a slow, manageable pace. He didn't think he'd be able to keep a rein on his emotions when she left.

He kept his head buried between her thighs until the walls of her cunt tightened. Then he pulled away, ignoring her disapproving moan as he licked her cream from his lips.

"Jerk," she said, slapping his chest.

"Easy there, darlin'." He grinned down at her, undoing the button of his jeans. "We're just getting started."

A slow smile spread across her face and she leaned back, resting her weight on her elbows. "Come on then. Show me what you got."

He laughed as he jerked his zipper downward and pulled his dick from the confines of his pants. Bracing his hands on either side of her body, he lunged forward, driving his cock deep inside her hot little pussy. She cried out and arched her back. He sucked in a deep breath as he drew back, then thrust forward again. Her cunt clenched around him and he closed his eyes, relishing the sensation. He wouldn't get this again for a while.

He steadied the motion of his hips and once they'd settled into a slow, rhythmic pace, he slid his hands beneath her shirt to play with her tits. The stiff nipples pressed into his palms and he pinched and rolled them. Jess's eyes widened and her lips clamped together. For about the millionth time since they'd first met in a hotel bar in New York, he wondered how the hell he wasn't in love with her. They were perfect for each other—the same views on life and how to live it. And she was perfectly at ease with his need for male-on-male encounters. Hell, she joined in whenever she could. But though the sex blew his mind, she wasn't the one. And he wasn't *her* one either.

"Faster, Cade, move faster." Her breathless demand broke into his thoughts. He gripped the edge of the table and thrust his hips forward, pulling out before she could blink. He fucked her hard, watching her at all times. Her legs were still hooked over his shoulders, leaving her completely bare to his hungry gaze. The sight of his cock disappearing inside her glistening pussy nearly did him in. He wanted this image stamped on his brain. The next few weeks would be full of long, lonely nights and this memory would keep his blood warm.

Jess's whole body stiffened, a tell-tale sign she was ready to come. He plunged inside her in quick, short strokes and groaned as her cunt contracted around him. He couldn't hold back. With one lurch forward, he spilled inside her.

"I'm going to miss you around here," he said when they'd caught their breath.

She grinned and stroked a lazy hand through his hair. "Me too. It's nice out here."

"How does ranch life compare with the city?"

She slipped off the table and helped him fix his pants. "How would I know?" she asked, waggling her perfectly shaped eyebrows at him. "We've spent the whole week in your bed."

"My bed, my bathroom, my kitchen table." He glanced over her head to check the clock on the wall and his gut twisted. "You better go tidy yourself up, darlin'," he said, forcing the words out. "It's getting late."

Sitting up slowly, she leaned forward and kissed the dimple in his left cheek. "I won't be long."

He watched her disappear into the hallway, feeling the loneliness trickle in on him again. Thirty minutes later, appearing fresh as a daisy and innocent as a virgin, Jess raced down the stairs. "Where's my stuff?"

"In the trunk."

It was a four-hour drive to El Paso Airport but the time flew as Cade milked the last precious moments he had with a friend. He didn't have many in town. He hadn't kept in touch with his high school buddies. Most of them had left Steeplecrest anyway. And Brett sure as hell wouldn't want his company.

His thoughts caught on Brett and a picture of the tall, well-muscled man formed in his mind's eye. Strong, rugged, sexy as hell. He had a mop of silky black hair, a chiseled face and a stern brow. Perfect, slightly full lips and eyes black as sin. Pity he was straight as a rake.

And pity he hates my guts.

Cade didn't know what the guy's problem was but he sure had one. Son of a bitch had made it plain as day over the past week that he wanted Cade gone, as soon as he handed over his half of the ranch.

Maybe that was part of the reason Cade was delaying the whole thing. He liked winding the guy up, enjoyed watching him seethe every time they'd happened across one another since Cade had come back to town.

"What are you thinking about?" Jess asked, her voice cutting into his thoughts.

"Brett."

"Ah, I see." She let out a wistful sigh. "Now he is a fine thing."

Cade lifted a brow in surprise. "How would you know?"

"I saw him in the distance a couple of times."

Cade smirked. "You should see him up close."

"Oh yeah."

"Yeah." He glanced at her out of the corner of his eye. "You'd cream your panties, sugar," he drawled, then chuckled as she punched him in the shoulder.

"I bet you're right, though," she admitted, twisting in her seat to face him. "Wish I could have met him."

Imagining how Brett would deal with a woman like Jessica who was as sexy as she was forward, Cade laughed.

"What's so funny?"

"Nothing." He winked at Jessica. "I wish you'd met him too."

Her eyes widened and she laughed. "Hey, who was on the phone this morning?" she asked after a while.

Cade grimaced. "Mike. He's getting impatient."

In typical Jessica fashion, she sniffed her disgust. "Well, tell him to go fuck himself." She never minced her words and Cade didn't think he'd ever find a friend as loyal as she was.

"Seriously, Cade," she continued, "you have the right to this time."

"I know, but they're losing business." Cade shrugged, keeping his eyes on the highway. Had he missed the exit for the airport?

"So what if they're losing business? You lost your mom and dad. Family wins out over business."

"I know." No, he hadn't missed the exit. Here it was.

Finding a parking space at the airport proved to be easier than he'd expected and he was soon walking Jess into the terminal. She left him with a long hug, more matronly than sexual. He breathed in her light scent of honeysuckles one last time, then stepped back and watched her disappear through the boarding gate. As soon as her blonde mane was out of sight, he felt a hard drop in his stomach.

He took his time going back to the car, a black Lexus he'd rented for his stay in Steeplecrest, and it was almost seven by the time he got home. As soon as he stepped inside the kitchen, he realized he hadn't eaten since breakfast. His stomach realized it too and growled loudly.

He pulled open the fridge and stared into it. Though he was hungry, moldy cheese and sour milk didn't exactly appeal. He emptied the fridge and threw the contents into the garbage. There was nothing else to do, he thought as he rambled back down the porch steps to the car. He'd have to face the world, or at least the salesperson at the grocery store. A man had to eat.

As he pulled open the car door, he glanced across the fields. In the distance, the Miller house stood proud, a large white-washed three-storey with a wrap-around porch. If Brett was home, maybe he could... Cade let the thought trail off and grinned. If there was one person in this town who'd be unwilling to give him some food, it was Brett Miller.

His eyes narrowed as he made out Brett's outline in the distance. He was with someone, probably Jimmy, the ranch's wrangler. The old man had worked on the ranch since before Cade was born and had called by every evening since the funeral to check on him. He was family, a solid man whose wife had died soon after they'd married. He'd struggled with alcoholism for years, a trait he had in common with Cade's father.

Cade stiffened as memories of drunken arguments and broken glass ran through his mind like a snapshot of a movie. He got into the car and put it in drive. Ken Armstrong had pulled himself together and gone sober a good ten years back, about the same time as Jimmy. But though Cade had a soft spot for the wrangler, he'd never fully been able to mend bridges with his father. Too late now, he guessed as he followed the long drive to the ranch gates. Taking a right for the town, he left the ranch and memories of his father behind.

It was a short drive into Steeplecrest, less than twenty minutes. He drove past the high school which was deserted at this time of the evening. His high school days had been some of the best of his life. Good grades, class president and captain of the basketball team had made him popular with both his teachers and his fellow students. The ladies too. He grinned as he turned onto Main Street. Girls had been a big part of his life back then. These days he was split between men and women, cock and pussy. What was that saying his mother had always used? *Variety's the spice of life.* If there was anything his years in New York had given him, it was variety.

He pulled to a stop along the curb outside Macy's Groceries and peered in the window. Didn't look too busy, maybe he'd make an escape before bumping into old friends. He got out of the car and headed into the store. As he wandered the aisles, he wished he'd made a list. What did he need? Potatoes, some milk. Sandwich stuff. Chips.

With his arms full of food, he approached the checkout. He loaded his purchases onto the conveyor belt and then grabbed a six pack from one of the shelves.

"Cash or card?"

He glanced at the girl behind the register and felt a rush of relief when he didn't recognize her. "Card."

"Okay, that's eighty-four dollars and fifty cents."

He handed her the card. Just as she swiped it, another voice sounded behind him.

"Cade?"

He cursed inwardly and turned. Tommy Dawes, owner of the betting shop across the street, stood in front of him with a basket that resembled pretty much what Cade had bought. Typical bachelor living. Tommy's father was town sheriff and had been a good friend of both Cade and Brett's fathers.

"How're you doing, Tommy?" he asked, taking his card from the checkout girl.

"Good." Tommy's expression became sober as he said hurriedly, "Uh, sorry about the accident. I didn't get a chance to say it to you at the funeral."

Cade shrugged. "Don't worry about it. I got out of there pretty fast."

"Yeah." A few seconds of uncomfortable silence passed before Tommy spoke again. "How long are you sticking around for?"

"Not sure yet."

"If you're still around on Friday, you should come down. A few of the guys are having drinks at Billy's, maybe a round of poker."

Cade nodded. "Might take you up on that."

"You should." Tommy's grin returned full force. "This might be a small town, but we sure do have our fair share of ladies."

"Sounds good to me." He gathered his bags and gave a mock salute. "See you Friday."

As he stepped out of the store, he wondered what he'd been so worried about. Sure, people were going to offer their condolences, but he could handle that. He'd grown up with these guys and they knew how to have a good time.

He drew in a deep breath of hot Texas air and then released it. He looked up and down Main Street, noting the familiar signs and store windows. His mouth suddenly watered for an iced tea from Delia's Diner.

Despite the shitty circumstances, it was good to be home.

Chapter Two

"You can take off now, Jimmy," Brett said as he ran his gaze over the result of their work. A hundred and sixty cattle moved from one pasture to another over a mile away in less than four hours. "I think we did good, old man," he said, wiping the back of his arm across his forehead.

Jimmy laughed croakily, a sound that came from one too many cigarettes. "You're a slave driver, boss."

Brett grinned, even as Jimmy's use of the word "boss" stung a little. He shook it off. Even when his dad had been alive, Jimmy had called him "boss". He'd used the term for both father and son. But since Henry had died it had taken on a new meaning for Brett. Now he really was the boss. There was nobody left to share the title with.

"I'll wash this girl down first," Jimmy said, patting the mare who'd done the brunt of the work today. "See you tomorrow."

Brett nodded, watching the old man lead one of Steeplecrest's quarter horses back to the stables. He turned and pulled the brim of his Stetson low over his brow to block out the evening sun as he headed for the house. His stomach growled and the muscles across his shoulders groaned. He didn't know what he wanted to do first—shower and let the jets of water ease out the knots of tension in his back, or eat and satisfy the hunger that had been building since he'd skipped lunch. His stomach growled again, this time longer and louder. He grinned. Looked like his body had made up his mind for him.

He kicked off his boots on the veranda and stepped into the kitchen. In less than a minute, he'd ripped off his shirt, raided the fridge and fixed a humongous sandwich of beef and tomato. He'd wolfed down half of it when the doorbell rang.

Swearing through a mouthful of bread and meat, he pushed to his feet. He strode out of the kitchen and through the foyer and groaned. On the other side of the screen door stood Cade, a six pack of Bud at his side. *Shit.*

Summoning all the patience he could muster, he took another step forward and pulled open the door. Cade looked up from where he'd been studying the porch floor and visibly jumped. Brett raised an eyebrow and waited.

"Thought I'd stop by," Cade finally said, pulling himself together. "Guess we have a few things to talk about."

"Guess so." Leaving the door open, Brett headed back into the kitchen and leaned against the kitchen counter-top. He folded his arms across his chest, watching Cade as he followed him in. At least he'd taken the damn suit off. Dressed in blue jeans and a white T-shirt, the kid almost looked like he belonged on a ranch. Even the dark blonde curls that had been perfectly slicked back at the funeral were hanging loose, almost reaching his collar.

Cade held up the beers and then placed them on the table. Without waiting to be asked, he sat on one of the chairs and slung his arm over the back of another. "Busy day?"

"We're always busy." Brett glanced at the remains of his sandwich that were sitting in the middle of the table and felt another stab of annoyance. With this guy sitting in his kitchen, he'd lost his appetite.

"Saw Jimmy on my way up here. Looked pretty tired."

Brett narrowed his eyes. Arrogant son of a bitch. What was he trying to say? That he worked the old man too hard? "Jimmy's tough as nails," he bit out. "If he thought I was working him too hard, he'd say so."

Cade frowned. "Did I say you were working him too hard?"

"Forget it." He pushed away from the counter and stood in front of Cade. Why did he always have to get so defensive around this guy? As kids they'd always gotten along okay, though they'd moved in different circles. A two-year age gap was a big deal in high school and he hadn't wanted Cade following him around every second of the day. He still didn't want that. "Could you get to the point already? I need to take a shower."

Cade seemed to stiffen in his chair and his blue eyes dropped to Brett's sweat-covered torso. Brett didn't know why but he felt a sudden urge to cover himself up.

"Take a shower," Cade said, his eyes returning to Brett's. "I can wait."

He scowled. What could he say to that? Besides, despite the fact that he wanted this kid out of here, they had a lot to figure out first. And he didn't want to be shirtless and sweating while they did it.

"Fine," he said, grabbing the remnants of his sandwich and throwing it in the garbage. "I'll be down in a minute."

Leaving Cade lounging in his chair, he headed upstairs, unbuckling his belt as he went. He removed his socks and pants in the bathroom and then stepped into the shower. For five minutes, he let the hot water blast the tension from his muscles, but as soon as he turned it off the tension hit back full force.

This was going to be a long night.

Cade didn't know what he'd expected when he'd rung the Miller doorbell ten minutes ago, but he definitely hadn't expected to be greeted with the sight of Brett's naked chest. As he'd stared openly at the expanse of sweat-slick muscle, he'd barely been able to string a sentence together and he could only thank the Lord Brett had been too pissed off to notice the thickening bulge in his pants.

Always the sucker for punishment, Cade glanced at the wooden counter-top where Brett had leaned against minutes before with his arms crossed over his solid chest. The position had made his well-formed biceps bulge and the angle he'd rested his hips against the counter had pushed his pelvis forward, accentuating the lines of muscle that disappeared beneath the waistband of his jeans.

Cade shook his head. The way his mind worked, no wonder he was still hard even though Brett had been out of sight for more than five minutes.

Clamping his left hand over his balls, he reached for the long-neck he'd opened with his right. He brought it to his lips and drank long and deep, letting the cold beer wash down his throat and soothe the burning within him. If he could just pull himself together before Brett came down…

Too late. Brett's footsteps on the staircase echoed in the foyer. Cade gripped his bottle, focusing on the label as Brett stalked into the kitchen. The clean, soapy scents of shampoo and shower gel swirled around him. Nothing fancy, simple and masculine. A perfect match to Brett's personality. Cade's grip on the beer bottle tightened as he held it up and forced a smile.

"Couldn't help myself."

Brett mumbled something under his breath as he went to the sink and poured a glass of water. With his back turned, Cade dared to sneak a glance in his direction. *Oh hell.* He was fully clothed but he still looked edible. His jeans were baggy on the legs but molded to the firm curves of his ass, an ass so tight you could shell walnuts on it. Cade gritted his teeth. This was not the way to be thinking.

He forced his gaze upward as Brett turned and tried not to salivate. The gray T-shirt Brett wore hugged his upper body like a second skin, outlining every line of muscle. Cade's dick throbbed in his jeans.

Brett swung into the chair opposite him and reached for a beer. "Why are you still here, Armstrong?"

Cade blinked as his thoughts shifted from sex to the matter at hand. He leaned back in his chair, holding Brett's stony gaze. He fought a smile. If Brett thought he could intimidate him into giving up his half of the ranch, he was gonna get one hell of a surprise.

"Where else do you think I'd be?" he asked casually, taking another sip of beer.

Irritation glittered in Brett's dark eyes. "Shouldn't you be getting on back to New York? I'm sure you've got a lot of important people waiting on you."

He did, but that didn't bother him. "They can keep waiting."

Brett was silent as he uncapped his beer and took a long draw. Cade's mouth dried as he watched the other man swallow. Did he have any idea what he was doing to him? Did he realize that just by sitting there drinking beer, he could give Cade a raging hard-on?

Again, Cade fought a smile. He could just imagine what Brett would do to him if he knew. He'd be lucky to walk out of here alive.

Brett's groan of frustration tore him from his thoughts. He looked on as the other man set down his beer and leaned forward.

"Let's cut the crap, Cade. You'll be going back to New York sooner or later. You don't need the ranch. Give. It. Up."

Give it up. Interesting choice of words. And if Brett had been talking about sex, Cade would give it up in a heartbeat. But not the ranch.

He leaned forward, resting his elbows on the table as he matched the determination in Brett's face. "I'm not giving it up, not yet anyway."

Watching Brett try to contain his fury was priceless. Cade glanced to the side for a second to hold back the laughter.

"Why?" Brett asked through gritted teeth. "What would you do with a ranch?"

Cade looked back at him and shrugged carelessly. "What do *you* do with a ranch?"

Brett's chair squealed as he pushed it back and rose to his feet. "You're not fucking serious."

"Why not? A few weeks ago three people ran this ranch— you, your dad and my old man. Now it's just you. Don't tell me you're not falling behind."

"I have help."

"Not enough, I'll bet."

Brett strode to the glass doors at the bottom of the kitchen and stared out. Cade could almost hear his mind searching for an argument.

"You wouldn't know what to do on a ranch," he said finally, facing Cade once again. "You wouldn't be any good to me."

This time Cade couldn't hold it in. He laughed, a loud chuckle that turned Brett's face to thunder. "You're forgetting I grew up on this ranch too. Your father took me to Kentucky every year to check out the horses. I picked half the animals in that stable out there."

A tic pulsed at the side of Brett's jaw and his eyes blazed with anger. Cade relaxed back in his chair, enjoying the sense of victory. Brett knew he couldn't argue. At a time like this, with roles changing and a larger workload, there was no one better to have around than someone who knew the ranch like the back of his own hand. And that was Cade.

The fire in Brett's eyes faded as he sank back into his chair. "This will be a temporary thing, right? You're not sticking around forever."

"Who knows?" Cade swallowed the last of his beer. "We'll have to see how it goes." He got to his feet, wishing they had a relationship that allowed them to relax and kick back with a few beers and some TV. He wished too that he could ask how Brett was doing since the accident, but he knew all the response he'd get would be stony silence. "I'll come over in the morning to help with feeding."

Brett didn't reply, just took another gulp of beer. Cade left him like that, sitting at the kitchen table, looking like the Dallas Cowboys had just lost the Superbowl.

That Friday night on the drive into Steeplecrest, Brett punched up the volume on the stereo so high he was sure even the goddamn cows would be singing along. The riffs and bass of the classic Aerosmith hit vibrated in the cab of his truck but it wasn't enough to drown out the thoughts circling his head.

The past week had been hell, plain and simple. The week following the funeral had been a long one but he'd been able to lose himself in the mountain of work that needed to get done. But these past few days had been a hell of a lot worse and he blamed Cade. Having that kid hanging around wound him up so tight, he couldn't believe he'd made it through the week without shooting his mouth off. It was bad enough Cade was determined to help out on the ranch, but what made it worse was the fact that he actually knew what he was doing. Watching him round up the cows and take care of the horses made Brett's teeth grind. The guy worked magic with the animals and from the way he kidded around with Jimmy and the other ranch hands, he obviously enjoyed the work.

It didn't look as if he'd be heading east anytime soon.

Brett gave his head a quick shake. He wouldn't think about Cade tonight. A round of beers and a game of poker would set him straight. He needed to unwind and have a few laughs. He didn't think he'd ever needed it more.

He pulled into a spot outside Billy's Bar and got out of the truck. Heads turned in his direction, people recognizing the Chevrolet and peering in the dark to see if it really was Brett Miller. Once they saw him, they either nodded stiffly or looked in the other direction. Brett drew in a deep breath and slammed the truck's door shut behind him. He needed to rip off the Band-Aid, face the music. Once he got past the door and saw the guys everything would go back to normal.

Ignoring the stares and the quick glances, he strode into the bar. The familiar mist of cigarette smoke and cheap perfume wrapped around him and he felt himself relax. Billy's was the same as it had been before the accident. Dark wood paneling on the walls, a large flat screen hanging to the side of the bar, tables and stools in clusters on the floors. Booths lined the walls and a small dance floor was off to the side where some of the ladies liked to show off their moves after one too many vodkas.

He carved a path through the crowd, already settling into the warm, loud atmosphere. A sea of people surrounded him, most of whom he recognized. He caught a few eyes but didn't stop to make conversation until he reached the bar.

"Hey, Karl, can I get a whiskey?"

The bartender turned and surprise crossed his face as he looked at Brett. Then he grinned, grabbing a glass from under the bar and getting to work on fixing the drink. "Good to see you, Miller."

Brett did a quick survey of the room but the mass of bodies made it hard to see anything. "Are the rest of the guys in yet?"

"Sure, they're over by the pool tables." Karl set the whiskey down in front of them. "On the house."

The gesture twisted his stomach, reminding him of the many free cakes and casseroles that had been brought into the house right after the accident. Nice people doing good deeds. They meant well but it only served as a reminder that things had changed.

Brett's cheeks ached as he struggled to keep the smile on his face. "Thanks, Karl," he said, taking the glass from the bar. As soon as he turned, he let the corners of his mouth drop.

"There you are, buddy." A hand came down on his shoulder and steered him through the crowd. "Wondered if you'd make it."

"Course I made it." Brett glanced at Tommy, his best friend since high school, and felt his face relax into a genuine smile. "You started without me."

"We're on round two." Tommy pushed the way through the last of the crowd and they slid into the booth occupied by the rest of the guys. A couple of them looked a little awkward at first and mumbled a few words of condolence, but as Brett kept the easy smile on his face they soon settled into the old, lighthearted banter. After a while, with the Jack Daniels warming his blood, Brett felt almost relaxed. But then his eyes caught on a familiar outline through the haze of smoke. Son of a bitch, he thought as he watched Cade lean down to whisper something in a barmaid's ear. *What the hell is he doing here?*

"Hey, there's Cade."

Brett turned to Tommy who was getting to his feet. It sounded like his buddy had expected Cade to be here tonight. And *damn it*, now he was gesturing for the kid to get over here.

Every muscle in Brett's body tightened as Cade headed their way, his long, lean body sauntering carelessly toward them. The girl he'd been talking to stood where he'd left her, her cheeks pink and her lips slightly parted as she watched him go. It was enough to make Brett hurl.

He was so focused on the horny bartender, he didn't notice Cade sliding into the booth until the bastard was sitting smack bang in front of him. Cade swapped greetings with the rest of the group and then faced forward. His brow furrowed as he held Brett's gaze, probably wondering what he'd done now to piss him off. For the sake of the rest of the guys, Brett tried to rearrange the scowl on his face to appear more welcoming. Cade's blue eyes widened and twinkled and his mouth twisted in a knowing smirk.

"Didn't know you'd be here, Miller," he said, leaning back in the booth. The friendly tone made it sound as if they were tight. Brett would have laughed if he hadn't been so ticked off.

"Where else would he be?" Tommy asked, bringing a hand down on Brett's back. "You should have rode in together. Then at least one of you could get wasted."

Brett shrugged. "Didn't know he was coming." *I sure as hell didn't invite him.*

Cade's grin widened and Brett noted the dimple in the guy's left cheek. Back in high school girls had dropped their panties for that thing. He couldn't count how many times he'd caught

Cade screwing some chick's ass off behind the barn. Couldn't count how many times he'd stopped and watched.

Shaking Cade out of his head, Brett looked down the table and focused his attention on Mitch who was bragging about a woman he'd scored with a few nights back, but after a few minutes his interest waned. And he couldn't relax with the "suit" sitting right across the table.

He got to his feet. "I'm going to get another drink. Anybody want anything?"

Orders were hollered in his direction and, as he wound his way back to the bar, he was glad the guys were relaxing around him. He didn't think he'd have hung around if it had been a night of awkward silence and somber glances.

Tommy sidled up beside him as he waited for the drinks. "You all right, Brett?"

Brett looked up at his friend and then back at the booth. "Since when are you and Cade so tight?" he asked and immediately regretted bringing it up at Tommy's expression of surprise.

"I met him at Macy's on Monday night. Didn't think it would be a problem." Tommy's forehead creased in a frown. "You and Cade not getting along?"

Shaking his head, Brett tried to brush it off. "We just rub each other up the wrong way, I guess." Then, changing the subject, he asked, "How's the folks?"

"They're good. Mom wants to have you over for dinner next week if that works for you."

"That'd be great."

With drinks in hand, they started back to the booth and found the whole table shaking with laughter. Brett had already set the drinks on the table before he realized they were laughing at something Cade had said. He lowered into his seat and took a long drink of whiskey, letting the amber liquid burn the back of his throat. When he put down the glass, he caught Cade watching him, waiting for a reaction. He looked away as a wave of tension tightened his body. He didn't think he'd ever been so uncomfortable around anyone in his life.

Chapter Three

Even though Brett spent most of the night sulking, Cade had a good time. He'd forgotten how easy this was—talking sports with the guys, checking out the girls by the bar, smoking the cigars Macy's had imported illegally from Cuba. A million miles away from a Friday night in New York. Sure he had friends in the city, more than enough. But he knew them through work. They were business associates. And he had no doubt that if any of them had half a chance to screw him over, they'd do it in a heartbeat.

Cade held up a hand as Tommy began to deal another round of poker. "No way. I've lost enough money tonight. My pride can't take it."

Tommy turned to Brett who was staring sullenly into his empty glass. "You in?"

Brett's head jerked up. "Huh?"

Tommy held up the cards. "You want in?"

He shook his head and turned back to his glass. "I need another one of these."

Cade raised an eyebrow. Brett was going through whiskey like water on a summer's day. "You sure about that, buddy?"

The glare he received could have cut through stone. He bit back a laugh and then reached out for one of the bartenders.

"Lilly, sweetheart, come here."

The redhead who'd made a beeline for him the second he'd entered the bar sauntered toward him, swinging her hips from side to side as she moved. Cade licked his lips. The come on was clear and he was pretty sure he'd be taking her up on the offer.

"What is it, sugar?" she simpered, batting her long eyelashes at him.

He stroked his hand along the curve of her waist. Her low-cut top was made of some clingy material, light enough for him to feel the heat of her skin through it.

He jerked his head toward Brett. "Would you get my friend here another drink?"

"He ain't no friend of mine," Brett piped up.

Cade ignored the slur but Lilly pouted. "Now that wasn't very nice," she admonished, glaring in Brett's direction.

The man shrugged carelessly, not lifting his gaze from his glass.

"Don't pay attention to him, sweetheart," Cade said, sliding his hand lower to skim the full curve of her ass. A sultry smile tilted her lips. "He's in a pissy mood. A whiskey will make it better."

She nodded slowly and pressed her ass into his hand. "I'll be back in a sec."

He watched her go and felt his cock twitch as the swing of her hips became more exaggerated, for his benefit he guessed. Though it had been less than a week ago, it felt like forever since Jess had left for the airport and his balls were suffering in the absence of a woman's touch.

His attention flickered back to the man in front of him. Of course, spending a few hours every day in the presence of this guy didn't help with keeping his lust to a manageable level. Brett worked hard on the ranch and his labor showed clearly in the ropy muscles down his arms and back and the golden color of his skin. He liked to get his hands dirty, liked to sweat. Cade shifted in his seat as his groin tightened. He liked to *watch* him sweat. Liked it too damn much. Catching a glimpse of Brett with his shirt off, perspiration glistening all over his chest, set his mind crazy with fantasies he'd rather not be having with Jimmy in such close quarters. Fantasies of following Brett into one of the fields and telling him to take his clothes off. He'd back him up against the fence, move so close to him he'd feel Brett's breath on his face. Then he'd kiss him, claim those firm, masculine lips with his own, thrust his tongue in his mouth and taste him. After that he'd make him turn around and brace himself against one of the fence posts, ass high in the air. Cade would fuck him so hard Brett would be screaming his name as his come sputtered into the grass.

Cade rubbed his hand over his jaw, painfully aware of how constricted his pants had become in the last twenty seconds. He shifted again and then gritted his teeth. *Shit.* The head of his cock pressed against the seam of his jeans and any move he made would only be friction he didn't need right now.

He glanced around the bar, searching the crowd for a head of red curls. Where was Lilly? She'd made it plain as day she'd take care of him tonight.

"What would that girlfriend of yours think if she knew what you were up to?"

Cade blinked and turned back to face Brett. The man was eying him, hostility plain in his dark, almost-black gaze.

"What?"

"The blonde I saw you with last week."

The blonde? Oh right. "That's Jessica." He shrugged,

imagining how Jess would react to being called a "girlfriend". It sure wouldn't be pretty. "She's just a friend."

"Right." Brett's mouth twisted into a humorless smile. "A friend you fuck."

"You got it."

"She's a hot little thing," Brett continued, his voice quiet but clear. "What the hell's she doing with a guy like you?"

The way he said "guy", he might as well have called him *asshole*. Cade smiled, holding Brett's glinting gaze. What would he do if he knew that each hard-edged glare and bitten-out word only served to turn Cade on even more?

The intoxicating scent of perfume and cigarettes teased his nostrils as Lilly returned with Brett's drink. She set the glass of whiskey down in front of him and then scooted over to Cade. He removed his elbows from the table so she could slide into his lap.

A couple of the guys looked up from their game to make some wisecracks. Lilly played up to it, pushing her barely covered tits into the crook of his neck and nipping at his jaw. He pulled her further into his lap and let her straddle one of his thighs. Curved in all the right places and she knew it too. The kind of girl who went after what she wanted, who did the sex-with-no-strings thing on a regular basis.

He lounged back in the booth and swallowed a groan as Lilly's long nails scratched a path down toward his belt buckle. Behind her, Brett was watching them, face expressionless as he nursed his drink. The one-man audience had Cade's dick rock-hard. He held Brett's eyes as he slid his hand beneath Lilly's skirt and stroked the smooth, baby-soft skin of her thighs. She shuddered.

"You cold, sweetheart?" he crooned, still watching Brett.

"Nuh-uh." She squirmed in his lap, her pussy seeking the

caress of his fingers. His hand slid upward, finding the lacy edge of her panties. He slipped his fingers beneath the material and found her wet and swollen.

"Very nice," he murmured as her breathing grew labored in his ear. He drew his thumb along her creamy entrance. "All this for me?"

"Mmm." She let out a small gasp as he rubbed the pad of his thumb over the small button of her clit. "You sure know what you're doing."

He grinned, glad to be able to focus his energy on her pleasure long enough to forget his own. Her hand, though still at his crotch, had quit its mission once he'd started touching her and as a result his erection had weakened slightly. Maybe he'd be able to walk out of here without the embarrassment of stuffing his hands in his pockets.

A glance over Lilly's shoulder told him Brett was still observing the show. His eyes were glazed over, a clear sign he was wasted, but Cade could make out the hunger in his dark pupils. Drunk or not, Brett Miller was horny.

Continuing to stroke Lilly's pussy, Cade wondered if he could help the guy out. Maybe that's what Brett's problem was—he needed to fuck and he needed it bad. And if Cade couldn't be the one to do it...

Slowly and reluctantly, Cade removed his fingers from Lilly's dripping cunt. She let out a tiny moan of protest.

"Shhh," he soothed, patting her thigh. "I need you to do me a favor."

Her eyes, glassy with desire, searched his. "Anything for you, honey."

He stretched his neck to the side to whisper in the ear. After telling her exactly what he wanted her to do, he got to his feet and made his way to the bar to buy another round.

Brett couldn't remember the details of exactly how it had happened. All he knew was that somewhere between his fourth whiskey and his sixth, the redhead who'd been grinding up against Cade earlier in the night had somehow fallen into his lap.

Her giggles echoed in his head as she wound her arms around his neck and stuck her tongue in his ear. His cock reared as she licked the shell with the point of her tongue. She was whispering something, he couldn't make out what through the loud buzzing in his head, but from the way her fingers curled into the front of his shirt and tugged, he guessed she wanted to get out of here.

He was up for that.

"Come on, darlin'," he mumbled, smacking her lightly on her Lycra-covered ass. "Let me see you walk."

She giggled again, a sound that grated, but he didn't complain. Hell, she could shriek the whole place down as long as she took care of the tent at the front of his jeans.

Holding her at the waist, he pushed her forward through the crowd. How the fuck did they get out of here? And why was the bar spinning? He blinked slowly and focused on a point straight ahead.

Through the pounding in his brain, he heard a couple of people call his name. He didn't stop, just kept on going until the redhead—*Lilly maybe?*—led him outside. The air outside wrapped around him like a suffocating mist, even more humid than inside the bar.

"Where's your ride, sugar?"

"The blue truck," he muttered, still holding her against

him. She had one hell of a fine ass, fleshy but firm.

"Ooh, I like it!"

"Huh?" He glanced past her and made out the outline of his truck. That was fast. "You coming home with me?"

She twirled in his arms and laughed. The pitchy sound made him wince. "You think you can drive in the state you're in?"

What state was he in? Of course he could fucking drive. He moved forward, stumbling slightly as he backed her up against the truck door. "I can do a lot of things in the state I'm in."

"Oh yeah?" Her voice turned coy as she reached down between them and stroked him through his jeans. "Wanna prove it?"

She didn't need to ask twice. He grasped at his belt buckle, fumbling with it until it came loose. Then he unbuttoned the fly and jerked the zipper down. His cock sprang free and jutted outward.

Lilly's moan of approval nearly brought him to his knees. But she was the one who dropped to the ground. She wrapped her hands around the base of his dick. Her breath blew lightly over his tight skin. Yes, this was what he needed, what his body was crying out for.

Bracing one hand on the side of his truck, he dug the other into her mass of red hair. Then her mouth, wet and wide, closed around the swollen head of his cock and sucked. Hard.

Sweet mercy.

He closed his eyes and tightened his grip on Lilly's silky mane. Her lips moved farther down his shaft, swallowing him, bathing him with her skilled tongue. He groaned, clenching the muscles in his thighs. Her head bobbed up and down beneath his grip, her rhythm steady and well-practiced. He tried to remember the last time a chick had given him head. More than a month ago. Too long.

His cock swelled dangerously as Lilly's hand stroked his balls through the denim barrier of his pants. *That's it, baby. Keep doing exactly what you're doing.* He kept his eyes closed, waiting for the haze in his mind and the burn in his body to melt his problems away. The struggles of the past couple of weeks retreated, all but one. Cade. With a grunt of defeat, Brett let Cade's pretty face swim in his mind as he pumped his cock into Lilly's mouth. And as the asshole flashed him a smile in his mind's eye, Brett groaned and shoved his dick down Lilly's throat as far as she could take him.

From the heavy throbbing in his cock and the way his balls had drawn tight beneath his body, Cade wondered if he'd come before Brett did. He knew Lilly's fire-engine red lips had to feel good as they slid up and down Brett's engorged cock, but that sensation couldn't beat the visual Cade was savoring from where he stood in the shadows.

Fuck, Brett was big. Really big. Bigger than Cade had remembered. He'd seen Brett naked before. Whenever he'd stayed at the Miller house while his parents were out of town, he'd always made it his business to get a glimpse, whether it meant walking in on Brett in the shower or, and much as it pained him to admit it, spying on him through the keyhole of his room. That's how far his crush had taken him.

Those memories of his horny teenage years faded to the back of his mind and his eyes drank in the reality of *now*. No need for a keyhole tonight. In long thrusts that were surprisingly steady considering how drunk he was, Brett drove into Lilly's welcoming mouth. Cade watched, transfixed as Lilly's lips stretched around Brett's impossible size and wondered what it would feel like to be fucked by that cock, to feel Brett's long, thick shaft pulsing in his ass.

He stifled a groan as he pressed his hand to his groin and touched himself lightly through his jeans. He ached to go over there and take over from Lilly, to feel Brett's hot shaft slide over his tongue.

Leaning back against the wall, he upped the pace of his self-soothing strokes. Brett's hips surged faster now, pushing his cock further down Lilly's throat. She made an excited sound, sucking him eagerly, accepting the relentless drive of his hips. Cade gritted his teeth. His cock strained in his jeans. All he could hear was the wet smacking sound of Lilly's lips on Brett's dick. His breathing shortened and then stopped altogether as Lilly's pink tongue snuck out and licked its way up the underside of Brett's shaft. She swiped the tip over the plum-shaped head before swallowing it again and, giving a low shout, Brett meshed his hips into her face and came.

Cade's legs shook at the sight of the other man losing control. Brett's large, muscled body shuddered as he filled Lilly's mouth with his release. Realizing he'd been holding his breath for a good twenty seconds, Cade released it on a heavy sigh. The sound caught the attention of both Lilly and Brett whose heads snapped in his direction. He swallowed thickly and stepped out of the shadows. Lilly's eyes brightened when she saw him and he winked at her. She smiled dazedly back. Brett wasn't quite so welcoming.

"You spying on us, Armstrong?" he asked, slurring a couple of words. With shaky hands, he adjusted himself and drew up his zipper. "This how you get your kicks?"

Oh, he had no idea.

Trying to ignore the hard-on that ached with each step he took, Cade ambled forward and held out a hand to Lilly. She took it and rose to her feet.

"It ain't spying," he told Brett, who'd propped himself against the hood of the truck. With a dazed expression in his eyes, he looked about ready to pass out. "Not when you're in the middle of a damn parking lot."

Brett muttered something under his breath. Cade thought he caught the word "bastard" but he couldn't be sure.

Cade turned to Lilly and quirked a brow. "You wanna get out of here?" She giggled and he wrapped an arm around her shoulders, pulling her tight against his body. She'd really helped him out tonight and he was determined to return the favor.

But Brett had other ideas. As he stumbled back against the truck, Cade released Lilly and grabbed Brett by the shoulder.

"I'm fine," Brett insisted, shaking him off. Then he stumbled again, this time nearly hitting the ground. Cade caught him just in time. He held him by the shoulders, trying not to let his erection make contact with Brett's denim-clad ass.

"I think we're gonna have to call it a night," Cade said reluctantly, glancing back at Lilly.

She shrugged. "Figures."

"Maybe another time?"

She grinned. "Count on it."

"Count on what?" Brett mumbled. Now his eyes were half-closed.

Lilly's laugh rang in the air. She winked at Cade and then swished her way back toward the bar. He watched her go, feeling a twinge of regret. What would have happened if Brett had stayed halfway sober tonight? Maybe all three of them would have gotten some.

"Seriously, man," Brett slurred, twisting against Cade's

grip. "Where's she going?"

"To find someone who can give her what she needs." Cade started to drag him away from the truck.

"Where're we going?"

"Home."

"But the truck..."

"You can get it tomorrow. You ain't in a fit state to drive."

"Why does everybody keep saying that? I can drive."

Cade chuckled. "You can barely even talk."

"Fuck you."

"Expletives don't count." Reaching his car, Cade helped Brett into the passenger seat and then walked around to the driver's side. "Think you can make it without puking all over my car?"

"Sure."

"You better. It's a rental."

Cade spent the ride home struggling not to laugh. Beside him, Brett fumbled with the car radio, pressing button after button and eventually settling on some rock and roll. He sang along, skipping some of the words and slurring the others. It was cute.

At the thought, Cade couldn't help himself. He let out a bark of laughter and then coughed to disguise it. He didn't think Brett would dig being called "cute".

As he maneuvered the car along the ranch's winding drive, he briefly considered just taking Brett home with him. But having Brett in the same house with him all night would be too darn tempting, especially when Brett wasn't fully in control of his senses.

Cade pulled to a stop outside the Miller house and got out

of the car. Getting Brett inside the house proved to be even trickier than getting him into the car had been. The twenty-minute drive had made Brett sleepy and he could barely hold his head up as Cade helped him up the porch steps.

"Where's the keys, Brett?"

"Huh?"

"Your keys." Cade took a guess and slipped a hand inside Brett's back pocket. His fingers stilled, pressing lightly against Brett's firm ass. Just as he'd thought, it was hard as nails. He swallowed, moved his hand in deeper and grasped the key.

"Hang on there a second, buddy," he said as he towed Brett into the foyer. "We're nearly there."

"We gotta get up the stairs."

"Yeah." Cade hesitated, calculating how difficult it would be to get Brett up the staircase. Hell, he'd take a whack at it. "Come on, hold on to me."

It took them the guts of ten minutes to reach the top of the stairs, not only because Brett had been weighing Cade down, but also because the closeness of their bodies had brought Cade's erection back full-force.

He led Brett to the bottom of the landing and kicked open his bedroom door. As he stepped inside, he tried not to focus on the bed in the center of the room. It was no mean feat. The bed was massive, plenty of room for two horny guys.

"You okay now?" he asked, pushing sex from his mind and helping Brett to the bed. "Think you can manage this yourself?"

His mouth dried as Brett lifted the hem of his shirt and pulled it over his head. Despite having been faced with Brett's bare chest almost every day this week, the sight still grabbed Cade between the legs. He swallowed and took a long step back. "I'll get going."

Brett grunted, hands already fiddling with his zipper. He hadn't bothered to buckle his belt back at the bar. Cade watched, dry-mouthed, as Brett worked the zipper down and then shucked out of his pants. He reached down and pulled off his socks.

Cade blinked. Now was the time to get the hell out. He didn't need to see anymore. He didn't need to watch Brett stripping out of his boxers.

But he couldn't summon the will to move. He felt as if he was stuck in mud. His feet rooted to the beechwood floor. As Brett stumbled to his feet and shoved down his shorts, Cade's cock leaped.

"Hey, sorry about your girl," Brett said as he reached for a pair of sweats. Cade held his breath, afraid to move a muscle until the man had covered himself up. Hanging limp between his legs, Brett's cock was still the hottest thing Cade had ever seen.

"Girl?" he croaked when Brett had settled the waistband of his pants safely around his hips.

"Yeah. Didn't mean to steal her or nothing. She was just so darn…" Brett trailed off and shrugged. "Anyway, sorry."

Cade's eyes widened and he gave a startled laugh. Brett was apologizing to him? Now that just didn't happen. If the slurred speech and the unsteady limbs hadn't been evidence enough, that apology would have proven he was drunk out of his mind.

"Forget it," he said, wondering what Brett would say if he knew Cade had asked Lilly to take care of him. He wouldn't like it, wouldn't appreciate Cade messing around with his business. Well, good thing he'd never find out.

"Okay, I'm going to head home now." This time he meant it.

"Whatever." Brett lay flat on his back, his eyes already

closing. By the time Cade left the house, he was certain the guy was snoring his brains out.

As he got into the car and revved the engine, Cade rummaged around in the glove compartment and came up with nothing. Why he'd let Jess throw out his last pack of Marlboros he didn't know, because right now he really needed a cigarette.

Chapter Four

The following morning Brett awoke to the heavy beat of a drum. Blinking slowly, he winced as the bright glare of the sun's rays stung his eyes. Why hadn't he closed the drapes last night? And who the hell kept banging those drums?

He sat up in the bed and groaned as pain flared between his eyes. The drums grew louder. Realization dawned and he cursed. He wasn't hearing drums. The sound originated inside his head, a heavy throbbing at the back of his brain. Jesus Christ, how much did he have to drink last night?

He cradled his head in his hands as he shifted to the edge of the bed and tentatively placed his feet on the ground. What the hell time was it anyway? Lifting his head, he squinted at his clock radio. *Shit.* It was almost noon. Dad was going to beat his hide.

He stiffened, stark realization hitting him square in the chest, holding him immobile for a few seconds. No, Dad wasn't around anymore to beat his hide. The only one he had to answer to now was himself and the reality check left a bitter taste in his mouth.

His limbs creaked as he stood shakily and stumbled from the bedroom to the bathroom. He stepped beneath the shower, letting cold water rain down on him, rousing his senses better than any wake-up call. Five minutes later, and feeling a lot less like the waking dead, he dried off and pulled on some clothes.

Jimmy was in the yard when he walked outside. The old man lifted a hand in greeting, a crooked smile spreading across his wrinkled face.

"You look like hell, kid."

Brett snorted. "I feel like hell too." He glanced around, noting the presence of Paul and Danny, their two ranch-hands who were carrying supplies into the tack shed. Cade was nowhere in sight. "Where's Armstrong?"

"Took a couple of the horses out to one of the paddocks." Jimmy lifted his Stetson off his head and wiped the back of his arm over his brow. "Kid sure knows what he's doing with those animals."

Brett nodded silently. Talking about Cade had brought back flashes of the night before, memories that included Cade half-carrying him up the stairs. Bad enough he'd gotten totally wasted but Cade picking up the pieces made it even worse.

"I'm glad he's sticking around," Jimmy continued. "Maybe you guys will put your differences behind you soon. He's a good kid."

Resisting the urge to roll his eyes, Brett grunted in agreement. Much as it bugged him, Jimmy was right. But Brett didn't feel like facing up to Cade just yet. Not when his head weighed down on him like a brick of granite.

Lucky for him, he didn't see Cade for the rest of the afternoon. Though his body was still stiff, he threw himself into the work, helping Jimmy load bales of hay into the barn. The old man headed off home at five and Brett returned to the house. After downing a liter of water, he grabbed a steak from the refrigerator. He hadn't even turned on the pan when Cade swaggered into the kitchen.

"Well, look who's still alive."

Instead of pissing him off, Cade's wry tone drew a sheepish smile. He turned from the stove and faced the amusement swimming in the other man's eyes. "Sorry about last night," he said, waiting for the inevitable hostility toward the other man to return. It didn't. "Guess I went a little overboard."

Cade's bark of laughter rang in his ears and Brett grimaced at the noise.

"Sorry." Cade threw his hat on the table and folded his arms. "But man, you should have seen yourself last night. Haven't laughed like that in a long while."

"Glad I amused you."

Cocking his head to the side, Cade made a face. "Though I gotta admit, I didn't find it so funny when you made off with my girl."

Girl? Red curly hair flashed in Brett's mind's eye and he groaned. "Uh, sorry about that."

Cade's eyes twinkled in good humor and Brett felt worse. "Forget about it."

He shook his head. "Guess I ruined your night."

"Hell, I'm just glad you didn't start a fight."

"Me too." Brett looked at the steak on the countertop and then glanced back at Cade. "You want something to eat?"

Surprise flickered in Cade's blue eyes and Brett fought a sudden grin. The guy probably thought he was still drunk.

"Nah," Cade said after a brief pause. "Already ate." He pulled out a chair and folded his long body into it. "Just wondered if you wanted to take a ride into town?"

Brett raised a brow. "Why?"

"To pick up your truck."

"Oh, right." Brett nodded. Another dose of guilt pricked him. He'd treated Cade like shit for the past few weeks, yet the guy had been decent enough to drive him home and help him upstairs. Hell, he hadn't even punched his lights out for macking on his girl. "You don't have to."

Cade shrugged. "Who else is going to do it?"

He had a point. Steeplecrest Ranch wasn't exactly the center of things. "You want to go now?"

"Eat first. I can wait."

"Thanks." Brett got the steak started and then grabbed a couple of sodas from the refrigerator. He slid one across the table to Cade and then pulled back the tab on his own. As the meat sizzled in the hot oil, he stood over it and took a long drink of cola. Damn, he was starving.

"Jimmy gone home?"

Brett nodded, flipping the steak over in the pan. "He's not looking too good."

"Well, he's working hard." Cade rested his elbows on the table and leaned forward. "And with the accident and everything..." He let the sentence trail off.

"Yeah."

Their respective fathers had done a lot on this ranch. They were big boots to fill and Jimmy was picking up the slack. For the first time, Brett realized how lucky he was that Cade had stuck around.

They fell into silence, a silence disturbed by the crackle of frying meat. Not an awkward silence, much to Brett's surprise. Who'd have guessed Cade would make such easy company?

After a few minutes, Brett transferred the steak to a plate and grabbed some bread. The first bite of meat melted in his mouth and with his appetite urging him on, he shoveled the rest in.

"Hungry?" Cade asked, a small smile lifting the corner of

his mouth.

Brett shrugged, still chewing. When he'd swallowed the last crust of bread, he sighed. He could have eaten another one of those.

"You ready to go?" he asked reluctantly, mind still on food.

"Sure." Cade rose from the table and grabbed his Stetson. His hair had grown out, a shaggy mane of dirty blond curls brushing his shoulders.

Brett frowned. Why the hell was he noticing a thing like that? Since when had he turned into a goddamn woman?

He looked away and dropped his plate in the sink. Then he followed Cade out of the house to the guy's car.

"Still using a rental?" he asked when they were on the road.

"For now. No point in buying one if I'm heading back to New York."

Brett blinked, an uneasy sensation tightening his stomach. "You're going back to New York?"

"I don't know." Cade slanted him a look. "I'm on a trial, remember?"

"Right." Brett faced forward, concentrating on the road. He didn't want to think about the possibility of Cade's departure. And he didn't like the sense of dread it roused within him. He'd spent weeks wishing Cade would get the hell out of Steeplecrest and suddenly he'd done a one-eighty. Overnight. Like he wanted Cade to stick around.

Change the subject. "I must have been still pissed this morning," he said, keeping his eyes on the barren land they drove by. "When I woke up and saw the time—" he laughed shortly, "—I thought for a second 'Dad's gonna fucking kill me'."

As soon as the admission left his mouth, he regretted it. Stupid thing to say, especially to Cade who'd no doubt read more into it than necessary. Heat crawled up Brett's neck as he felt Cade's gaze studying him, picking him apart. If the atmosphere had been strained a minute ago, it was ready to snap now.

When Cade remained silent for a couple of minutes, relief eased the knot of tension in Brett's stomach. Maybe he'd let it go.

But then Cade opened his mouth. "I don't think it's hit me yet," he said quietly, slowing as they approached a junction then steering the car to the left. "I've been gone for seven years. Not used to seeing them every day."

Brett suddenly found it hard to swallow. He *had* seen them every day. "Sometimes it's like they're on vacation." His lips twisted in a bitter smile. "Except they didn't do vacation."

Cade laughed and the rich sound was warm to Brett's ears. "They sure didn't." There was a pause before Cade asked, "Does it feel really different without them around?"

Thinking about his dad's way of overanalyzing the procedures with Jimmy and Ken's short fuse with the bulls, Brett nodded. "It's a lot quieter." Then he added, "Not so quiet with you here though." The words made it sound as if he liked having the guy around and he wished he could take them back. But then again, maybe he did like having Cade around. If anything, the time passed more quickly and the workload decreased faster with an extra person on board.

If Cade had taken his words to mean more than he'd intended, he didn't show it. "You saying I'm loud?" he asked instead, slapping a palm on the wheel.

"Louder than Paul and Danny."

Cade snorted. "That's not hard, is it? Those kids just don't talk."

Silence drifted over the car again, but this time Brett

relaxed into it. Soon, Cade pulled up outside Billy's.

Seeing the parking lot brought back another rush of memories from the previous night. "Jesus Christ," Brett moaned, remembering how Cade had half-carried him across the tarmac-covered surface. "I haven't been that wasted since high school."

"Then you're not living right."

"Maybe not." Brett got out of the car and rested his hand on the door, looking back in at Cade. "And, uh, thanks for the ride."

Cade's dimple winked at him. "No worries." He shifted the clutch. "See you tomorrow."

He nodded and watched the Lexus roll away, leaving a cloud of dust in its wake. He turned back to the parking lot, vacant except for a couple of cars and his blue truck. He trudged toward it, sneaking a glance at Mrs. Blackthorn's upstairs window that overlooked the lot.

He could only hope to God she hadn't caught the show last night.

Over the next couple of weeks Steeplecrest Ranch really started to feel like home again. Cade got up at dawn every day, letting the morning sun act as his alarm clock. He started out feeding the cattle and the horses, then moved on to whatever big tasks they had that day. A couple of times, he took the four-wheel drive out to check out the land. And he'd spent a couple of evenings fishing in the creek at the other side of the ranch. It was a far cry from a day at his New York office.

To make things even better, the whole dynamic had changed between him and Brett. They'd slipped into an amicable working relationship and Cade had been invited over more than once to watch a game on Brett's flat screen. It wasn't easy hiding his attraction to the other man, especially when Brett lounged on the sofa wearing nothing more than a pair of sweatpants slung low on his narrow hips.

"Christ, Jess, sometimes I think he's going to stand up and his pants are gonna fall down," Cade said on the phone one night after an evening at Brett's. "And I'm sitting there praying it'll happen."

Her laugh tinkled down the line. "If it does, please take a picture."

"Will do."

They'd come so far Cade now felt he could mention their folks without turning Brett to stone. They didn't talk about them often—dead parents didn't really work well with replacing horseshoes—but when it came up they handled it and Cade was getting to grips with just how much pain Brett had to work through. Problem was that knowing how much grief the other man felt made Cade want him even more.

"We got him," Brett shouted on one stifling afternoon. "Hold him there."

They were on the dry land above the pastures where the gradient became really mountainous, Brett on horseback, Cade on his feet. One of the bulls had strayed from the herd and Cade couldn't figure how an animal as large and stupid looking as this one had gotten so far. Brett had roped him and the bull stared dopily at them with the loop around its neck.

Cade jogged toward it and shook his head. "You going somewhere, big guy?"

Brett rode up behind him and dropped down from the horse. "You got him secured?"

"Sure do." Cade pulled on the rope, leading the animal

back to where he'd come from.

"We need to get them branded."

"Why? There's no other livestock around here."

"Yeah, but they could get stolen."

"Who'd want to steal one of these?" Cade asked, glancing at the bull whose big brown eyes gazed into the distance.

Brett grinned. "They're smarter than you think."

Sure. They strode down toward the grassy meadows and Cade drew in a breath. Brett had visited their parents' graves last night and Cade had been searching for a way to bring it up all day. "Jimmy said you went to the cemetery last night," he said on a rush of breath, grateful to finally get the words out.

There was a brief pause before Brett confirmed it. "That's right."

Cade nodded, not sure what to say next. He wanted to know what it had been like standing over the graves. He hadn't ventured down there yet, hadn't worked up the courage.

"No big deal," Brett said, answering the unasked question. "Just a cemetery."

"A cemetery where our folks are buried."

"Yeah."

Even though he'd brought it up, desperation to get away from the subject of their dead parents swept through Cade. He hunted his mind for something to say, something different. Remembering the phone call he'd received that morning, he faltered. One awkward topic to the next. "My boss called me today," he said, glancing up to catch Brett's reaction.

The man lifted a brow. "I thought I was your boss."

Cade snorted. "In your dreams."

"What did he say?" Brett's tone was even, but Cade

detected an edge to the casual enquiry.

"Wants to know when I'm coming back."

"Why? He thinks your vacation has gone on long enough?"

"Vacation?" Cade gestured to his boots that were caked in dirt. "If this is a vacation, I'm going to kill myself."

Brett laughed shortly. After a few seconds, he picked up on the conversation. "Do you like your job?"

"Sure." Cade thought about the hard work, the competitive environment, the unbeatable buzz after landing a big client. "I'm good at it and I like the work."

"Then why are you still here?" This time the edge in Brett's voice was clear.

Cade glanced at him, noting the stern set of his jaw. "I like this place too."

Brett didn't question him further. He kept his gaze fixed on a point ahead and neither of them said a word until they reached the pastures.

"Want to come over to my place tonight?" Cade asked once the adventurous bull was back in its pen. "I've got two rib eyes and a couple of cans in the refrigerator."

Brett turned, brow still furrowed. But he nodded, accepting the olive branch. "I'll come by about seven."

"Great."

Three hours later, bellies lined with the best kind of steak, they lounged in Cade's living room watching baseball on ESPN.

"This place looks different," Brett mused.

Cade glanced around the room, remembering how he'd ripped the house apart on one lazy Sunday after the funeral in an effort to make the place feel more like his. "I moved some stuff down to the basement—picture frames and Mom's antiques." He took a sip of beer and shrugged. "It was too feminine in here."

"Guess I should do the same," Brett said quietly.

Cade frowned. He'd forgotten Brett hadn't lived with his folks at the time of the accident. When Cade had left home seven years back, Brett had still been living in the Miller house, but a couple of years later, he'd moved into the town. A two-storey off Main Street, if Cade was remembering his mother correctly. "Do you still have your place in town?"

"Yeah. I'm going to put it on the market. No point hanging onto it."

The conversation dimmed, but shouts and thuds from the TV set created a buzz in the room, preventing the silence from becoming deafening. Their lives had changed a lot in a short space of time, Cade realized—they'd both led lives separate from their families. Now they were living at home again, this time without any parents around. It left a weird energy floating around the place. He and Brett were responsible now. The ranch rested on their shoulders alone.

"You know what would really piss my mom off about dying?" Brett said, cracking a smile as he looked away from the TV set.

Cade leaned forward to rest his beer on the coffee table. "What?"

"She never saw me get married." Brett shook his head in wonder. "Not a day went by when she didn't shoot a hint my way. She tried to set me up with every damn girl in Steeplecrest before I hit twenty-one and that's no lie."

Cade laughed, thinking of his own mother. "Mom hated any girl I brought home."

"Oh yeah?"

"Yeah. I don't think there's a woman in this world she would have been happy to have as a daughter-in-law."

"But she wanted you to get married eventually. She used to go on about you and your New York girlfriends all the time."

"She did?" Cade struggled to absorb this nugget of information. "It must have been the distance. She probably hoped my taste in women would improve in the city."

There was a moment's pause before Brett said, "Well, now she doesn't have to worry about it."

"No, guess not." The smile faded from Cade's face as the reality struck home. No girl would ever have to impress his mother again. And he'd never be forced to reveal his ambiguous sexual preferences to her. A relief. "Ever come close to getting married?" he asked, leaning back against the leather sofa.

"Nope." Brett glanced his way and smirked. "And it ain't happening any time soon."

"You don't want to settle down?"

Brett hesitated, his eyes narrowing as he thought about it. "Not yet," he said finally. "The girls I've been out with—I haven't found the right fit."

"Same here." Except he hadn't found the right fit with girls *or* guys. As Brett turned his attention back to the sports channel, Cade studied his angular profile and wondered what it would be like if he and Brett were the right fit. If they crossed the line and became lovers, would they be able to hang out like this, chilling with a couple of beers? Or would they be too busy screwing each other's asses off?

If he had his way, it would be the latter.

Cade grabbed his can and gulped down the last of his beer. This had to stop. Fantasizing about Brett while he was sitting a few feet away screamed bad idea. One of these days Brett was going to turn around and catch Cade ogling him. Or God forbid, he might notice the erection Cade suffered ninety percent of the time when Brett was near. Brett would have him on the first plane back to New York if he got wind of the thoughts circling Cade's mind.

"I'm heading to El Paso tomorrow," he said, changing the subject in an effort to distract himself. One of the ranch's suppliers down in the city had a horse he wanted Cade to check out.

"I forgot about that." Brett turned and glared at him. "Don't buy anything without me knowing about it."

Cade grinned and shook his head. "No, sir."

"Fuck off."

He laughed and got to his feet. "Want another beer?"

"Nah. I better get going." Brett rose from the armchair and stretched his arms behind his neck. The move lifted the hem of his T-shirt enough to reveal a strip of tan, muscled stomach. Cade's cock twitched and he turned abruptly.

"I'll see you when you get back," Brett said, walking down the hallway.

"Sure." Cade waited for the door to close behind the other man before dropping the empty Budweiser cans on the hall table and racing up the stairs. He had his jeans unzipped before he got to the bathroom. He tore the rest of his clothes off and reached into the shower stall to turn on the water. With a sigh of relief, he stepped beneath the hot spray and wrapped his hand around his dick. For fuck's sake. This was what two hours spent in Brett's company drove him to. Jacking off in his damn shower. What the hell age was he? Sixteen?

He closed his eyes as he pumped his hand up and down. His skin stretched tight over his shaft, the head bulging, drops of come already seeping from the slit. He dipped his head and breathed in, imagining Brett's naked body as his strokes quickened. Smooth golden skin. Flexing muscle. Powerful thighs and an enormous cock he knew would drive him to pleasure as he'd never known it before.

The jets of water drowned out his strangled gasp as his dick swelled further. His balls drew tight beneath him. *So fucking close.* With a ruthless grip, he pulled his hand up his cock and swiped his thumb over the broad head. In his mind, he conjured up Brett's face, the full lips that so often pressed into a harsh line of disapproval. He could almost hear the man's voice telling him exactly what he was doing wrong. He tried to manipulate what Brett had said in the past into what he ached to hear now. "Bend over," he imagined Brett saying hoarsely. "Bend over. Let me fuck you."

Cade let out a long moan as his climax exploded, his balls emptying all over his fist. He pictured Brett on his knees before him and watched the mirage lick up his sticky release. His whole body shuddered, his skin tingling with excitement. He rested his forearms against the stall's tiled walls and sucked in a deep breath.

He needed to get laid. Fast.

Chapter Five

The following morning dragged as Brett got to grips with paperwork he'd been pushing aside since the accident. The tedious work had his brain working overtime and it was darn typical that Cade had chosen that day for riding down to El Paso. Back in New York Cade dealt with paperwork all the time, so why the hell wasn't he looking after this crap?

At noon, Brett passed the halfway point and pushed back from the desk. Enough for now. He'd head into the yard, see what needed doing. Nothing like manual labor to relax his mind.

The midday sun beat down on him as he worked, searing through the thin material of his shirt. He didn't mind. He thrived on the heat, loved how it made him sweat. Cade was different that way. He liked the sun well enough but when it shone this hard he kept to the shade.

Remembering the man's mention of New York the previous evening, Brett frowned. He couldn't figure the guy out. Did he want to go back to New York or would he stick around? He didn't seem to know himself and it was starting to piss Brett off.

He stepped back from the four-wheeler he'd been washing down and placed his hands on his hips. If he was honest with himself, it bothered him that Cade was even entertaining thoughts of leaving. Since the night at Billy's he'd started to really like the guy. Their minds worked the same way and Brett had been caught off-guard once or twice when Cade had said the exact words he'd been thinking. They had the same goals for the ranch. Without their fathers around they could focus on modernizing the ranch, letting go of the old tried-and-tested ways and bringing in something new. Cade's enthusiasm for the project had rubbed off on Brett and, as he stared out at the rolling meadows and steep hills of the ranch, he saw more potential in the land than he had in a long time. Besides Cade's enthusiasm and ideas, he worked hard and he worked well, which earned a lot of respect from Brett. He cooked a mean steak dinner too. Shaking his head, Brett tried to imagine the ranch without Cade's presence. He couldn't. But he was damn sure it would be different.

He'd have Jimmy, of course, and they got along well. They were family. And Paul and Danny did their bit. But Cade brought something that had been missing before—an energy and a sense of humor that kept them all on a balanced level. It seemed he was always in good spirits, laughing and kidding around even as he worked. Without him around, Brett was willing to bet the atmosphere would get pretty damn depressing after a while.

"Hello," a voice, a *female* voice, called warily somewhere out front. "Anyone home?"

Brett grabbed his Stetson from where he'd left it on the vehicle and placed it on his head as he jogged around the house. The sight of a slender blonde woman in a short pink dress greeted him. If her Eastern twang hadn't been enough to negate her of a Texan background, her four-inch stilettos did the trick.

Spotting his approach, she pushed her sunglasses up into her hair and her red lips stretched into a smile.

"Hi there," he greeted, wiping his greasy palms on the front of his jeans. "You lost, ma'am?"

Her smile widened and a perfect set of whites flashed at him. "Nope. I'm not lost." Her gaze drifted over the length of his body, resting for a second at his groin before working its way back up to his face. She tilted her head to the side and her blonde hair fell in a curtain over one shoulder. "Though I wouldn't mind being *your* damsel in distress."

The blatant come-on in her honeyed voice made him laugh. "Can't say I'd mind that either." He folded his arms across his chest, recognition setting in. "You're Cade's girl."

She laughed and the fun-loving throaty sound tugged between his legs.

"Cade's girl?" she asked, humor drenching her tone. "I'm no one's girl."

He raised a brow. "Glad to hear it."

She ran the tip of her tongue over her bottom lip, drawing his eyes to her mouth. He let his gaze linger there before meeting her knowing eyes again.

"Why don't you come on in?" he said, backing up toward the house. "Cade's in El Paso. Won't be back till late tonight."

"That'll give us a chance to get to know one another," she said silkily.

He grinned and gestured for her to follow him inside. She was a firecracker, this one.

"You want something to eat?" he asked when they stepped inside the kitchen.

"What have you got?"

He pulled open the refrigerator and peered inside. "Not much." His thoughts turned to Delia's Diner and he faced his guest again. "Feel like some good Southern cooking?"

"You're on."

Heat enveloped them as they headed back into the sun and Brett's eyes widened at the sight of the red Beamer sitting in his drive. He'd been so focused on the chick, he hadn't noticed her ride.

"You rented this at the airport?" he asked, running his hand over the shiny red hood.

"Yeah. Expensive but worth it."

He grinned. That sounded about right. She came across as the kind of girl who liked to indulge herself.

"But can we take yours instead?" she asked, teetering across the drive to his truck. "I've never taken a ride in a pickup before."

They'd reached the gates to the ranch before she introduced herself.

"I'm Jessica Lawson," she said, twisting her body on the bench seat to face him fully.

"Brett," he replied.

"I know. I saw you once or twice the last time I was here."

"And you never came by to say hello?" He glanced at her, feigning an expression of dismay.

She giggled. "Believe me, I wanted to. You were just so intimidating."

He frowned, not sure whether to laugh or to worry. He didn't want to be scaring off the ladies. "Intimidating?" He couldn't imagine this girl being intimidated by anybody.

"Sure. You stormed around the place like an ogre, a very *sexy* ogre. After bumping into you in the fields, Cade would come inside and tell me how you nearly bit his head off." She shook her head in amusement. "He used to break his heart laughing."

Brett gave a reluctant smile, imagining Cade cracking up after one of their encounters. "Guess I wasn't the best neighbor back then."

Her eyes widened. "So things have changed?"

He shrugged. "He's a good kid."

They were quiet for a few minutes but he could feel her eyes on him. Her inquisitive gaze had prickles of awareness spreading over his skin. "So how long have you known Cade?" he asked, breaking the silence.

"Since college. We took an English class together."

"What do you do?"

She flicked a fly off her knee with one red nail. "I'm an executive at a beauty company based in New York."

Ah, she was a high flyer. "You like it?"

She nodded. "Don't get me wrong, it can be stressful, but I suppose I thrive on that."

Brett focused on the road ahead as Jessica admired the various nooks and crannies in the cab. After a while, he took a left turn and started down Main Street. The truck trundled to a stop outside the diner.

"Mmm, that was fun," she said when he pulled open her door. He took her hand and watched her dress flare as she jumped down. The flash of creamy thighs made his mouth water.

"Hey, honey," Delia greeted him as he walked through the door. Warm and matronly, Delia always made her customers feel at home. And she'd been a good friend to his mother. In the run up to the funeral a mountain of Delia's pies and cakes had weighed down his kitchen table. "Comfort food", she'd told him with tears in her brown eyes. "It's good for the soul."

"Hi, Delia," he said, stooping to kiss her weathered cheek.

"This here is Jessica Lawson. She's Cade's friend."

Delia beamed at Jessica and then clapped her hands together. "I hope you two are hungry. The fried chicken is good today, if I do say so myself."

"Fried chicken?" Jessica cried, sliding into one of the booths. "I need some of that. God, I'm so hungry."

"Same for you?" Delia asked Brett.

He nodded and then watched her bustle toward the kitchen.

"That's good service," Jessica noted, folding her hands on the table. "She's really sweet."

Feeling a surge of pride for Delia, he grinned. "She sure is."

Ten minutes later their food arrived along with two vanilla milkshakes, on the house.

Jessica grabbed her straw and slurped noisily. She wasn't like the many diet-addicted girls he'd been out with. Unafraid to exhibit her hunger, she tore into her fried chicken with gusto. The sight of her uninhibited hunger turned him on, and the pure ecstasy in her expression at the first taste of Delia's crispy batter turned him on even more. "Is this how she looks during sex?" he wondered.

Cade would know.

After devouring most of her chicken, Jessica rested her head on the edge of the booth and rolled her eyes up to the heavens. "That was the best meal I've had in years."

"Hunger's a damn fine gravy."

"Mmm." She looked at him through sleepy eyes as he continued to eat. "So tell me, cowboy, how's Cade doing?"

He gave a bark of laughter. "How the hell would I know?"

"You see him every day."

"Yeah, but I'm not his babysitter. I don't keep tabs on him."

"But how does he seem to you?" she prompted, eyes fixed on his face. She had that inquisitive expression again. He didn't like it. "Is he happy?"

"I don't know. I guess he kids around a lot. That's a good sign, right?"

She nodded. "When bad shit happens, he doesn't like to talk about it. But I think being here with you has helped him a lot." She smiled softly, sassy chick gone and replaced with a concerned friend. "I'm really sorry about your parents, by the way."

He looked at her in surprise. "Uh, thanks."

She shook her head. "It was a really bad thing to happen."

"Yeah." Grief grasped his chest and for a long moment he couldn't breathe. Then, as air filled his chest again, he forced a smile. "Life goes on, I guess."

Understanding warmed her eyes. "It must help to have Cade around."

He hesitated, not sure what to say to that. As the truth of her words hit home, he nodded. "It does."

They were silent for a few minutes and Brett looked out at Main Street as his food digested in his system. In just two hours he already had a pretty clear picture of who Jessica was and he liked what he saw. Behind the sharp wit and sexual persona, she read people fast. And from the way she talked about Cade she was a really good friend. Brett had known for a while now that having Cade on the ranch was a good thing in terms of the ranch and having a buddy to hang out with. He just hadn't realized that his own grief process had been made a hell of a lot easier by Cade's presence. They faced the same loss, felt the same emptiness. Brett hadn't seen it before but over the past few weeks a bond had developed between him and Cade, a bond he didn't think would be easily broken.

"Anyway," Jessica started after Delia left two cups of coffee on the table for them, "you're exactly what I expected, you know?"

Her earlier "ogre" comment popped into his mind and his brows drew together. "What do you mean?"

"You're a funny guy, way sexier than any person should be. But you're so controlled." She leaned forward, deepening the line of her cleavage. He swallowed hard and forced his gaze upward to meet her eyes.

"Controlled, huh?"

"Yeah. All restrained." She licked her lips and winked. "We'll have to loosen you up before I leave."

He liked the sound of that. So did his cock judging by the way it jumped in his pants.

"Do you think he's going to come back to New York?" she asked, her tone somber, her eyes watching for his reaction.

He paused. The familiar pit of dread opened up in his stomach. He shrugged, hoping she couldn't see past his relaxed façade. "I don't know. It doesn't come up in conversation much."

"Okay."

As she sipped the hot drink, he studied her serene expression and wondered if something bubbled beneath the surface. Maybe she missed Cade. Was that what she was here for? To get him back?

"Do you want him to go back with you?" He asked the question straight out, no games.

Her eyes widened in surprise and she put down her cup. "I miss him," she said after mulling it over. "But from our phone calls, he seems to feel at home here. I guess that makes sense, it's where he grew up." She scrunched up her face, not happy with her answer. "You know what? If he's happy here, I want him to stay. I think the ranch suits that cowboy smile of his." Her face broke into a grin. "And I wouldn't mind visiting him down here every now and then. Especially if you're hanging around."

He grinned back as warm lust rolled over his body. He liked this woman. There was one thing he had to say about Cade— the guy had good taste.

"You want to get out of here?" he asked, digging into his pocket for some cash.

"Yeah." She slid to the edge of the booth and stood. "Can we go for a drive around town?"

"We can do whatever you like, darlin'". He got to his feet and threw a few notes on the table to cover the bill. Then, shouting a goodbye to Delia, he led the city girl outside.

"The air is really dry down here," she said as they walked to the truck. "And freaking hot. I'm going to have to work on my tan before I head home."

Imagining her stretched out on the grass in his backyard, wearing nothing but a tiny bikini, he bit back a groan. "I'm sure that'll be possible," he said stiffly, giving her a hand up into the truck and trying to resist peeking up her dress.

He drove along Main Street and turned right for the road leading out of town. "There's some scenery up here you might want to see," he told her.

"The only scenery I need is sitting right here in this truck."

He laughed at her outrageous flirtation. "I've never come across a girl like you before, sweetheart."

"Oh no?" She sounded genuinely surprised at this. "Am I really so bad?"

"Bad? I didn't say bad." He glanced down and watched her hand slide over his thigh. "Not bad at all," he finished thickly.

He took a left turn on the main road, turning onto what was basically a dirt track. He followed it, his dick hardening with every stroke of Jessica's hand. Her fingers curled between his thighs, the long nails dangerously close to grazing his erection. He gripped the wheel and focused on not crashing into a tree.

The dirt track led to a dusty clearing, a make-out spot he and his friends had made use of as teenagers. He pulled the truck to a stop in the middle and got out.

"Wow," Jessica whispered, shielding her eyes with her hand as she stepped toward the edge of the clearing. Behind them stood bushes and trees. In front of them the land dipped in a deep canyon. There had to be at least a mile between them and the other side. A narrow creek, blue as the sky, trickled between the rocks along the bottom of the canyon. The water shimmered beneath the sun, creating a jeweled effect that could blind.

"That's amazing," Jessica said, stepping closer to the edge where the land began a dangerously steep decline. She turned to him, a mixture of awe and desire darkening her eyes. "You boys have it good out here."

"We sure do." He leaned back against the hood of his truck and watched her. While she admired the rugged beauty of their surroundings, he admired the curve of her fine ass, her shapely legs and her slim ankles. She turned, smiling wickedly when she caught him staring.

She approached him slowly with the slinky moves of a coyote. The subtle sway of her slender hips captivated him. As she closed in, the spicy scent of her perfume coiled around him. Seduction personified.

So close to him he could feel her breath on his neck, she lifted her face and pressed a kiss to his jaw. He gritted his teeth, blood pounding in his veins. Her arms slipped around his body trapping him against the Chevrolet.

"I really like your truck," she said, her tone low and sexy. "Every time we drove over a pothole or uneven road the whole seat vibrated." She pressed up against him so their bodies aligned. The slight hitch of her breath told him she was aware of his erection.

She hooked one of her legs around his waist, supporting her knee on the front grate of the truck. Then, in one slow move, she dragged her crotch along his dick. He sucked in a breath and held it as she repeated the action. He held her to him, pressing his palm into the small of her back, urging her to do it again.

Murmuring her approval, she started to ride him, rubbing her pussy against him. She gave a tiny moan, obviously finding the right friction, and then she abruptly stumbled back.

"You know what?" she asked, slightly out of breath. "We could do the foreplay thing, but I don't want to hang around." Hooking her fingers beneath the straps of her sundress, she pulled them down over her shoulders. The light material pooled around her ankles, leaving her naked except for a tiny white thong.

Brett's cock leaped in excitement as he drank in the dark berry nipples standing out like chocolate centers on each of her small, creamy breasts. He licked his lips and then dropped his gaze as she shimmied out of the thong. *Fuck.* Her pussy was hairless, the pink skin smooth, the tiny bud of her clit peeking out.

A deep hunger roared through his body. He lunged forward and grabbed her to him, holding her buttocks as she wrapped her legs around his waist. He swiveled and backed her up against the truck. Her hands slid down between them and tore open his belt.

"Come on," he pleaded with his jeans as the zipper refused to budge. "Fuck it, come on!"

The scrub of metal on metal resounded in the air as she finally got it down. The head of his cock nudged out of the opening. She reached in and pulled him out.

"Oh, you're big," she murmured, gliding her hand up and down his throbbing skin. "Very big." She shook her head and glanced up at him, pupils dilated with lust. "Put it inside me," she demanded, pushing her hand between her legs and parting the juicy lips of her pussy. "Please."

No part of him wanted to resist. He bent at the knees and drove upward, spearing her flesh with his cock. She arched against him, her cunt stretching for him. He pulled out and lunged forward again. Her sheath fit snugly around him, hot and drenched with her cream. He set a furious pace, needing to fuck her, to make them both scream. At the back of his mind he knew they were playing with fire. Anyone could come along. Not only was this a make-out spot, it was part of a walking trail, it was the perfect area for a picnic and it was a sunny day.

Dipping his head, he claimed Jessica's red lips, forcing his tongue inside her mouth. Her tongue wrapped around his as her nails dug into the front of his chest. He groaned into her mouth as her pussy clenched around his cock. She was close. He could feel it in the urgency of her kiss and the bucking of her hips.

Out of nowhere, Cade's face swam into his mind. Did he fuck her like this? Hard and fast and with the risk of being caught?

Brett adjusted the angle of his hips, letting his cock hit

Jessica differently. Her cry of pleasure, muffled at the back of his throat, assured him he'd hit the right spot, the point that made any girl melt. Did Cade know how to reach that pillowed zone? Could he make her writhe like this, naked and sweating beneath the sun? Brett didn't understand why, but he ached to know the answers.

Another thought crept into his mind and he ripped his mouth from Jessica's. "What about Cade?" he rasped in her ear.

"What about him?" Her voice sounded far away through the rush of blood in his ears.

"Would he mind us doing this?"

"What? Fucking?" Her breathless laugh vibrated in her belly and nearly did him in.

He clamped his jaw together and held on. When the desperate urge to come passed, he nodded. "Yeah, fucking."

She laughed again and her pussy tightened deliciously around his cock. "No, he wouldn't mind," she said, the pitch of her voice rising with every syllable. "He's the sharing kind of guy."

He's the sharing kind of guy. Those words rolled across Brett's mind over and over as Jessica's cunt rippled and then clutched him. She screamed, her whole body stiffening as she came. Burying his head in the crook of her neck, he followed her over the edge, allowing the spasms of her cunt to milk him dry.

It was past seven by the time Cade's car rolled through the gates of Steeplecrest Ranch. Keeping one hand on the wheel, he dragged his other over his exhausted face. Eight hours on the road in one day was hell, even in a car as sleek as this one. He had the air con on at full blast but his shirt stuck to his skin and the leather of his seat burned in the stifling heat. Only now, as the sun disappeared below the horizon, did he feel any measure of relief.

The hellish day had been worth it though, he was forced to admit, remembering the excitable mahogany bay mare he'd bought before leaving El Paso. A beautiful animal. Her dark eyes and glossy mane had stolen his heart at first glance. She was excitable, but he'd have her trained fast and she had plenty of potential. He'd had the pleasure of taking her for a short ride around her paddock and had felt her power beneath him.

A thrill of anticipation shot through him. She'd be here within the week. Now all he had to do was break the news to Brett. He knew she was worth every penny he'd paid for her, but convincing Brett that the money had been spent wisely wouldn't be easy.

Figuring he better get it over with, he continued on to Brett's house instead of taking the turn for his place. As he approached, he spotted a red car in the yard out front. He got even closer and realized it was a Beamer. Hot damn, who was Brett entertaining in there?

He parked alongside it and got out of his car, admiring the beautiful red vehicle as he headed toward the house. He climbed the porch steps, opened the screen door and pressed the doorbell. Brett pulled open the door in less than a second, barefoot and looking more relaxed than Cade had ever seen him.

"Hey," he greeted, stepping past the other man into the house and catching a whiff of his cologne, a woody scent that haunted Cade's dreams. His wet dreams, at least. "Who owns the car?"

Brett didn't answer, just cocked his head toward the

kitchen. His relaxed expression had tightened into wariness.

Cade walked on and stepped through the open door of the kitchen. There, curled up on one of the kitchen chairs, sat Jess. She glanced up from her coffee, caught his eye and squealed.

"There you are," she cried, jumping out of the chair and pouncing on him. "What the hell took you so long?"

He blinked in amazement and then started to laugh. "What are you doing all the way up here?"

"I wanted to surprise you."

"Well, you sure did that." He wrapped his arms around her, holding her against him. It seemed like a hell of a long time since he'd had a woman in his arms. Dipping his head, he brushed his lips over hers. "When did you get here?"

"This afternoon." She peered over his shoulder and grinned. "Don't worry, Brett took care of me."

From the mischievous sparkle in her blue eyes, Brett had done a lot more than take care of her.

"I'll bet he did," Cade laughed, turning to glance at the other man. Shifting from foot to foot, gaze fixed on a point on the floor, Brett looked as if he wanted the ground to open up and swallow him.

"Uh, you want me to get your stuff, Jess?" Brett asked, lifting his head but still adorably shamefaced. He didn't wait for an answer, just turned and headed out of the kitchen.

A giggle fell from Jess's lips and she shook her head. "He's so proper."

"Old-fashioned values."

"Oh." Jess's face fell and her eyes turned pitiful. "So no luck for you yet?"

"Nope." He shrugged. "Not expecting it to happen, to be honest."

"Hey, don't give up hope yet." She leaned in, dropping her voice to a whisper. "He is *seriously* good."

Cade groaned, jealousy rising within him. "Lucky bitch."

Brett's return cut the conversation short. He handed Jess a bag and looked at Cade almost defensively. "She needed to use my shower."

The desperate guilt swimming in Brett's eyes had Cade biting the insides of his cheeks to keep from laughing. "That's very nice of you, Brett," he said when he could speak without breaking into hysterics. "I really appreciate you looking after her so good."

Brett's gaze darted away, his whole body stiffening. Cade choked down a laugh and grabbed Jess's arm. "Say goodbye, sweetheart."

"'Bye, Brett," she called as Cade dragged her down the hallway. "I'll see you soon."

The two of them fell out of the house. Once the door shut behind them they dissolved into laughter.

"I've never seen anyone look so guilty before," Jess said when they'd pulled themselves together. "Even when we were fucking, he felt bad."

"How could anyone feel bad about fucking you?" he asked, walking her to her car. "You're too darn gorgeous."

She lifted her shoulders in a shrug and slid into the Beemer. "It's the first time a guy has ever asked me about another guy during sex," she said, looking at him meaningfully.

"What do you mean?"

"He had me against his truck, his cock was inside me and he wanted to know if you'd be okay with it."

"Ah, he's just that kind of guy."

"Even so—" she turned the key in the ignition and the

engine purred, "—you were on his mind. That's gotta mean something."

He hesitated, his mind processing her meaning. Then he shook it off. "You women always overanalyze everything."

"Fine then, don't listen to me." She winked at him. "I'll see you back at yours."

"Yeah." He watched the red car shoot down the drive toward his place. Her words stuck in his mind, playing on repeat in his brain. *"You were on his mind. That's gotta mean something."* He glanced back at Brett's house and sighed. With all his being, he wished Jess was right.

Jessica rested her tush on the hood of her car as she waited for Cade to arrive. Funny how the day had panned out. When she'd boarded the plane at JFK, she'd been looking forward to a few days of wild, hedonistic sex. She hadn't counted on starting the vacation off with Brett, and boy had he set her off with a bang. She couldn't wait to fill Cade in on all the juicy details, from the veined thickness of Brett's cock to how his calloused fingers had felt digging into her waist.

Besides the sex, Brett had turned out to be quite the surprise. She'd expected arrogance, coolness, a blunt tongue. But he'd been the perfect Southern gentleman, ensuring she was fed and watered and comfortable before he'd given her the ride of her life. He cared about Cade too. She'd noted that pretty fast. Though he'd never come out and said it, she'd seen the warmth in his eyes while they'd talked about Cade. And when Brett had asked her about Cade mid-sex, she'd known the guy's feelings for her friend ran a hell of a lot deeper than she'd initially believed.

As Cade's black Lexus finally came into view, she stood and watched him park. When he got out of the car his face was a mask of concentration. His brows furrowed into a deep V and he was slapping his Stetson against his thigh in an even rhythm. She didn't need three guesses to know where his mind was. It was right back at Brett Miller's house.

"Did Brett feed you?" he asked, when they entered the house.

She dropped her bag on the floor while he stood her suitcase by the stairs. "He did. More than once."

Cade slanted her a teasing look. "I'm not talking about sex."

She laughed, glancing around the hallway. Cade had taken down the majority of picture frames, vases and decorative pieces since her last visit. The house now looked reasonably masculine, except for the floral wallpaper covering the walls. She took the changes as a sign he was making this place his home. He was settling in.

She walked through the hall and into the spacious kitchen. "You tired?" she asked, swiveling on her heel to face him.

He was watching her the way he always did before they fucked. His blue eyes darkened to the color of a deep ocean and swept over her body. His gaze, so intense she could feel it piercing through her clothes to her skin, roamed from her feet to the top of her head, then returned to her eyes.

"Did I tell you how good you're looking, Jess?"

She smiled, knowing there was no way he'd want to wait. She couldn't figure how he could live so close to Brett, spend so much time with him, and not lose his mind. His sexual frustration was probably at a level that she couldn't imagine. She couldn't wait to tap that.

With her insides clenching in anticipation, she walked

toward him and then ducked around his body. "Let's go upstairs," she said, taking his hand.

His eyes flared as he followed her out to the hall. She turned away from him and began to ascend the staircase, then gasped when his hand touched the back of her knees. Pausing between steps, she closed her eyes, letting his hand stroke upward, caressing her inner thigh.

"Keep moving," he ordered, his voice thick with desire.

She forced herself forward, climbing slowly as his hand rose farther beneath her dress. He knew her body better than anyone, knew exactly how to touch her. They reached the top of the stairs and the backs of his fingers brushed her damp panties.

The way he propelled her forward into his bedroom so she stumbled and fell onto the end of the king-size bed told her how badly he wanted her. And as he dragged his fingers back and forth along the strip of material between her legs and said "Spread open for me, baby" in a voice husky with sex, she wondered how many times he'd imagined Brett growling those exact words. Pressing the length of his middle finger against her seam, he pushed the thin cotton between the swollen lips of her pussy. He caught the material and drew it along her opening, creating a friction that had moisture pooling in her cunt.

She rose up on hands and knees and blew out a long breath. "You're taking your time."

"I want to draw it out." He paused. "It's been a while."

"No pussy around these parts?" she asked, then bit her lip when the material of her panties caught on her clit.

"Brett keeps me busy."

She smirked. "Not the way you want him to."

"No," he agreed.

He pushed her dress over her hips and air flowed around her thighs, cooling her skin. He removed his hand from between her legs and the delicious sounds of buttons popping and his belt being unbuckled permeated the silence.

"You want me to suck you?" she asked, staring straight ahead at the dark mahogany headboard.

"Later." The bed dipped behind her as he climbed onto the mattress. "I want to be inside you first."

She whimpered, shifting her knees on the covers so her legs spread farther apart. He settled himself behind her, the hair on his thighs tickling the smooth skin of hers. The heat of his cock burned her skin, the swollen head probing the line of her buttocks.

More moisture sluiced through her pussy and her inner muscles clenched in hunger. He leaned over her, his hard chest pressing against her back. Bracing his hands on either side of her shoulders, he dipped his face into her neck. He inhaled deeply and let out a groan of anguish as his cock leaped insistently against her ass.

"You smell like him," he ground out at her neck. "You used his shower gel?"

The strain in his voice caught her off-guard. Christ, he wanted Brett bad, more than she'd realized. "Uh huh." Her whole body shook as his erection pulsed against her bare skin. Cream seeped from her cunt. "I used his shower gel and then I dried off with his towel." She pushed her ass back, rubbing herself along his dick. "Does that make you hot?"

His low chuckle lacked any trace of humor. "What do you think?"

She squirmed beneath him. "Come on, Cade, you're killing both of us here."

He lifted one hand from the bed and wrapped it around his

cock. Slowly, he guided himself inside her pussy. She held her breath as the broad head invaded her, followed by his impressive length. He slid right to the hilt and stilled.

"How many times did he fuck you?"

She closed her eyes, his question setting her body on fire. "Once," she answered.

He pulled out and then entered her again, inch by sweet inch. His breath tickled her ear as he whispered, "Where?"

"Just outside town. He said it was called Johnston's Point." Cade's cock swelled inside her and she shuddered. "He fucked me against his truck."

"You were outside?" Cade's breathing grew labored, thrusting his hips forward again. "Someone could have caught you."

Her juices trickled down her thigh and she nodded. "I know."

Cade bit her shoulder, a groan rumbling in his chest. "Tell me how he did it," he said, voice strained. "I need to know."

She gripped the sheets as memories of the afternoon tryst flashed in her mind. "It was fast," she gasped, remembering the powerful snap of Brett's hips. "And hard."

Cade drew back and then drove inside her, making her cry out with the abrupt change of pace.

"Like that?" he asked.

She bit her lip and shook her head. "Harder."

He thrust inside her again, the force making her arms and legs tremble.

"Even harder," she gasped.

This time the power behind his entry made her head spin. She could barely hear her scream through the pounding of blood in her head. Her arms collapsed as Cade fucked her as hard as Brett had earlier that day, their thrusts almost identical in speed and force. She rested her cheek on the bed, her cunt squeezing Cade's cock in ripples of pleasure.

"Was it like this?" he asked, his tone urgent.

"Yes, just like this." Beads of sweat dripped down her neck and between her breasts which were flattened against the mattress. "He doesn't do gentle." She swallowed, her throat parched. "He knows how to fuck a girl."

"What did he say to you?"

Her vision blurred, pressure building in the pit of her stomach. "Not much. He's quiet during sex—" She broke off as her orgasm exploded inside her, the waves of release fanning outward through her body. Cade stayed with her through her climax, his cock still rock hard as he pumped his hips in an unrelenting rhythm.

Eventually, the waves eased and she could speak again. "The only words he—" She gasped for breath as Cade's cock stroked her tender flesh. "The only time he spoke during the whole thing was when he—when he asked about you."

"What did he say?"

"He wanted to know if you'd mind, if the two of us fucking would bother you." She cut off as a second orgasm took hold inside her. Feeling Cade's harsh breaths against her neck, she forced herself to finish. "He never—he never said my name." She swallowed thickly, a haze clouding her head. "But," she whispered, hoping he could hear her, "he said *yours*."

Cade's tortured groan filled her ears and this time as she rode the wave of her orgasm, Cade followed her over the edge, coming harder than he ever had before with her. When he finally collapsed over her spent body, anguish radiated from his skin.

"What is it?" she asked, twisting beneath him. Reaching

up, she stroked his cheek. "What is it, honey?"

He shook his head and fell onto the bed beside her. "I don't know," he said quietly. "Sometimes I just—sometimes I want him so bad I can't handle it. It eats at me. I can't make it stop."

She rolled onto her side and rubbed his defined stomach, wishing she could take his pain away. Knowing nothing she could say would be of any help, she curled up against him and hoped the heat of her body would help him to sleep tonight. Maybe in his dreams he'd have what he wanted so badly. Brett.

"You did what?" Brett demanded, unable to believe what he was hearing. He stared at Cade whose relaxed stance aggravated him even more. "You handed over that much money and you didn't think to tell me about it?"

"I'm telling you now," Cade drawled, his gaze following Brett as he paced the length of the stables. "She's a real beauty, Brett. Worth every penny."

"I don't care what she's worth," Brett seethed, fists clenching into balls at his sides. One of the horses whinnied, obviously picking up on his rage. He took a deep breath in an effort to calm himself. "You should have called first," he said through gritted teeth. "You should have held off on the deal until you talked to me."

"Yeah," Cade sighed. "I know."

Brett's eyes widened. He hadn't expected the other man to back down so fast. But then again, Cade already had what he wanted—the horse.

The anger flared inside him again and he stormed into the yard, muttering curses under his breath. He didn't need this right now. Cade sneaking around behind his back left a bad taste in his mouth. Coupled with a sleepless night, all he wanted to do was throw his fist into something hard.

He rubbed a weary hand over his jaw and stopped in the middle of the yard. He'd tossed and turned all night, unable to get a wink of sleep when the wheels of his mind had refused to quit turning. His imagination had run riot, conjuring up images of Cade and Jessica together, doing whatever the hell they were doing while he lay awake in his bed. Fucking torture. And when Cade had rambled into the paddock that morning, later than usual and wearing the satisfied expression of a man who'd gotten well and truly laid, Brett's fury had hit him full-force.

Fury? he wondered now as he stared blindly ahead. *Or is it jealousy?* Whatever he was feeling, it made him pathetic. He had no reason to be jealous. Hell, he'd fucked Jessica yesterday afternoon and Cade hadn't raised an eyebrow.

The thud of boots on the ground behind him cut into his thoughts.

"Listen," Cade started, tone apologetic. "What happened yesterday won't happen again."

Is he talking about the horse or Jessica? Brett sincerely hoped he was referring to the horse.

"Forget about it," he said stiffly. He yanked his hat from his head and faced the other man. "Why don't you take off? I'm sure your guest would appreciate some company."

Cade broke into a grin. "I'd bet my bottom dollar she's still in bed. Jet lag and all that."

Brett narrowed his eyes. *Jet lag or a long night?*

Cade's grin widened as if he was reading his mind. "She's really something, ain't she?"

Feeling slightly uncomfortable that Cade knew he'd fucked his girl, Brett looked at the ground and nodded. "Yeah."

"Hey, don't look so guilty." Cade brought his hand down on his shoulder. "No hard feelings."

"Sure." Despite the assurances, Brett still couldn't bring himself to look him in the eye.

"You should come over tonight?"

"Huh?" Taken aback, he glanced up. "Come over?"

"Yeah. I'm going to fire up the barbecue, cook a couple of steaks, nothing fancy." Cade waggled his eyebrows. "Jess sure would love your company."

Brett's brow furrowed as he studied Cade's friendly expression for a hint of hostility. Was this guy serious? He wanted the three of them to eat together tonight even though both he and Cade had fucked Jessica in the past twenty-four hours?

"Okay, I'm going to take your silence as a yes," Cade decided, backing up toward the stable. "I'm going to set up a stall for Marci. I'll catch you later."

At the mention of Marci, their new acquisition, Brett's insides tightened in frustration again, distracting him from what he'd just been signed up for. He shook the feeling off, then felt a tension of a different kind settle in the pit of his stomach. Dinner tonight with Cade and Jessica. He couldn't think of a more uncomfortable scenario.

Chapter Six

That evening as the sun lowered in the sky, Brett trekked across the fields of Steeplecrest Ranch, shortcutting a path to Cade's house. Armed with beer and a heavy dose of caution, he felt more confident than he'd expected to, though he still had the uneasy suspicion he was walking into a warzone.

He approached the house from the back and soon the sounds of cutlery, chatter and sizzling meat reached his ears. Once he jumped over the last fence, the backyard came into view. Jessica lay sprawled out on a lounger, sunglasses perched on the top of her head. In just a tank top and a denim mini-skirt, she looked good enough to eat.

His gaze roamed her bare legs from the hem of the skirt to her red toenails, then skipped back up to the swell of her breasts that were covered by the white cotton of her top. The top stopped just below her navel, exposing a strip of smooth, tanned midriff. His mouth watered at the thought of tasting her skin.

He shoved past the bushes and into the backyard. Seeing his approach, Jessica sat up and waved, a bright smile curving her lips.

"Hey there, cowboy," she greeted, whipping her long legs over the side of the lounger and slinking to her feet. "Cade," she called, keeping her sparkling eyes on Brett, "our guest is here."

Cade appeared at the kitchen door, plates in hand. He jumped down the veranda steps and left the plates beside the barbecue.

"Take a seat," he said, gesturing to the garden chairs that surrounded a patio table. "Food's almost up."

The aroma of barbecued steak teased Brett's nostrils and his stomach growled. He smiled sheepishly and lifted the beers. "Where do you want these?"

"I'll take one," Jess said, selecting a bottle.

He watched her uncap it then take a long sip. Her delicate throat worked as she swallowed and he felt his jeans tighten. Sitting, he took a beer for himself. Here less than two minutes and he already needed a cold drink.

"I hope you're hungry," Jess said, bottle dangling from her fingers as she took the chair beside him. She sat, twisting her body toward him and then crossed one leg over the other. The move displayed a flash of black panties and he downed another gulp of beer.

"Yeah, I'm hungry," he said, answering her question.

As if on cue, Cade set a plate of steak in front of him. "Dig in."

Brett nodded. "Thanks." He grabbed a fork and knife from the center of the table and cut into the meat. "How did you spend your day?" he asked Jessica after he'd swallowed his first bite. "Bored?"

"Not at all." She leaned back in her chair, stretching her legs out in front of her. Her colorful toes brushed his boots. "I sunbathed and read for a while."

"Jess doesn't take a lot of vacations," Cade explained, bringing over two plates of food for him and Jessica and pulling up a chair. "So when she gets a break she does zilch."

"Zilch?" she questioned, slanting a glance in Cade's direction. "Is that what I was doing last night?"

"Or yesterday afternoon?" Brett wondered. Trying to ignore the images of Jessica's naked body that flashed across his mind, he focused on his food.

They ate in silence for a few minutes, each focusing on the tender steak. After ingesting the last bite, Brett hooked his arm over the back of his chair and sighed. "I have to admit," he said lightly, "that was good, Armstrong."

Cade gave a bark of laughter. "Do you have to sound so surprised?"

Brett shrugged, grinning. With food lining his stomach and alcohol buzzing in his bloodstream, the tension in his stomach was slowly dissipating.

Shifting his attention back to Jessica, he watched awestruck as a morsel of steak disappeared between her lips. "So how long are you sticking around for?" he asked her, ignoring the heaviness in his balls.

"A couple of days."

He frowned. "You came all the way down here for a couple of days?"

She smiled and patted Cade's knee. "I had to check on this guy, see if you're treating him okay."

Brett glanced at the other man in surprise. "And am I treating him okay?"

Cade smirked and met his eyes as Jessica tapped her finger to her chin thoughtfully. "I think so," she said after a few moments of pondering. "But he's so tense these days." She slid out of her chair and moved around Cade, rubbing his shoulders. "You could bring him out on the town one of these nights, help him get laid."

Brett choked on a mouthful of beer and Cade chuckled.

"I don't need any help getting laid, sweetheart," he told Jessica, pulling her in front of him and slapping her on the ass. "As a matter of fact, I've had to help him out a couple of times."

Jessica swiveled to face Brett, humor shining in her eyes. "Oh really?"

Remembering the redhead from Billy's, Brett squirmed in his seat. "That was one time and I was wasted."

Jessica giggled, shaking her head in mock despair. "I don't know what I'm going to do with you boys."

"How about you feed us?" Cade suggested, looking up at her. "I think it's time for dessert."

"Mmm. I think so too." She danced out of his embrace and skipped up the steps into the kitchen. Less than a minute later she reappeared with pie.

"It's apple," she said, slicing a knife through the golden pastry. "Cade had some apples in the kitchen so I thought I'd bake something sweet."

She passed Brett a slice and he dug hungrily into the dessert. At the first sweet taste, he closed his eyes. "This is real good, darlin'," he said, barely glancing up from his plate. "Thanks."

"You're welcome."

A few seconds later, Cade added his thanks. "Where the hell did you learn to bake?" he demanded through a mouthful of pie.

"I took a class in New York."

"You took a class?"

Brett laughed at the disbelief in Cade's voice.

"Yes, I took a class," Jessica said defensively. She shrugged. "The teacher was really cute."

"Now that explains it," Cade said, a smug expression on his face. He winked at Brett. "She can't help herself. She's a fucking nympho."

Brett didn't say anything, but he wondered if he'd get to see the nymphomaniac streak tonight. He sure as hell wanted to.

They sat enjoying the evening heat for another hour or so. They talked about the World Series, Jessica's job and her family. Brett settled into the easy atmosphere, unable to help laughing at Jessica's outrageous stories. She was a wild cat, lived life on the edge. It became clear as crystal to him that a girl like this would never settle down, hence her commitment-free relationship with Cade.

At nine, Jessica jumped to her feet and gathered the dishes.

"Here," he said, getting up too. "Let me help you."

"No need. I'm just going to stack these in the sink." She carried them toward the kitchen, calling out as she went, "Cade, why don't you take Brett into the living room and turn on the TV. I really want to catch that movie."

"You game for a movie?" Cade asked, stretching his arms over his head.

"You don't want me to get out of your hair?"

"It's good to have you here."

Deciding to take the guy's word for it, Brett stayed. In the living room he took the sofa by the window while Cade and Jessica curled up on the one opposite the TV. The movie, an action thriller full of violence and graphic sex, barely held his attention. He was aware of the couple sitting so close at all times. He had no idea what they were doing in the dark and he itched to turn his head and find out. But he refused to give in and stared straight ahead.

When the credits rolled he turned slowly and found Cade and Jess innocently reading the list of actors.

"I knew that was him," Jessica said, putting a bowl of popcorn onto the coffee table. "I really liked that movie. What did you think, Brett?"

He shrugged, barely able to remember the main character's name. "I guess it was okay."

Cade shook his head. "I thought it would be better. The ending sucked." As he spoke, Cade's arm dropped from where it had been casually draped across the back of the sofa to the other side of Jessica's body. He stroked the curve of her waist and then lifted his hand to her breast. As he squeezed the small mound, Brett held his breath.

"Uh, I should go," he said, rising to his feet and tearing his gaze from Cade's hand.

"Oh, stay a while," Jessica pouted. She let her knees fall open suggestively while sliding her left hand between Cade's thighs. Brett's cock stiffened in his pants. "It's still so early. We haven't even gotten started yet."

We haven't even gotten started yet. Did he even want to know what she meant by that? He took in Jessica's pleading expression and then glanced at Cade who was still watching the credits as he fondled Jessica's breast. They both looked completely at ease, as if this was normal.

Maybe it's normal for them.

As his pants became even more constricted, Jessica's statement repeated in his mind. *We haven't even gotten started yet.*

He wanted to know what she meant. He wanted to know more than anything.

Slowly, he backed up to the sofa at the window and

resumed his seating position. *What the hell am I letting myself in for?*

Warm lust threaded Cade's veins as out of the corner of his eye he watched Brett sit back down on the sofa, shoulders squared and feet flat on the floor. He looked as if he was ready to jump up and dart out the door at any second. The typical fight-or-flight response. Despite his obvious apprehension, he'd decided to fight and the victory sent little thrills up and down Cade's spine.

The man he'd been lusting after for as long as he could remember had agreed to stay, to take part in the sexual games they had planned for the evening. He hadn't dared to dream Brett would agree to stay. The man saw things in black and white. One woman and one man. Cade and Jessica were going to smash that illusion to pieces tonight and Cade couldn't wait.

Keeping one hand on Jessica's breast, he reached for the remote control and clicked the off button. The picture on the TV screen faded to black and they were plunged into silence, a silence punctuated by Jessica's unsteady breaths. He circled her nipple through her tank top and then pinched the hard tip. A soft sigh fell from her lips and she smiled up at him. A question lighted her eyes. *You want to start now?*

He gave a curt nod. Of course he wanted to start now. Did she think he could hold out any longer with Brett sitting so close? He wasn't made of steel.

Her hand continued to stroke the thickening bulge in his pants. "Take off your shirt," she said, loud enough for Brett to hear.

With his free hand, he popped open the buttons of his shirt one by one. When he'd slipped the last button out of its eyelet, Jess removed her hand from his dick and lifted her body into his lap. She straddled his thighs, digging her knees into the cushions on either side of his body. Parting the lapels of his shirt, she ducked her head to taste his skin. Her tongue, warm and wet, licked a trail down his chest. As she sucked at his belly button, he was painfully aware of Brett's eyes on them. Did watching the foreplay turn him on? Was his dick as hard as Cade's? Was he touching himself?

Unable to help himself, Cade's gaze darted toward the other man. Brett's eyes met his, and even from across the room Cade could see how dilated the pupils were. Just about to drop his gaze to Brett's crotch, he almost groaned as Jessica straightened in his lap and blocked the view.

A knowing glint sparkled in her eyes and she looked over her shoulder. "I think Brett could use a hand," she sang, sliding from Cade's lap.

With his cock battling against the tight prison of his jeans, Cade watched her saunter toward the other sofa. She lifted her skirt another inch up her thighs and climbed on top of Brett.

"What about you, honey? You going to take off your clothes?" she asked, bracing her hands on his shoulders. Cade shifted on the sofa to get a better view. He watched a smirk twist Brett's lips as the man clasped his large hands around Jessica's waist.

"You first," he drawled.

Cade's cock jerked in his pants.

"Okay then," Jess agreed, her voice full of laughter. She lifted the hem of her top and whipped it over her head. Cade drank in the smooth lines of her back and wondered how hard her nipples were. Then Brett leaned forward and pressed his head to her tits. A sucking sound rose in the air.

Unable to bear the discomfort, Cade ripped open his belt and tugged his zipper down. He reached into his jeans and pulled out his cock. A few quick strokes eased the need to empty his balls. Keeping his hand wrapped around his shaft, he settled back and let Jess's breathy moans tease his ears.

At the rasp of another zipper, he straightened, his gaze catching on the gap between Jess's ass and Brett's thighs. Knowing what Cade needed to see, Jess lifted her ass farther as she released Brett's cock from the confines of his pants. The thick stalk of Brett's dick came into view and Cade clamped a hand to his balls. He ached to get up, to cross the room and push Jess to the side. To suck that cock down his throat, to feel Brett's shaft pulsing on his tongue. He swallowed as Jess rose even higher and gathered her skirt around her hips. The entire length of Brett's cock filled Cade's eyes and a groan stuck in his throat. In the well-lit living room he appeared even bigger than he had that night in Billy's parking lot. Thick, straight and plum-red in color. The stalk flared outward at the head, reminding Cade of a large lollipop, a lollipop his mouth watered to suck on.

He held his breath as Jess pushed her panties to the side and lowered her hips, her pussy swallowing Brett's cock inch by inch. It was almost painful to watch but it struck Cade as the most beautiful thing he'd ever seen. He gripped his own dick in one hand and ground the other against his balls. He didn't want to come. Not yet, not until he saw Brett come first.

Jess's moans of delight grew louder as she rode Brett's cock. He let her set the pace at first, a lazy ride that gave Cade a perfect view of her pink cunt parting for Brett's shaft. But then Brett's hands lowered to her ass and gripped her buttocks as he started to jerk his hips upward. Jess's moans became cries as Brett's cock met her pussy on the down stroke and witnessing the power in Brett's thrusts nearly did Cade in. He clamped his jaw together, summoning all his strength to hold back from the edge. Jess had been right, Brett was quiet during sex. Unable to see the other man's face, Cade couldn't guess how close he was to coming.

He had to know. He had to go over there.

Shaking legs carried him slowly across the pinewood floor to the other sofa. He could see Brett clearly now. The man's face was tight, controlled. His eyes were fixed on Jess's face as she slammed down on his dick. Cade circled them and gave his dick another quick stroke. Brett's gaze flickered to Cade's cock and the motion of his hips slowed. Not wanting to distract the guy, Cade was ready to step back but then Brett's hard thrusts resumed as he looked back at Jess.

"Looks like Cade here needs a little help," he muttered, his voice matching his tight face.

Hearing his name on the other man's lips had little shocks of pleasure darting down his spine. Cade stood at one end of the sofa and shifted his focus to Jess. Her face was a mask of pleasure—glassy eyes, bottom lip caught between her teeth, a sheen of sweat covering her skin. She met his eyes and smiled shakily.

"Can we switch positions, Brett?" she gasped, stretching out a hand to Cade.

"Sure, darlin'." With an ease that came as a surprise to Cade, Brett lifted Jess off him and set her down at the end of the sofa. Only the armrest separated her from Cade.

She maneuvered herself onto her knees and braced her hands on the armrest. Cade watched Brett settle behind her, his cock probing between Jess's thighs. He lifted her slightly and then plunged inside her pussy. Her head jerked back and she cried out.

"Easy, sweetheart," Cade soothed, cupping her face in his hands. Her head dropped and her gaze cleared. She was eyelevel with his cock and her eyes widened when she saw how hard he was.

"Poor Cade," she whispered, running her tongue over her lips. "Let me take care of you."

He stepped forward and held her head steady as he pressed the head of his cock to her mouth. Her lips parted immediately and he slid across her tongue into the warm cavern of her mouth. She started to suck, keeping her lips locked tightly around his shaft. He began to move his hips, sliding back and forth over her tongue. His gaze shifted from where Jess swallowed his cock to where Brett's dick was disappearing inside her cunt. So close now, he could see the veins on Brett's cock each time he slid out. They ran alongside the shaft, bulging with the heavy thrum of blood. That cock had to feel good inside Jess, those ridges would stroke every inch of her flesh. Cade wished he could feel it too, pushing past the barrier of his ass.

A prickle of awareness crept up his neck and he tore his gaze from Brett's cock to find the man watching him. He swallowed thickly at the black desire in Brett's eyes. Did he know what was going through Cade's mind? Did he know how badly he wanted him?

"She feels good, doesn't she?" he forced the words out, studying Brett's face for a reaction.

A small smile appeared at the corner of his mouth as he nodded sharply. "Sure does."

Cade closed his eyes as the combination of Brett's harsh voice and Jess's hot mouth undid him. He tunneled his hands into her silky hair and let out a low moan as his come spurted into her mouth and down her throat. She continued to suck him, swallowing the last of his essence. He forced open his eyes, needing to see Brett's end. His hips still pumped against Jess's, but more erratically now. His face tightened further. He was going to come.

Cade's cock leaped back to life in Jess's mouth as Brett's fingers dug into her hips. Abruptly, she released Cade from her mouth and screamed as Brett entered her in a powerful thrust. As her body jerked, Brett went completely still. Cade watched hypnotized as Brett buried his head against Jess's neck. Not a sound escaped his lips as he came. The only evidence of his climax was a short snap of his hips a couple of seconds later. Cade waited for Brett to lift his head, breath leaving his body in heavy rasps. His whole body shook, his cock pulsing again. Jess's hand found his and she squeezed. Finally, Brett pulled back and shifted into a sitting position on the sofa. Jess lifted her head, a satisfied grin playing on her lips. She winked at Cade and then slid into Brett's lap, patting the space she'd just vacated for Cade to sit. With his cock stretching outward from the opening in his jeans, he walked stiffly around the armrest and sank onto the cushion.

Their breathing gradually steadied as the minutes ticked by. Then Jess pushed to her feet, shimmied out of her skirt and stretched her arms right above her head. The move lifted her breasts into two tempting mounds. "Okay boys, I need the little girls' room. Be back in a sec." Bare-ass naked, she danced out of the room leaving the two men alone.

Cade snuck a glance at Brett out of the corner of his eye. The man's head rested against the sofa, his eyes staring straight ahead.

"You do this often?" he asked, not meeting Cade's gaze. "Bring in someone else, I mean."

"Yeah."

"Why?" This time Brett's eyes slanted in his direction.

Taking in the mix of curiosity and uncertainty in Brett's expression, Cade shrugged, playing it cool. "It makes Jessica hot," he said simply, stretching his arm over the back of the sofa. "What makes Jessica hot, makes me hot." He left out the fact that he usually fucked the third too. Brett wasn't ready to hear that yet and Cade wasn't sure he ever would be.

He looked down at his left thigh. Only a hair's breadth separated him from Brett. He could feel the man's body heat radiating off him and his cock twitched. He wondered what Brett thought of the fact that Cade had a hard-on even though Jess had carted her naked ass upstairs. Did he even notice? If he did, was it bugging him?

Cade let his gaze drift over Brett's thigh to his groin. The tip of his half-hard cock peeked out of his jeans. He wasn't limp either.

Cade didn't get the chance to mull that over. Jess returned to the room and dropped a small bag by the sofa. She smiled wickedly at him and he leaned back against the cushions. She had plenty more in store for them and he couldn't wait to find out what she had up her sleeve.

Anticipation buzzed in Jessica's veins as she drank in the sight of her two lovers sitting side by side. Cade's expression matched her feelings—excited, curious and aroused. Brett's expression was darker, more restrained, but she detected the lust in the depths of his black eyes and she didn't miss the twitch of his dick as she sashayed toward them.

They sat so close together she could rest her knees between each of their denim-clad legs. She sat back, one buttock on Cade's knee and the other on Brett's.

"I thought you boys would need more rest time," she said, eyeing Cade's hard cock and Brett's stiffening erection. "I see I was wrong."

Brett rubbed his calloused hand over her thigh. His rough

touch provoked a heavy rush of desire inside her and she squirmed. His hand slid higher and cupped her pussy.

"You're ready to go too," he said, surprise lacing his tone. He slipped one long finger inside her dripping cunt. "What do you want to do now?"

She sensed the courage it took for him to ask that question. A battle of wills roared in his eyes. Part of him hated the lack of control, despised it. The other part, the *larger* part she guessed, wanted to stay, to discover what other pleasures she and Cade could introduce him to.

She tilted her head to the side and reached out to touch his mouth. Running the pad of her thumb along his full bottom lip, she sighed. She knew what she wanted to do.

She slithered to the floor and settled herself directly in front of Brett. Placing her hands on each of his knees, she pushed them apart. "I wanna taste you," she whispered, leaning in to his bobbing cock. She opened her mouth and closed her lips around the plum-shaped head. The salty taste of his skin made her tongue tingle and his musky essence mixed with her juices filled her mouth as she slowly slid her lips down his shaft. It was a potent combination, one that had cream coating her pussy.

She took him to the back of her throat and then angled back to take even more of him. When her nose brushed the wiry curls at the base of his sex, she inhaled his masculine scent. She loved sucking cock, loved it almost more than she loved being eaten out. The sense of power it gave her as she licked and sucked a man dry thrilled her very bones. And this particular cock, so long and thick, was a particularly tasty treat.

She bobbed her head up and down rhythmically, laving her tongue along the veined underside then swirling the tip around the swollen head. Brett's fingers weaved into her hair, holding her head in place as she sucked him greedily. She moaned around his cock as he tugged on her hair. He wanted her up. He didn't want to come yet.

This time she decided to let him have his way. Reluctantly, she drew her lips up his cock and released the head with a wet-sounding pop. Looking up into his fiery eyes, she licked her lips. Her gaze danced to Cade, whose hand was wrapped tightly around his erection. "How hard is this for him?" she wondered, taking in the raw desire glittering in his blue eyes. Barely an inch separated his body from Brett's, they'd already taken part in a threesome tonight, but the glaring rule remained—Cade couldn't touch the other man and she was willing to bet it was killing him.

In time with her thoughts, Cade rose wearily to his feet. "I'm going to get something to drink," he said, quirking an eyebrow at her. She caught his drift. He needed a break.

She watched him go, admiring the view of his behind. Though leaner than Brett, his muscles were equally defined. His legs and arms were powerful. His whole torso was smooth while Brett's had a line of coarse dark hair stretching from his navel to his cock. He was deliciously fair while Brett was dark as sin. They made an extraordinarily appealing match and she ached to see them together, to watch the conflict as each man battled for the upper hand.

As Cade disappeared into the kitchen, she returned her attention to Brett and gave him a coy smile. "Why don't you throw me some cushions?" she suggested, scooting back into the center of the room. "And then come join me."

Brett's eyes sparked as he gathered some cushions and tossed them onto the floor. She arranged them in a pile around her as he approached.

"Take off your jeans," she told him, settling her head on one velvety cushion. Stretching her legs out in front of her, she watched Brett shove his pants down to his ankles. Long muscled legs dusted in dark hairs came into view and her blood hummed with excitement. His cock hung between his legs, heavy and rock-hard.

He stood over her, hands on his hips and a small smile quirking the corner of his mouth. He was starting to relax again.

"Where do you want me?" he drawled.

She patted the floor beside him. "As close to me as possible."

"I can do that, darlin'." He stretched out on the floor beside her and smoothed a palm over her belly. Her skin tingled and a rush of fresh moisture pooled in her cunt. "I don't think I've ever been this turned on," he admitted, gliding his fingertips over her hairless pussy.

"Really?" she asked, watching his face as he touched her. "Why's that?"

"I don't know." His eyes met hers and he smiled helplessly. "Like I said before, you're not like the girls round here."

"Are you sure it's me?"

His finger stilled. "What do you mean?"

"Maybe it's the kink," she said, studying him for a reaction. "You've never tried this before, have you? A threesome."

His lips pressed into a thin line. "You think it turns me on to have a guy in the room?"

Well, doesn't it? She longed to push him on the subject but she didn't want to scare him off. "Not at all," she laughed, threading her fingers into his silky black hair. "I just mean that it's a different scenario. I'm twice as hot as I would be if there was only one of you. My horniness is probably rubbing off on you."

He seemed to accept that and his fingers resumed their mission. He brushed a fingertip over the stiff button of her clit and she sucked in a breath.

"You sure know how to touch a woman, Brett Miller."

A grin curved his lips. "Well thank you, ma'am. Always happy to please."

She giggled and spread her legs wider to give him better access. He sank two fingers inside her pussy and began a slow pumping motion. Closing her eyes, she gave herself over to his hand. He strummed her pussy like a musician strummed a guitar, hitting all the right notes and making her blood sing. Hooking one finger back inside her cunt, he stroked the spot that made her writhe. Her hips jerked off the floor and her pussy rippled.

A couple of minutes later, the withdrawal of his fingers made her eyes snap open. He held her hypnotized as he brought his hand to his mouth and sucked her juices off each finger, one by one.

"You have the sweetest honey I've ever tasted," he told her, leaning over her body. "Anyone ever tell you that?"

"Cade tells me all the time." She knew she shouldn't tease him, but each time she mentioned Cade's name Brett's expression grew defensive. The change fascinated her.

To put him at ease, she lifted her head and pressed her lips to his. He hesitated for a second and then brushed his mouth back and forth over hers. The tip of his tongue probed the barrier of her lips and she opened for him, twining her tongue with his.

He kissed her softly at first, then harder, more urgently, as he rolled her over and pulled her on top of him. His cock throbbed against her stomach as his tongue thrust alongside hers, mimicking the act of sex. Moaning into his open mouth, she tried to shift her body upward so her pussy could catch on his cock. He slapped her lightly on the ass and broke the kiss.

"You're insatiable," he told her, his eyes hazy with desire.

"Me?" She sat up and glared pointedly at the erection that stretched to his navel. "What about you?"

Brett opened his mouth to reply and then paused. He looked past her shoulder and his eyes darkened. She didn't need to turn around to know Cade was standing behind them.

She fought a smile as she stumbled to her feet and twirled around to face Cade. "You're wearing too many clothes," she complained, pressing her body against his and tugging on the waistband of his jeans. "Take 'em off."

"Yes, ma'am." Cade kicked out of his jeans and stood, his erection jutting proudly from between his legs. His eyes sparkled with equal measures of lust and humor. The breather in the kitchen had done him good.

Spotting the bottles of water he'd left on the coffee table, she grabbed one and uncapped it. After downing half the bottle in one go, she passed it to Brett. As he guzzled the rest of the water, she slipped her arms around Cade's waist and rose on tiptoe to kiss his lips.

"You know what we haven't tried since I got here?" she asked, reaching between their bodies to stroke his burning cock.

His hand snaked around her waist and dropped to her ass, caressing it suggestively. He raised an eyebrow and she grinned. He knew exactly what they hadn't tried yet.

Untangling herself from his embrace, she took his hand and led him to the pile of cushions. Brett had vacated his spot on the floor and was standing by the coffee table where he'd started on another bottle of water.

Leaning back onto the cushions, she pulled Cade on top of her. His mouth claimed hers as his cock pressed against her pussy. She drew up her knees and rubbed herself against him as his tongue swept through her mouth. Then his lips left hers to trail kisses over her chin and down her throat. His cock jerked against her and realization struck.

"You haven't had any pussy yet," she said, tugging at his blond curls.

He raised his head and shot her a look of mock disapproval. "Ain't that the truth?"

She hooked her legs around his waist and drew him closer. "Well come on then," she teased. "Get it while it's hot."

He grinned at her choice of phrasing and then plunged inside her, all the way to the hilt. She bit her lip as her pussy contracted around him and he let out a groan.

"Easy, sweetheart."

She squirmed against him. "I can't help it."

He waited for her to settle and then started to rotate his hips, hitting her in the spots he knew so well. Her head rolled to the side and she caught Brett watching them from beneath hooded lids.

"Sit up, Cade," she urged him. "Brett can't touch me when I'm under you like this."

The mention of Brett's name made Cade's cock jump inside her. She shuddered and then followed his body as he rose onto his knees. Kneeling in front of him, she clutched his shoulders as he continued to thrust upward inside her. Cade's face turned to the side and he addressed Brett.

"Come here," he said, his steady voice belying the furious throbbing in his cock. "I'll show you how to touch her."

Brett's footsteps padded on the floor behind her as he approached. She caught her breath as she felt him kneel behind her, his body heat reacting with hers.

"Play with her ass," Cade instructed, his dick thickening even further inside her cunt. "She loves it."

Brett remained silent as his rough hand palmed her ass and she wished she could see his face. He squeezed the cheeks of her ass lightly, then slipped a finger between her buttocks and she jerked against Cade, biting at his jaw as Brett's finger sought out her puckered hole. He found it and circled the bud. Her juices gushed over Cade's cock.

"Put your finger inside her," Cade said, sounding slightly less in control as her cunt squeezed his dick. "Fuck her ass with your finger."

The head of Brett's cock, hot as hell, brushed the small of her back as he inserted the tip of his finger inside her hole. She pushed back against him, taking more of his finger inside her. Then her orgasm broke in her stomach and she cried out. Brett's finger slipped from her ass as she shook in Cade's arms. Still rock-hard, Cade withdrew from her body. When she could breathe again, he gave new instructions.

"Turn around, Jess. I want to show Brett something."

Breathing heavily, she turned and fell forward on her hands and knees. Brett got to his feet and took a step back, waiting. Staring at the hard length of his cock, she swallowed and found her throat was like sawdust.

"You ever tried anal sex before, Brett?" Cade's voice broke through the buzzing in her ears as his hands skimmed along her waist.

Brett's eyes flared and he shook his head. "Can't say I have."

Cade's hands lowered to her ass. He parted her cheeks and

then reached beneath her body to gather cream from her pussy. She sank her teeth into her bottom lip as he drew the moisture back up to her hole, preparing her for his entrance. Satisfied she was ready to take him, he positioned his cock against the cleft of her buttocks and gripped her hips.

The heat of his skin burned into hers as he propelled forward slowly, entering her with just the tip of his cock. A shiver passed through her as the familiar pressure built and then released as he slid another inch inside her. She hadn't taken a guy this way since the last time she'd visited the ranch and the delicate muscles of her anus were tighter than usual, but Cade took his time with her, easing himself into her body. Then he began a very slow pumping motion with his hips. A sweat broke out across her brow as her muscles gradually relaxed. Warm, aching pleasure rippled outward from where he fucked her and a throb started deep inside her pussy.

"Feel good?" Cade murmured in her ear, his cock sliding deeper with each gentle thrust.

Unable to form words, she gave a small whimper of approval. As the minutes passed, strength returned to her limbs. She lifted her head, her hair falling around her shoulders in chaotic fashion. Her eyes snagged on Brett's erection, encased firmly in his fist. The head bulged, ready to erupt. Her gaze drifted higher, over Brett's muscled torso and up to his harsh face. Every muscle in his face was rigid and a tic pulsed at the side of his jaw.

She forced her eyes up further, meeting his gaze. A gasp fell from her lips and she pushed a hand between her legs, finding her clit and capturing it between two fingers.

In the past she and Cade had experienced two or three different guys at a time, sometimes with a couple of girls thrown in for variety, but Jess had never been as aroused as she was now. It was the look in Brett's eyes that made the difference, she decided as she rolled and pinched her clit. A strange combination of confusion and raw, carnal desire. His gaze fixated on where Cade's cock pushed into her ass and she knew what he was thinking. He was imagining Cade's dick sliding into *his* ass. He was imagining getting fucked by a man, giving himself over to Cade's powerful body. It terrified him, threw him off his game. She understood his dilemma, almost felt the battle she was certain raged within him. But the throbbing cock between his legs proved how turned on he was by the idea.

As Cade's thrusts quickened, she wondered if he saw it too. Was he watching Brett as he neared the edge? Or was he too caught up in the sensations her ass elicited within him that he was blind to what was happening less than five yards away.

She kept her eyes trained on Brett as she circled her clit. Flames of desire licked from her knees to her breasts and Cade's unrelenting cock had her teetering over the edge before she could grind out his name. Her pussy convulsed in another orgasm as her ass rippled around Cade's dick. The tips of his fingers dug into her skin, his hips jerking against hers one last time. His shout of pleasure echoed in her ears as his seed exploded deep inside her ass. Her arms and legs collapsed beneath her and she fell to the floor. Closing her eyes, she let the wooden floor bite into her breasts and thighs, soothing the scratchy heat that crawled over her skin. *What a night.*

Brett didn't know whether to stay or go. Jessica lay face down on the floor across the living room, her gorgeous ass pink and white from where Cade's fingers had dug into her flesh. Cade lay a couple of feet away from her, his long body sprawled on the cushions. One arm covered his eyes as he got his breath back.

Brett watched the guy's muscular chest lift on each inhale and swallowed. He should go now. A golden opportunity to make his escape lay in front of him, the chance to leave this mind-bending night behind. He could go to bed, sleep off the combination of lust and alcohol. In the morning, he'd wake up and the emotions that warred inside him would be in the past. Gone.

But he wasn't ready to walk out the door. Blood still thrummed in his veins. His cock reached up to his belly button, aching for release. He knew he'd get it if he stuck around.

Slowly, Jess lifted her head from the floor and her eyes peeked from between strands of blonde hair. She pushed her hair out of her face and her swollen lips tilted in a wicked smile.

"What are you doing all the way over there?" she whispered, rising onto her knees and sitting back so her ass rested on her calves. She stretched out her arms to him. "Come lie with us."

He moved toward her, his cock bobbing with each step. Rolling onto her back, she grabbed some cushions for him to lie on. He lowered himself to the floor and stretched out beside her, very aware that Cade, the first man to ever give him lessons on touching a woman, lay on Jessica's other side.

"You really never tried anal sex?" Jess asked, propping her head in her hand and staring down at him.

He shook his head as a visual of Cade's engorged cock disappearing between the cheeks of her ass flashed in his mind. "Never," he said hoarsely.

She walked her fingers up his torso and then circled the flat disc of his nipple with her fingertip. "I'd offer it to you now but I'm going to need a while."

He smiled and then hissed a breath through his teeth as

110

she pinched his nipple.

"You know," she said thoughtfully, leaning in to nip his shoulder, "I think I have something you might like."

"What is it?"

"A toy." A glint of mischief entered her eye. She rubbed her hand down over his stomach and curled her fingers around the base of his dick. "It would really help with this."

"Oh yeah." Whatever it was, it sounded good to him. Her hand slid up his cock slowly, pulling on his tight skin. "Go get it."

She released his cock and sat up. "Wait here."

He watched her scramble to her feet and dart across the room. Beside him, he sensed movement and stiffened.

"You don't know what you're letting yourself in for, man," Cade said huskily, getting to his feet.

Brett found himself noticing the strong lines of Cade's back and the firm curve of his ass as the man ambled to the coffee table, his muscles flexing with each step. Realizing he was staring, Brett tore his gaze away and gave his head a quick shake. What the hell was wrong with him? He focused on Jess who was bent over at a delicious angle in the corner of the room, sifting through a bag. But as if drawn to a magnet, his eyes kept returning to Cade's lean physique. He watched the other man down a bottle of water and swipe a hand over his mouth. Brett swallowed, suddenly thirsty too.

"Here we are," Jess said triumphantly, strolling toward him. He rose on his elbows and squinted. What was the little temptress holding? It was dark in color and shaped like a cylinder.

She stood over him and tapped the object against the palm of her hand. Peering up at it, he frowned as he tried to distinguish the shape. It wasn't a cylinder. It curved at the top. It was a... His eyes widened in shock. *Dildo.* What the hell did she need one of those for? Two real cocks not enough for her?

His eyes widened further and dread coiled tight in the pit of his stomach. She didn't need a dildo, she knew that. It wasn't for her. His gaze darted from the toy to her eyes and then back again. Surely she wasn't planning on... She didn't mean... He swallowed thickly. She wasn't going to use that on him, was she?

He dared to meet her gaze again and the light in her eye told him she most certainly *was* going to use it on him. Scooting back on the cushions, he shook his head dumbly.

She pouted. "Oh come on, it's no big deal." Placing one foot on the other side of his body, she lowered herself until she straddled his stomach. Her cream spread over his skin like warm honey. Damn, this game really turned her on.

Leaning over him, she licked at the pulse at the base of his throat. "I promise you'll like it," she murmured.

He closed his eyes, his erection pressing into her stomach. Tension strained in every muscle of his body. He wanted to run, he wanted to hide. He wanted to turn around and let her use that dildo on him.

"You've come so far," she told him, nuzzling her nose against his jaw. "Let me do this for you."

"You want it that bad?"

She nodded, holding his gaze. Her determination and confidence were contagious. If it had been the beginning of the night, he would have stormed out the door. But now, with his head swimming and his cock begging for mercy, he couldn't say no. He didn't want to say no.

"What do I need to do?" he forced out, his stomach rolling with anxiety.

112

A smile spread across her lips and she slid from his body. "Turn around, honey."

A slight tremble shook his limbs as he rolled over and rose on hands and knees. He'd never been in a position like this, not with someone behind him—someone wielding the equivalent to a cock.

He shuddered as fear and excitement churned in his stomach. He tried to control his breathing, tried to take his mind out of the situation. Footsteps approached and he went rigid as Cade towered over him, his erection a mere few inches from Brett's face.

"Here," Cade said, passing something to Jess. "He'll need that."

Brett released the breath he'd been holding as the other man retreated. He stopped a couple of meters away beside one of the sofas. His body faced Brett, his cock extending from his thatch of golden curls, deep red and bulging. Heat crawled up Brett's neck. He couldn't bring himself to lift his gaze, to meet the other man's eyes. He was terrified of what he'd see there.

Jess's fingers slipped between the cheeks of his ass and coated his hole with a cold jello-like substance.

"This might hurt a little at first," she warned him, stroking his ass tenderly. "Give it a minute and it'll get really good."

The hard tip of the dildo pressed against his hole and he tensed.

"You need to relax, Brett," she cooed, circling his opening with the dildo. "Just breathe."

He inhaled deeply and focused on relaxing. Jess pressed the dildo against his hole again and pushed the tip inside. His ass protested at the invasion, the tight ring of muscles closing sharply around the toy.

"Easy," Jess soothed. "Let me in."

He took another breath and held it as she pushed the dildo in farther. Pressure bore down on his passage as the toy slid forward and then a sharp pain flared within him. He gritted his teeth and Jess rubbed her free hand down his back.

"That's it," she whispered, "it'll be over in a sec."

He waited out the pain as she withdrew the dildo and then propelled it forward again. Gradually, the pain lessened and the light flick of her wrist converted the sensation into an aching, burning pleasure. Sweat beaded across his forehead as the dildo sank deep inside him. His arms shook with exertion and his breath left his body in sharp bursts. The movement of the dildo grew more assured as his muscles relaxed. The head of his cock burned into his belly as his balls drew up beneath his body.

"Touch yourself."

The harsh order penetrated his mind and he peered through bleary eyes at Cade. The man, still standing a few feet away, was fisting his cock in sharp strokes. Brett's own cock leaped in response.

"Touch yourself," Cade repeated slowly. "It'll make you feel better."

Brett blinked and lifted one hand from the floor. He reached between his legs and grasped his cock. The grip of his hand elicited a groan from his lips. He closed his eyes briefly. When they flickered open again they fixated on Cade's pulsing dick.

He didn't know why he found the image of the other man jacking off so hypnotizing. He couldn't understand the fierce reaction he was experiencing to the sight of Cade's pleasure. But it was happening. And his mind was too fuzzy to worry about it. He could only feel, only see.

A groan choked in his throat as Jess's weapon sank even deeper inside him, brushing nerve-endings he'd never known existed. He pulled at his cock, twisting his fist around the bulbous head and swiping away the drops of come seeping from the slit.

Cade was close to coming too. The veins along his cock stood out, throbbing thickly. The head glistened with pre-come and Brett's mouth watered. Why did he suddenly feel so thirsty, so hungry? Why did his jaw ache to stretch around something long and thick?

Heavy emotion clogged Brett's throat as he let his gaze drift upward to meet Cade's eyes. The blazing desire he saw there shocked him, twisted his gut and tugged at his balls. His whole body shook as his hand pumped faster up and down his cock. He needed to come. And he needed to see Cade come too.

Seeming to sense his need, Jess slid the dildo in and out of his ass in quick, short strokes and, as the walls of his ass clenched, his dick exploded and white semen spilled over his fist. His eyes dropped from Cade's to his dick. In two harsh swipes of his hand, Cade came too, his cock erupting like a fountain. Brett let out a hollow groan, his hips still jerking in orgasm. It seemed forever before his balls were dry. The last thing he saw before he passed out was Cade collapsing onto the sofa.

The thumping of his brain inside his skull woke Brett the following morning. His eyelids flickered open and he blinked rapidly until the blurry vision cleared. Gradually, he became aware of his position—he lay spread-eagle on the floor of Cade's living room, stomach down. He breathed in and the air tickled the back of his dry throat, making him cough. Clamping his hand over his mouth to mute the sound, he slowly pushed to his feet. His legs shook as he found his balance. He glanced around the room, his gaze settling on the tangle of naked limbs on the sofa. Cade and Jessica, wrapped around one another, slept on, completely oblivious to his stare.

As memories of the previous night flooded his mind, he stumbled across the floor and grabbed the pieces of clothing he recognized as his own. Without looking at Cade and Jessica again, he shot out the door and dressed in the hall.

His mind didn't stop as he pulled open the door and raced across the yard, shirt hanging open. Images of Jessica's mouth wrapped around his cock sluiced through his brain. Then images of his dick disappearing inside her pussy.

He could handle those memories if they only stopped there.

He was halfway up the field that backed onto Cade's yard when he stopped and pressed the heels of his hands into his eyes. Behind his eyes he saw Cade's cock, thick and long, sliding between Jessica's buttocks. Then he saw Cade's eyes, glittering with raw desire. Brett groaned, remembering how those eyes had held his as Jessica had inserted that goddamn dildo in his ass.

What the fuck had he let himself in for?

Not wanting to think about what last night could mean to the ranch, to his relationship with Cade, to his own fucking soul, he started to run. His boots dug into the grass and then sprang back up as he sprinted toward his house. He didn't stop until he was safe inside his kitchen.

He raced up the stairs, tearing off his clothes as he went, and jumped into the shower. He turned the jets on full blast and let the hum of water drown out the voices in his head.

Chapter Seven

"Okay, slugger," Jessica called as she flipped the last pancake onto the stack on the plate before her. "I sure hope you're hungry." She carried the plate to the table and set it down in front of Cade. "Eat up."

He smirked. "You don't need to tell me twice." He caught a pancake between two forks and dragged it to his plate. "Looks good, sweetheart," he told her, pouring on the maple syrup.

"I know." She helped herself to a couple of pancakes and snatched the syrup bottle out of his hand. "I'm freakin' starving."

They ate their breakfast in silence, a silence heavy with things left unsaid. When they'd woken less than an hour ago all traces of Brett had been gone. Jessica didn't know what Cade thought about that but she was pretty sure it was a bad sign. They'd freaked him out, pushed him too far. Guilt gnawed at her gut with the knowledge that it was her fault.

She forked her last bite of golden, syrup-soaked pancake into her mouth and sighed. Cade was staring blindly at the back of a cereal box. She didn't know what to say.

"Stop it," Cade said, shifting his gaze to hers. "Quit blaming yourself. Nobody forced him to do anything he didn't want to do."

Jessica's eyes widened. Irritation lined Cade's tone. He was pissed at Brett. Now that was interesting.

She leaned forward, the silk lapels of her robe falling open, and studied his expression carefully. "So you're not heartbroken that he ran out of here before we woke up?"

Cade's warm laugh filled the kitchen and she relaxed back into her seat. When he laughed like that the dimple in his left cheek creased and she longed to kiss it. "What's so funny?"

He shrugged. "Brett was going to freak out. I knew that." He carried their plates to the sink and then turned and waggled his eyebrows at her. "Can't wait to see what he does when I see him later on."

She smiled, bringing her coffee cup to her lips. She sipped the nutty drink, letting it soothe her throat which still ached after the oral favors she'd performed the night before.

"He was more into it than I expected him to be," she said, placing her cup on the table. "I mean, I thought he'd walk out of there after I started sucking your cock while he was still fucking me."

"I thought he would too." Cade braced his hands on the edge of the table and leaned down to her. "But then again, Jessica Lawson, you could talk a guy into anything."

Her eyes narrowed as she folded her arms beneath her breasts. "You think it was just me who convinced him to stay?"

Cade's bark of laughter resounded in the kitchen. "What? You think me and my dick had something to do with it?"

She looked him straight in the eye and gave a curt nod. "Absolutely."

Amusement twinkled in Cade's blue eyes as he shook his head. "In my dreams, Jess."

"I'm serious." Remembering the confusion etched into Brett's expression the night before and the hunger in his dark eyes as he'd watched Cade's cock fuck her ass, Jess knew she had it right. Maybe it had simply been the fact that he'd never seen anal sex in action before, but instinct told her otherwise, and she *always* trusted her instincts.

"He couldn't take his eyes off you," she said, rising from the table and slipping toward Cade. She wrapped her arms around his waist and released a sigh as the disbelief remained in his expression. "I know I'm right," she said, glowering up at him. "I saw it in his face. He wanted you."

Cade's face twisted and he let out a groan. "Quit teasing me, Jess. I don't need to hear this."

Letting her arms drop to her sides, she backed down. Nothing she said would convince him.

"Fine," she muttered, tightening the sash of her robe. "Don't believe me." She spun on her heel and started for the door. "I'm going to take a shower and then I'm getting some shuteye. Say hi to Brett when you see him."

The rich sound of Cade's laughter followed her all the way up the stairs.

Cade didn't know what he'd expected when he ambled into the stables later that afternoon, but finding Brett standing in front of Dixie's stall sure as hell wasn't it. His footsteps faltered as he blinked to make sure he wasn't seeing things. After Brett's disappearing act in the small hours of the morning, Cade had felt sure he wouldn't show his face on the ranch for a couple of days. Hell, he'd half expected Brett to pick up and take off as fast as his truck's wheels could spin.

He cleared his throat, shifting his weight from one foot to the other. Brett didn't look his way.

"There's something wrong with her," he said, his voice low. "Take a look."

Concern brewed in Cade as he strode forward to inspect the mare. It took a few moments for him to notice the stiff movement of her neck and her awkward stance.

"Did you call a vet?"

"Yeah, Rob Daly's coming up to check her out." Brett turned from the stall and as he passed, Cade inhaled his masculine scent of soap and fresh sweat. He closed his eyes briefly, blocking the lust that threatened to sweep through him, and then returned his attention to the horse.

"She's got plenty of water in there?"

"Yeah."

Cade turned and found himself staring at Brett's squared shoulders. Remembering the intimacy of watching the guy get his ass fucked for the first time, Cade's chest filled with emotion.

As if sensing Cade's eyes on him, Brett started toward the door. "I want to check out the land past the pastures," he said, setting his Stetson on his dark head. "I know it's dry, but with some irrigation I think we could use it for crops."

Cade nodded. Sounded like a practical way to escape his company. "I'll hang around here till Rob arrives."

He watched Brett stride across the yard and tried not to notice the way the muscles in his ass flexed with each step. When Brett's frame disappeared from view, Cade turned back to Dixie and reached out a hand to stroke her mane. She was a damn fine horse and probably the oldest they had. The stiffness in her muscles could be a symptom of old age but he was glad they were making sure.

"At least he's talking to me like a human," he muttered,

referring to Brett as he trailed his fingertips along Dixie's silky hair. "I sure as hell didn't expect that."

His thoughts flickered once again to the previous night and his gut twisted. He understood Brett being shook up about it. Jess had really pushed his boundaries last night. What Cade didn't understand was why *he* was so shook up. The muscles across his shoulders strained tight. The pancakes he'd devoured that morning rolled around in his stomach. His mind kept replaying the events of the previous night, torturing him with vivid memories of Brett's mouth-watering body, of the pure sexuality in his dark eyes.

He'd loved every second of watching Brett lose control. Hell, he'd savored the sight of Jess's dildo penetrating Brett's virgin ass. But even as his dick had exploded in his hand, he hadn't felt satisfied. He wanted more, needed more. In pain he'd listened to Jessica's moans as she took all Brett had to give. Cade didn't think he'd ever been more jealous in his entire life.

The strong emotions scared him. He didn't know where they came from, what brought them on. Brett stirred something inside him, something no one else could touch, and it made Cade sweat. If he'd thought for half a second he'd find Brett on the ranch today, he'd have stayed the hell at home. Safe from the unfamiliar feelings that were set to drive him crazy before the sun went down.

He patted Dixie on the muzzle one last time and then headed back into the afternoon sun. The squeal of tires on the gravel out front reached his ears and he strolled across the yard to greet the vet. If he could distract himself with the workload they had on their hands, maybe the knots in his stomach would go away.

The knots in Cade's stomach didn't go away, but they relaxed slightly over the following few days. He focused on the work through the day, then Jessica through the night. He only saw Brett on the brief occasions when their paths crossed in the yard or the fields, but their eyes never met and only a grunt of greeting passed between them. Neither Cade nor Jessica came into contact with Brett after hours and despite the uneasy feelings that still clawed at Cade, a longing to be near the other man again took over.

"We should invite him over tonight," Jess said on Thursday night, four whole days after their tryst.

Cade shot her a look of warning and she lifted her shoulders in an innocent shrug. "Just for dinner."

His eyes returned to the paper he was reading. "He'd say no."

"Well, I think I'll ask him anyway."

Cade tried to appear unfazed as he flipped over a page, but the black and white words blurred on the paper. He waited, holding his breath as Jess punched a number into the phone. She held it to her ear. After a minute it became clear Brett wasn't picking up.

"I really wanted to see him before I go home," she said, flinging her body into a chair. "Are you guys talking yet?"

"Nope."

"Could you start please?" She lifted her feet into his lap and wiggled her toes. Today her nails were painted crimson. "I'm sure he misses me."

"I'm sure he does." Cade put down the paper and wrapped his hand around her ankle. "Why don't you go up there on Saturday before your flight? I've got to pick up some supplies in Steeplecrest. It'll be just you and him."

She leaned forward, her eyes softening. "But I want it to be the three of us. It's so much hotter that way."

Laughing, he shoved her foot off his lap. "I don't think that'll be happening again," he said, getting to his feet. "Not any time soon, at least."

"I really screwed things up for you, didn't I?" she said quietly, a sheen of guilt covering her eyes.

The smile faded from his face. "No, sweetie, of course not." He leaned down to kiss her forehead. "The guy just needs some time. So do I, if I'm honest."

"You're really into him, aren't you?" she said, making the question sound more like a statement.

His gaze dropped from hers as he shrugged. "Nothing I can't get over."

"I wish you didn't have to get over it." Her lips curved in an optimistic smile. "Maybe you won't have to."

He shook his head, trying to control the flare of hope her words elicited within him. "Can we talk about something else?"

"Of course."

As she launched into a recap of a telephone call she'd received from an editor at some big-shot New York magazine, he zoned out, his mind stubbornly set on thoughts of Brett. Why hadn't he picked up his phone? Was he out tonight? Picking up chicks at Billy's? Living a life completely separate to Cade's?

His stomach churned. He couldn't lose his relationship with Brett. Though it was strained and full of unfulfilled desires on his part, Brett was too important to lose, even if that meant they could only be friends. Somehow he had to figure out a way to get their camaraderie back or else life on Steeplecrest Ranch wouldn't be worth living.

The days following the night at Cade's place dragged as Brett struggled to keep his mind busy. The nights, without the distraction of ranch life, felt even longer. His bed was in a constant state of disarray—covers bunched at the foot of the bed and sheets twisted in a tangled mess. But the lack of sleep wasn't wearing him out. His mind was fully alert and his body sizzled like a livewire. He didn't know what Jessica and Cade had set off inside him but it felt like a ticking bomb just ready to explode in his veins. Every muscle in his body throbbed for something he couldn't put his finger on. He knew in his gut that Cade would know how to ease the ache and, in the dead of the night when Brett's cock jutted out angrily from between his legs, it was all he could do not to swing his legs over the side of the bed and take a stroll down to the Armstrong house.

On Friday morning, confident Cade would still be in bed with his body curled around Jessica's soft curves, Brett wandered out toward the pastures to check Paul had fed the cattle. He'd take the four-wheel drive out on the plains today just for the hell of it. Imagining the warm breeze on his face as he bound across the land, dust flying through the air behind him, he already felt the tension in his muscles relax. But as he rounded the corner of the barn and faced one of the paddocks, he stiffened, stopping in his tracks.

In the center of the paddock a horse he didn't recognize jerked and whinnied, its legs lifting in the air. Brett cast a brief glance at the animal, but what commanded his attention was the man the horse was trying to throw off.

Cade sat on the horse's back, his hands gripping the animal's dark mane as he struggled to stay upright. His denim-clad thighs locked around the beast, the heels of his boots digging into its sides and his bare chest, golden beneath the sun, glistened with sweat. A Stetson sat on his head, casting his eyes in shadow but Brett knew Cade's gaze was trained on the horse, his sole focus. Behind him, beneath the brim of his hat, shaggy blond hair curled outward, trailing over his muscled shoulders each time his head tilted back with the force of the horse's movements. Brett's gaze roamed over the other man's face, noting the clenched jaw, the tendons standing out along his neck—a result of the exertion it took to control the animal. Dropping his eyes to Cade's thighs, he felt his insides clench as he watched the muscles flex, clamping around the horse's body.

The whinnies began to lessen in strength. Beneath Cade's body, the animal's efforts to throw off its load eased. It continued to buck, its movements weakening until finally it gave up and stilled, giving an angry snort. A cheer penetrated the silence and Brett blinked, glanced to the side and spotted Jimmy. The old man opened the gate to the paddock and jogged toward the horse.

"That was magic, son," he said, his craggy voice loud with excitement. He patted the horse's muzzle, shaking his head in amazement. "Look at her. She's tame as a kitten."

Brett held back as Cade swung his leg over the horse and dropped to the ground. He pulled the hat from his head and shook out his hair. Before Brett thought to make a getaway, Cade's blue eyes, twinkling with excitement, found his. Holding his breath, Brett waited for the excitement in Cade's gaze to fade into wariness. After all, they hadn't made eye contact in days. But Cade's expression remained triumphant as he jerked a thumb toward the horse.

"What do you think of her?"

He looked at the horse, appreciating for the first time the strong, well-proportioned body and the glossy mahogany coat.

"I'll have to see her in action first."

Cade's shout of laughter rang in Brett's ears. "Did you hear that?" Cade demanded, looking to Jimmy in disbelief. "What does he need to see after that?"

Jimmy shook his head, looping a piece of rope around the horse's neck. "Don't listen to him, boy. He ain't never satisfied."

Letting out a chuckle, Brett felt himself relax. Even as Cade approached the fence, he stayed put. But the moment Jimmy led the horse away he regretted the decision to stay. Alone again.

Cade grabbed his shirt from the top bar of the fence and shrugged into it, leaving it unbuttoned. "Should have put a saddle on first," he said, swiping his hand over his ass.

Brett's gaze darted to where Cade's hand brushed his backside before he tore it away again.

"Where's Jess?" he asked, needing to break the silence. As soon as her name fell from his lips stark reminders of their night together pooled in his mind's eye. *Damn it.*

Cade didn't miss a beat. "Still in bed," he said casually, lifting a bottle of water from the ground and twisting off the cap. "She leaves tomorrow night."

"Right." Silence descended again and this time Brett couldn't think of anything to break it. "I'll see you later," he muttered, turning from the fence and starting toward the pastures. A couple of yards later Cade's shout had him turning back.

"Aw, come on Brett," Cade called from behind him. "Would you just get that stick out of your ass and get over it?"

His mind begged him to ignore the question, to keep on going, but he knew he had to deal with this some time. He stalked back to the fence, glaring at Cade as the guy leaped over the bars.

"Get over what?" he asked, folding his arms over his chest.

Cade's chuckle riled him up even more. "You're acting like the kid in the locker room. The one with the small dick."

Brett's eyes widened as fury tightened his fists into balls at his sides. "Are you saying I have a small dick?"

Cade raised an eyebrow, eyes still brimming with laughter. "Not at all." He leaned his elbow on the fence and crossed one foot behind the other, tapping the hard dirt ground with the toe of his boot. "I just can't figure out why you're so pissed that I saw you naked."

Brett's eyes bulged. "Are you fucking serious?" Even as he uttered the demand, heat crept up his neck. He held Cade's gaze, hoping he wouldn't notice how uncomfortable he'd made him.

"Well, then you tell me what the problem is." Cade looked at him expectantly, boot still stubbing the ground.

For a moment Brett was too mad to speak. "I don't have a problem," he bit out eventually, resisting the urge to lash out at Cade's smirk of disbelief. "Forget it," he said, wishing he could press rewind on the past couple of weeks. "I guess I just don't like sharing women, that's all."

Cade's eyes pierced into him, giving Brett the uneasy sense he was being interrogated. He struggled to maintain a deadpan expression. What he really wanted to do was sucker-punch Cade in the stomach or maybe even...

He didn't let the thought finish in his mind. He didn't want to know how it ended. Because despite his protests, he knew Cade was right. He hated that the other man had seen him naked. Every time Cade looked in his direction now he felt as if he was being stripped. It didn't make sense. He knew Cade was into girls. Hell, the guy hadn't been able to get enough of

127

Jessica's sweet body the other night. So why did he make Brett feel this way? And why the fuck was his traitorous mind suddenly noticing things about Cade he shouldn't be noticing. Like the curve of his lower lip. The way his blue eyes hardened when he was pissed. The goddamn definition of his stomach muscles.

Realizing he'd been staring at Cade for God knows how long, he backed up, ready to run. Cade's gaze followed him, the challenging glint in his eyes fading to confusion. Nausea swelled in Brett's stomach. He turned and headed blindly in the opposite direction. He didn't care where he was going. As long as it was as far away from Cade as possible.

He managed to avoid Cade for the rest of the day and for the whole of Saturday morning. At noon on Saturday he returned to the house to grab a bite to eat. He stood at one of the kitchen windows that overlooked the backyard as he munched on a sandwich. A few yards of patio sloped downward from the veranda across to the line of cedar trees guarding the end of the house. Beyond the trees lay a rectangular swimming pool, the blue water barely visible from the kitchen through the gaps between the thick green foliage.

Brett's eye caught on a movement through the trees and his jaw stilled. Now who was sneaking around out there?

Leaving the remains of his sandwich beside the sink, he headed out onto the veranda and jumped down the steps. In a few quick strides he crossed the patio and followed the narrow path, still lined with pots of his mother's flowers, to the swimming pool.

The midday sun reflected off the surface of the pool and beamed into his eyes, momentarily blinding him. He blinked until his vision cleared and then blinked again. There, stretched out on a sun lounger, lay a very topless Jessica. With her arms straight at her sides and her face pointed upward, she painted a picture of relaxation. He drank in her long, tanned limbs and the small swells of her breasts. The hard berry nipples jutted toward the sky. A scrap of purple material covered her mound.

His dick immediately reacted to her practically naked state, twitching inside his boxers. He adjusted himself in an effort to make himself more comfortable and managed to catch her attention in the process. Her head turned to him and a catlike smile spread across her glossy lips. Rising up on her elbows, she pushed her sunglasses into her hair.

"Hey there, stranger," she greeted, her tone light and teasing. "I was wondering if I'd get to see you before I go."

He held out his arms. "You're seeing me now."

"Yes, I am." She sat up fully, her tits bobbing with the movement. Swinging her legs over the edge of the lounger, she patted the empty space her feet left open. "Come sit with me."

"Nice of you to offer," he said, taking a seat and grinning at her. "It's not like it's my lounger or anything."

Her expression was immediately apologetic. "Oh, I'm sorry," she said, leaning closer to him, so close her nipples were a hair's breadth from his arm. "Cade said you had a pool and I couldn't resist."

"It's no problem," he said, eyes fixed on the hard tips of her breasts. "What time do you leave at?"

"Five," she replied, her lovely mouth twisting in a grimace. "I'm sure going to miss this place."

He glanced up into her regret-filled eyes. "You'll come back, right?"

A wicked smile curved her lips. "Are you going to make it worth my while?"

The meaning behind her words had him looking away. He didn't want to think about that night. Not ever.

"You know," Jessica started thoughtfully, running the back of her finger along the inside of his arm. Her light touch made his skin tingle. "If you've got a few minutes now we could..."

Her suggestion tugged him right back into the mood. He twisted on the lounger to face her fully and reached out to tease one brown nipple.

"What could we do?" he asked, rolling the bead between his thumb and forefinger.

She gave a soft sigh and smiled. "Anything you want."

He hesitated, palming the underside of her breast. She was so feminine with her curves and her tiny whimpers of pleasure. A sudden longing to be surrounded by a woman flared within him. Keeping one hand on her breast, he skated the other down over her belly. He needed pussy and lots of it.

He slid from the lounger and dropped to his knees at the bottom edge. "Move up to me," he ordered, gaze fixed on the apex of her thighs.

Catching his line of thought, she scooted her little ass along the lounger until she sat on the very edge. He held each knee and pushed them apart, opening her to him.

"Lie back, sweetheart," he told her, mouth watering for a taste of her honey. Reaching between her legs, he ripped the purple material from her pussy and uncovered her ripe pink flesh. He buried his head between her thighs and licked from the bottom of her seam right up to the throbbing bud of her clit. The first taste fuelled the flames that blazed inside him. Unable to control his hunger, he devoured her, digging the length of his tongue into her cunt and lapping up every drop of cream she had to offer. Her musky scent and sweet taste flooded his senses, making his mind spin as he licked and sucked on her soft flesh. Her fingers wove into his hair, holding him in place. He wanted to tell her he wasn't going anywhere, but he couldn't bear to lift his head for even a second.

This was what he wanted, what he needed, he told himself. Only a woman could satisfy him like this. Her breasts, her pussy, the soft curve of her thigh. No man could make those tiny noises of pleasure, no man could *purr*. Men were hard, rigid, unrelenting. They didn't whimper when they came, they roared. *Cade* roared. The sound still haunted Brett's dreams.

No. He closed his eyes against his thoughts. He wasn't supposed to be thinking about Cade. Not with his face between a woman's legs.

Continuing to draw his tongue through her folds, Brett lifted her legs and hooked them over his shoulders. The shift in position gave him better access and his tongue delved deeper inside her, tasting more of her essence. Her scream of pleasure rang in his ears as her pussy started to quake around his tongue. He drank up the cream that sluiced through her cunt as she orgasmed, breathing her in while he still could.

He continued to lick at her long after her grip on his hair had loosened. When he finally lifted his head he found her watching him, fondness warming her heavy-lidded eyes.

"You are one hell of a guy," she said softly, wiping some of her moisture from his bottom lip. "And you do that extremely well."

"It's a pleasure."

She grinned and then shivered as he dropped his head once again and swirled the tip of his tongue around her clit.

"I want to talk to you about something before I go."

He looked up again, his shoulders stiffening when he saw the serious expression on her face. *Don't say Cade.* He didn't want to talk about Cade.

"I hate seeing you boys like this," she said, her eyes searching his. "You have a really strong bond. I'd hate to see you lose it."

He stood abruptly and faced the pool. "We work together. There's no bond."

"Oh, of course there is," she said, moving up behind him. "You might refuse to see it but it's plain as day to everyone else."

He turned on his heel and glowered down at her. "What exactly is plain as day?" he asked through gritted teeth. He didn't know what had possessed him to ask the question. Something inside him needed to hear her answer, needed to know what she was seeing.

She stood before him naked as the day she was born, her eyes intent on his. "I don't think it's my place to say," she said eventually, her tone soft. "I just hope you won't get all caught up in that black-and-white world of yours. If you do, you'll miss out."

He opened his mouth to say something but the breath choked in his throat. He swallowed, suddenly drained from this encounter.

"Have a good flight, Jess," he said, looking down into her knowing eyes and feeling the irritation in his body dissipate. He was too tired to hang onto it. "I'll miss having a girl around here."

A sad smile flickered on her lips and she wrapped her arms around his neck in a brief hug. "Be good," she told him, turning back to the lounger. "And take care of Cade for me."

His stomach clenched at her words but he didn't respond to them. He gave a small wave and headed back toward the house, his steps weighted down by the emotion clutching his gut.

Chapter Eight

Saying goodbye to Jessica was a lot harder this time round than it had been after her first visit. Cade drove her to the airport, the atmosphere in the car somber and downright depressing. She'd tried to bring up the subject of Brett again before they'd left the house and, between the dread Cade felt at the prospect of her departure and the feelings for Brett that clogged his throat, he'd lost it for a second and snapped at her. They hadn't spoken since and they were twenty minutes away from the airport.

Jessica heaved a sigh as he took the exit for the airport. "Listen," she started, reaching a hand out to touch his leg, "I'm sorry. Please don't let me leave without forgiving me."

He fought a smile at her pleading tone and when she squeezed his thigh he cracked a grin. "Fine, you're forgiven."

"Really?"

"Yes, really." Glancing at her, he laughed at the suspicion in her eyes. "I mean it. I'm going to miss you, sweetheart."

"Me too. I just wish Brett would get over himself already."

His hands tightened on the steering wheel. "You're seriously not going to start with that again, are you?"

She paused and then tutted under her breath. "I guess not."

He nodded. "Glad to hear it."

They said their goodbyes in the terminal. After a long kiss that was to last him for God knows how long, Cade watched her blonde head disappear into the check-in queue, then headed back to the car.

When he stepped inside the house four hours later, it didn't feel like home. Silent and empty. *Fucking depressing.* He kicked off his boots and went into the kitchen to rummage up something to eat. A week ago he could have called Brett and invited him over for a game of pool and some beer. Grabbing a microwave meal from the fridge, he jammed it in the microwave and hit start. He was still feeling sorry for himself ten minutes later when the phone rang.

"Hello," he said into the receiver, pushing the remains of his mac and cheese around the plate.

"Cade, it's Tommy Dawes," a voice boomed down the line.

"Hey, Tommy, what's up?" Cade shoved his chair back from the table and got to his feet. "Anything I can do for you?"

"Just wanted to let you know a few of the guys are getting together again Friday night at Billy's. You're welcome to come along."

Cade smiled to himself. If Tommy was going to be there Brett would be invited too. Did Tommy have any idea how pissed off Brett would be to find Cade sitting in their booth?

"Sounds good to me," he said. "I'll be there."

That week was slow as hell, and just as hot too. Without Jessica to distract him, Cade spent more than twelve hours a day on the ranch. Jimmy, the two ranch hands and the animals provided his only company. On the rare occasion he bumped into Brett the other man pretended he didn't exist and each brush off was a sucker-punch to Cade's stomach.

When Friday finally rolled around, he'd had enough. At nine that night, instead of driving straight to Billy's, he headed up to Brett's house first. Seeing the blue Chevrolet was still in the drive, Cade grinned. He was still here.

Cade darted up to the porch and pulled open the screen door before pressing on the doorbell. A couple of minutes later he heard heavy footsteps trudging along the hallway. The door swung open and Brett's face appeared. His lip curled once he saw it was Cade.

"What do you want?"

Cade fought a grin as he jerked his head toward his car. "Figured you might need a ride."

Brett's expression grew thunderous. "You're going to Billy's?" he asked flatly.

"Yeah. And after last time I thought you might as well ride with me." Cade shoved his hands in his pockets, wishing Brett's furious eyes didn't turn him on so much. "I don't want to have to cart you back into Steeplecrest tomorrow morning so you can pick up your truck."

Boy, did he wish he'd brought a camera to capture the look on Brett's face. As the man struggled to find an argument, Cade turned and jogged down the steps to his car.

"You ready to go?" he called, pulling open the driver's door. He glanced back at the combination of rage and utter disbelief in Brett's eyes and nearly choked on a laugh. "I want to get a parking spot before the lot fills up."

After a five-minute wait in the car, he wondered if Brett's stubbornness would get the best of him. But the guy had too much pride to make a fool out of himself, Cade realized as Brett appeared by the passenger door. He opened it and slid inside the car. His broad shoulders and long legs commanded the small space and when Cade inhaled, he breathed in Brett's clean masculine scent.

He revved the engine and started down Brett's drive. Already his jeans were starting to feel too tight with his thickening cock.

This was going to be one long ride.

As usual for a Friday night in Steeplecrest, Billy's Bar teemed with people. Cade parked at the very back of the lot and Brett jumped out of the car and stalked toward the bar as soon as the engine died. He didn't know why, but he hadn't been able to breathe for the twenty-minute ride. He'd been too aware of the other man's presence, of his body. Not a word had passed between them as Cade had maneuvered the car along the twisting roads that led into the town and the silence had nearly suffocated him. He'd tried to distract himself with the car's upholstery, the CD collection stacked beneath the car stereo, the fields they were zipping by, but nothing worked. His eyes had kept flickering to Cade's hands where they gripped the steering wheel firmly and to the muscled length of his thigh. Even now, as Brett pushed his way into the bar, his pulse still pounded in his wrist. He made a note in his head for future reference—he wouldn't enter an enclosed space with Cade Armstrong again. *Never.*

"Brett!" someone shouted over the din of voices and country music. "Over here."

He scanned the crowd and finally pinpointed Tommy who was waving from one of the booths along the side of the bar.

"Hey," he greeted the guys when he reached the booth. He

slid along the bench and then realized he should have gotten a drink before fighting all the way over here. "Damn, it's busy in here tonight."

"More women than usual," Mitch agreed, his expression appreciative as his gaze roamed the room. "Did you see the sign outside?"

"What sign?"

"Billy's started making these fancy-shmancy cocktails to pull in the ladies," Tommy explained, wrinkling his nose in disgust. "Who the hell would want to drink one of those pink things is beyond me."

Brett laughed, thinking of Jessica. She was probably sipping a pink cocktail right now in one of New York's exclusive clubs. Whether she had a guy by her side or not, she wouldn't be going home alone tonight.

The smile dropped from his lips as Cade appeared through the crowd, two beers in his hands. He set one down in front of Brett and then sat on the other side of the booth. Typical that the bastard had to sit right opposite him, Brett fumed. As if he needed Cade's face in front of him while he got wasted.

Another thought occurred to him and unease crept over him. Maybe getting wasted wasn't such a good idea. Who knew what he would do if he lost control of his senses? And he had a sinking feeling Cade would be in no hurry to stop him making an ass of himself.

"So where's that girl of yours, Armstrong?" one of the guys at the end of the booth asked, a note of jealousy in his tone. "You didn't bring her?"

"What?" Tommy jumped in. "Are we not good enough company for the city girl?"

Cade swallowed a mouthful of beer and shrugged. "She's gone back to New York."

A chorus of "hell no's" rose from the table, a couple of the guys clutching their hearts in mock despair.

"We didn't even get to meet her," Tommy complained, glaring at Cade across the table.

"Maybe next time."

Tommy turned to Brett and jerked a finger toward Cade. "Can you believe this guy? Bet even you didn't get to meet her."

Cade's chuckle did things to Brett he didn't want to acknowledge. He shifted on his seat and clasped his hand around the cold, dewy bottle of beer, focusing on it until the tightness in his pants relaxed.

"Yeah, I got to meet her," he said, then grimaced at the strain in his voice.

He caught Cade's eye and looked away as the man added, "He got to do a whole lot more than meet her."

"Whoa there, Armstrong," Mitch bellowed, turning his meaty face to Brett. "You banged Cade's girl?"

Brett stared at the astonished expressions covering all the guys' faces and faltered. He wanted to speak, to laugh it off, but he couldn't find the words.

Finally, Cade broke the silence. "Ah, she's not really my girl."

"Yeah, but sheesh," Tommy said, still staring at Brett. "Since when do you go around stealing other men's women?"

A rush of frustration rose within Brett as he glared into Cade's twinkling eyes. *Son of a bitch.* "I didn't steal anything," he bit out, his grip nearly breaking the glass bottle in his hand. "Not my fault Cade here can't keep a woman satisfied."

Another round of hoots and hollers went up, but Brett kept his eyes on Cade, waiting for his reaction. It wasn't what he expected. Instead of getting pissed over the dig, he appeared even more amused, a crooked smile playing on his lips. Brett's stomach clenched again and he shot his gaze down to the surface of the table. Nothing fazed this guy. Anything Brett had to say spurred him on more.

Suddenly feeling weary, Brett got up from the table. He muttered something about getting another drink and then forced his way back to the bar. He'd finished off another beer when a warm, curvy body sidled up to him.

"Hi, Mary Ellen," he said, looking into her heavily made-up eyes. "It's been a while."

Her lipsticked mouth widened into what he guessed was supposed to be a sultry smile. "It sure has, stranger." Her hand curled around his wrist which rested on the bar. She tugged it away and turned him to face her fully. "I thought you were going to call me."

He frowned. Had he said he'd call her? He couldn't remember. "Sorry, I guess I've been busy."

She nodded and the sympathy she'd expressed at the funeral filled her eyes. The reminder of the day he'd buried his parents was not a turn on but, as she brushed up against him, her breasts pressing into his chest, his cock still managed a quiver.

"Of course you've been busy," she cooed, flattening a small palm to the front of his shirt. "I knew I should have stopped by to check on you. I'm sure you could have used some—" her hand trailed suggestively down the line of buttons, "—company."

He nodded. Maybe she was right. Some female company right after the funeral might have staved off the confusion he was experiencing now. He moved around her until she had her back against the bar. Bracing his arms on either side of her, he stepped forward until the heat of her body mingled with his.

"Want a drink?"

Her pink tongue trailed over her lips. "I'd love one."

Two hours later, Brett was still at the bar, his body wrapped around Mary Ellen Sanders. Cade tried his damnedest not to stare at them. He even managed to half-listen to the conversations around him and throw in a couple of words to save himself from coming off as a jerk. But his gaze kept snaking back to the bar, catching the way Brett's lips brushed Mary Ellen's ear and the glide of her small hands over his tight butt. Cade's body locked in jealousy as he watched the scene play out. The more Brett drank the further he went. His hips melded to the blonde's, so close they may as well have been fucking right there at the bar. He didn't know why he cared so much. He hadn't felt this way while watching Jessica with Brett. Seeing them together had turned him on. Probably because he'd been very much a part of the whole deal. But tonight something had snapped inside him. He wanted Brett and he didn't want *blondie* over there to get her hands on him first.

"I need another beer," he said, sliding out of the booth. "Back in a minute."

He pushed his way up to the bar and reached Brett just as Mary Ellen took off toward the ladies.

"Where'd you find her?" he asked, leaning against the bar.

Brett glanced in his direction, annoyance darkening his features. "What the hell is your problem?" he demanded, leaning in so close Cade could smell the alcohol on his breath.

"There's no problem."

"No problem?" Brett demanded incredulously. "Are you

fucking kidding me?"

Cade lifted a brow in response and watched Brett's eyes blaze with fury.

"You're always around," Brett said, "always there."

"We're neighbors, Brett, and we work together. What do you expect?"

Brett looked ready to lay his fist into Cade's face as he shook his head furiously. "It ain't just that, you're always..."

Cade straightened and crossed his arms over his chest. If Brett wanted a fight, he'd have to acknowledge the issue first. "I'm always what?"

The challenge seemed to throw Brett off and, as the anger dulled in his eyes, Cade felt a rush of guilt. He was doing this to Brett, confusing him. He wasn't being fair.

"Look," Cade said quietly, "it doesn't have to be like this."

"Like what?"

"Tense and shit." Cade took a step back in an effort to give them both more breathing room. "We could forget the past couple of weeks, put them behind us if they make you this uncomfortable."

Brett didn't look convinced, but his eyes remained calm and Cade decided now was as good a time as any to ask the question that had been keeping him awake at night.

"Why are you uncomfortable?" he asked, searching Brett's face for clues. "That night with Jess, it was just a bit of fun, nothing serious."

Confusion flashed in Brett's gaze before the anger returned. "Why can't you leave it the hell alone?" he seethed, bringing his beer bottle down on the bar with so much force Cade expected the glass to smash to pieces.

Returning his attention to Brett, he replied with a question of his own. "Why is it bugging you so much?"

"Maybe because it doesn't seem to be bugging you at all," Brett said, fists curling at his sides. Realizing they were drawing attention, Brett moved forward, his body heat enveloping Cade as he spoke again, this time in a much lower voice. "You liked it."

Cade gave a small laugh of surprise. "Of course I liked it. It was sex, what's not to like?"

"No." Brett shook his head. "Not just Jessica. You liked...even when she wasn't around, you liked..."

Tired of beating around the bush, Cade groaned his frustration. "Liked what?"

Brett couldn't say it but his thoughts were clear in his desperate eyes. "You were hard the whole time," he ground out eventually. "I saw you, I saw you looking."

Cade's gut twisted. This wasn't how he'd expected the conversation to go. He knew Brett had suspected this. Hell, he'd made a poor show of hiding his feelings for the man, especially that night. But when he'd thought about this confrontation over the past few days, he'd dreaded it, dreaded the accusation and disgust Brett was bound to display. What Cade hadn't counted on was the mix of confusion and desperate need in Brett's eyes he was facing now. And he'd be damned if that wasn't desire burning beneath all that emotion.

They stared at one another in silence and Cade finally let himself acknowledge the fact that Brett felt something too. No matter how small it was *something*.

"Brett, honey," a female voice simpered.

Brett's eyes dimmed once again and he turned his back on Cade. Glancing over the other man's shoulder, Cade watched Mary Ellen practically rub herself up against Brett. She was a piece of candy, this one—all candyfloss smiles and sugar-coated tones. Not his type at all.

It became clear as Brett slipped his hands down around her tiny waist he was putting an end to the conversation he'd been having with Cade. The high of anticipation and hope Cade had been feeling swooped downward, the anti-climax almost unbearable as he turned away from Brett and his piece of sugar. He would have walked straight out of the bar if his cell hadn't started buzzing in his pocket.

He pulled it out and flipped it open, not recognizing the number. "Hello," he said into it.

"Cade, it's Jimmy here."

Frowning at the strain in the old man's voice, Cade pressed the cell tighter to his ear. "Everything okay, Jimmy?"

"I tried to get Brett but he ain't answering his phone," Jimmy rushed on. "You boys need to come home. It's Dixie. She's not doing so good."

A sinking feeling weighted down Cade's stomach as he glanced back at Brett. Of all the horses, losing Dixie would break his heart. "Did you call the vet, Jimmy?"

"Yeah, Rob's on his way now."

"Okay, we'll be there in twenty." He snapped the phone shut and strode back to Brett. "We need to get out of here."

Brett didn't look away from his doting friend as he asked, "Why?"

"One of the horses is sick. Jimmy just called me."

This got Brett's attention. He untangled himself from the blonde who pouted up at him. "Sorry, Mary Ellen," Brett said, not sounding particularly sorry at all. "I gotta go."

Cade almost felt sorry for the girl who stood forgotten at the bar as Brett headed for the door. But noting the way the guy behind her was staring at her ass, eyes glinting with interest,

143

Cade shrugged off the sympathy and followed Brett outside. Mary Ellen wouldn't go home alone tonight.

The atmosphere in the car on the ride home was as strained as it had been on the way to Billy's. But the tension in the air was a different kind of tension—worry, fear.

"What horse?" Brett asked tersely as they left the town behind them.

Cade held his breath and then released it slowly. "Dixie."

They didn't utter another word until they reached the ranch. As soon as Cade pulled up in Brett's drive, whinnies of pain reached his ears. With Dixie at the front of his mind, he got out of the car and jogged to the stables with Brett right beside him.

"There you are," Jimmy said when they stepped inside the darkened stables. He stood outside one of the empty stalls beside the stable doors. Or at least it had been empty until now. When Cade reached the stall and saw Dixie inside, Rob Daly standing beside her, the pit of dread in his stomach deepened. They'd moved her down to this stall so she was right beside the exit. That way if she gave out it wouldn't be such a difficult task to move her.

"How is she?" Brett asked flatly and Cade knew he'd figured out why they'd moved her too.

Now they were closer, Cade could see the weariness in Jimmy's weathered face as he shook his head. "Not doing too good."

"The stiffness that was there when I came out last week is much worse," Rob said from the dark stall. "And she's sweating buckets."

"She went into convulsions about an hour ago," Jimmy added, grimacing at the memory. "Poor thing fell on the ground. That's when I called Rob."

"Convulsions?" Cade asked, looking at the vet for confirmation. When Rob nodded, he didn't just confirm the convulsions, he confirmed Cade's suspicions. "Tetanus."

Rob nodded again. "I'm almost sure. Between the stiffness and the spasms." He dropped to his knees and pointed to her front right hoof. "There's a cut just here on her leg. I missed that last week."

"Tetanus?" Brett asked, his brows drawn together in a frown. "But we have all the horses vaccinated every year, surely it can't—"

Rob cut him off. "Vaccinations aren't a hundred-percent guarantee against the disease," he reminded him gently.

There was a tense silence. Then Brett asked another question Cade had been dreading.

"So what's the next step? What treatment does she need?"

Rob ran his hand over the horse's mane and shook his head. "She's too far gone, Brett. Tetanus can lie dormant for months but once the symptoms set in, the disease progresses quickly."

Another silence and Cade could almost feel Brett's heart breaking.

"So we wait?" He directed his question at Rob as Brett stepped inside the stall.

Rob didn't reply as Brett ran a loving hand over the horse's stiff flanks, and Cade had to fight every instinct he had not to go in there and reach for him.

After a few moments, Brett turned his face away from the horse and looked at the vet. "Are we waiting?"

Rob hesitated and then slowly shook his head. "I think it'd be best if we put the old girl out of her misery."

A lump formed in Cade's throat at the dooming words. He

145

watched with an aching heart as Brett continued to pat down the horse, the usual harsh tone in his voice replaced by something softer as he soothed the distressed animal. Losing Dixie was a blow he didn't need to face right now.

Cade shifted his focus to Rob as Brett continued to whisper in the horse's ear. "What happens now?"

"I have what I need in the truck," he said somberly. "When Jimmy called and told me what was going on I thought I might need it."

Cade nodded stiffly. "And what about the—" he faltered and then took a deep breath, "—what about the body?"

"I can take it away on my trailer. There's a removal service I deal with just outside Steeplecrest. I can take care of all that."

Sensing the vet was trying to make it as easy for them as possible, Cade made a mental note to thank him later on. Right now he didn't think he could speak as he watched Brett, usually so hard and unyielding, stroke the horse gently, saying goodbye.

While Rob went to get his supplies from his truck, Cade turned away from the stall and swallowed past the lump in his throat. Jimmy was having a hard time of it too, rubbing at his eyes and clearing his throat with a cough.

"I'm glad I was here," Jimmy said hoarsely. "I just came by to pick up something I'd left behind and I heard her."

"Glad you were here too," Cade forced out, summoning the strength to face the stall again. Despite Brett's soothing strokes, the horse's pain was palpable. Her eyes, which had always been so soft and intelligent, were watering. The lockjaw had set in and she didn't appear to be able to move her face. She looked like a different animal from when he'd seen her that morning. She'd been stiff then too, but he'd put it down to old age. He wished it had clicked in his mind, but even if it had and they'd called Rob then, it probably wouldn't have made a difference. *Probably.*

Rob returned with a bag in his hand. He walked into the stall and got to his knees, unzipping the bag. Brett didn't turn from the horse but Cade didn't miss how his shoulders tensed further, the muscles bunching beneath his T-shirt.

With a needle in hand, Rob stood and approached the horse. "Are you ready?" he asked, looking to Brett for permission to continue.

Brett's curt nod was the only answer he got and, as Brett continued to whisper to Dixie, Rob inserted the needle beneath her skin and pulled back the syringe. Dixie didn't seem to feel the prick and Cade supposed she probably couldn't feel anything through the pain she was already experiencing. He looked on as her eyelids drooped. Slowly, her legs folded beneath her body and she dropped to the floor. Her eyes closed fully as if she were drifting into a sleep. Two minutes later, Rob stepped forward to check for a pulse.

"She's gone," he confirmed, getting to his feet. He turned sorry eyes on Brett and then glanced at Cade. "We can wait a while before taking her out, but not too long or rigor mortis will set in."

"Thanks, Rob," Jimmy croaked out. "But maybe we should get this done now, right boss?"

Brett turned and Cade had to look away from the raw pain swimming in his dark eyes.

"Yeah," Brett said quietly, "let's get it over with."

Moving the animal from the stall to Rob's trailer was no mean feat. Her weight bore down on them as they half-carried, half-dragged her across the yard. It made Cade's stomach turn to see the beautiful horse be treated this way, but he had to remind himself she was gone and what they were carrying now was dead meat, soulless.

He stood with Brett as Rob drove away, carrying what was left of Dixie with him. Jimmy left too and when the lights at the back of his old pickup faded into the distance, Cade couldn't stop himself. He reached out and put his hand on Brett's shoulder. To his surprise and relief, Brett didn't shrug him off. They stood like that for long minutes until Brett turned and started back toward his house. Cade didn't hesitate. He followed him.

Chapter Nine

Brett didn't turn on the lights when they stepped into the kitchen. There didn't seem to be a point to illuminate the room. His eyes were tired and the thought of brightness made his head throb. He turned to the window where shards of moonlight were slicing through the glass and casting shadows over the floor and walls. That was enough light. They didn't need more than that.

He stared at one triangle of silver that illuminated a picture frame on the wall. In the frame sat a picture of his parents, taken just after their wedding. As if their death had occurred only yesterday, the grief struck him between the ribs, a knife digging deep into his body and twisting cruelly. They were gone, he realized. And Dixie was gone too.

Swallowing hard, he dropped his gaze to the floor. His vision blurred, his throat burned. The thud of boots on the floor behind him reached his ears and he lifted his head. At the back of his mind he knew he should ask Cade to go but he couldn't bring himself to form the words. If there was one thing he was sure of, it was that he needed Cade here. If the man walked out of the house and left Brett alone, he didn't know what he'd do.

"Do you want something to drink?" Cade asked quietly, his voice close. "Or eat?"

Brett shook his head wordlessly. If he spoke his tight rein

on his control would crumble. Cade brought his hand down on his shoulder like he had before in the yard and he closed his eyes as the warmth of the large palm seared through his T-shirt. The warmth spread from his shoulder, down his arms and over his chest, soothing away the chill in his bones. Cade's grip on his shoulder tightened and he released a shaky breath. Inside him something shifted and a shiver of awareness tripped down his spine. He was treading thin ice here, he knew it. He just couldn't bring himself to care.

Slowly, he turned to face Cade and inhaled sharply when he found the man stood mere inches from him. Their eyes met and Brett's throat tightened further when he saw the tenderness in Cade's blue gaze. There was a shimmer of pain there too, a shared pain. Cade felt what he felt. They'd both lost so much already. They were coming through it together. It made so much sense now why they should comfort each other. Who else but Cade could understand what he was going through?

That thought repeated in his mind as his lips sought out Cade's in the dark. The other man's sharp intake of breath reached Brett's ears before he covered Cade's mouth with his own. The kiss started out soft at first as they tested the waters, little tremors of electricity passing between them. Brett lost himself in the texture of Cade's lips, smooth and firm, as they worked over his. And then Cade opened for him and the moist undersides of his lips pressed against Brett's mouth. He opened his mouth too and let the tip of his tongue glide along Cade's fuller bottom lip. Cade gave a quiet moan and his tongue touched his. Feeling the effects of the contact between his legs, Brett slid his tongue along Cade's, exploring the man's velvety mouth with a mix of curiosity and desire. Kissing him was completely different to kissing a woman. The firm pressure of his lips, the steady thrusting of his tongue, the warm taste of beer and mint on his breath. Nothing feminine about it. And when Cade stepped closer, closing the distance between their bodies, the difference became even clearer. Blood raced in Brett's veins, thick and fast, as he acknowledged the thick bulge in Cade's jeans, accepted that it was for him. He felt a tremor of fear, of wariness, but the building need within him washed the emotions away. In his pants, his dick strained against his boxers and, needing Cade to know how aroused he'd become, he sucked the man's tongue into his mouth and pressed his hips to Cade's. As their clothed erections rubbed together, a delicious friction building through the double barrier of denim, Brett groaned into the back of Cade's throat. He could come this way, just rocking his hips against Cade's. He could already feel his balls tightening, aching for release.

But abruptly, Cade ended the kiss, tearing his lips away. Brett waited for him to speak, fear gripping him. It wasn't the earlier fear of the unknown that surged through him. This time he feared Cade wanted to stop, to put an end to what passed between them, and Brett didn't know what he'd do if Cade walked away now. His lips burned, his cock throbbed heavily in his pants. He needed a release that he was certain only this man could give.

He held on as Cade's eyes, navy with desire, searched his.

"Are you sure you want to do this?" he asked eventually, his voice shaking. "We don't have to."

Relief washed over Brett and he would have smiled if he hadn't been so worked up. "I don't want to stop," he said, moving against Cade again. He drew in a deep breath, barely able to believe what he was about to say. "Come upstairs with me."

Cade's eyes flared though uncertainty remained in their blue depths. The desire won out and he nodded, expelling a long breath. "Okay."

As they climbed the stairs, Brett's mind travelled back to a few weeks ago when they'd done the very same thing. Of course, that night he'd been pissed out of his mind and Cade had been forced to half-carry him up the stairs. Wondering if Cade had felt this way back then, Brett's breathing grw shallow. Remembering how he'd led Cade into his bedroom and stripped out of his clothes, he felt his cock lurch in his jeans. Cade had backed away respectfully and left the room, hiding any desire he might have felt.

Tonight wouldn't end that way.

When they stepped inside his bedroom Brett stared down at the king-sized bed for a few moments before turning to face Cade. Tendrils of dark blonde hair, damp with sweat, hung around his shoulders. His lips were set in a hard line. His eyes glittered with need. This time it was Cade who reached for Brett, claiming his mouth, thrusting his tongue past his lips. He walked Brett to the bed until the backs of Brett's knees met the edge. Sitting, he leaned back on his elbows and let Cade and his firm lips take control.

Before he knew it he was on his back and Cade was on top of him, teeth nipping at his bottom lip. Plenty of times before, he'd had a girl ride him, bouncing around in his lap. But having a man on top was a whole different ball game. Cade's body, long and heavy with muscle, covered Brett completely. They were equals in height, in strength, and they could match one another's needs and desires. Brett didn't have to be gentle with Cade, and from the way Cade scraped the edge of his teeth over Brett's chin, he sure as hell wasn't going to go easy on him either.

"You're wearing too many clothes," Cade said huskily, pulling at the hem of Brett's T-shirt. "Sit up. I need to get this off."

Brett straightened and yanked the T-shirt over his head as Cade slipped out of his own shirt. Cade's crotch rested in Brett's lap and he felt Cade's cock jerk as he threw his T-shirt on the floor. The evidence of the effect he had on Cade's body had Brett choking back a groan. Then, as Cade's teeth closed around the tiny bud of his nipple, he lifted his hips up off the bed.

"You ever thought about this before?" he rasped out, and Cade's lips curved against his skin.

"Hell, yeah," was Cade's muffled reply as he kept his mouth on Brett's chest. "All the fucking time."

Blood surged straight to Brett's cock at Cade's words and he ran his hands over the smooth skin of the man's shoulders, feeling the muscles ripple as Cade lowered his head to Brett's ribs. Cade nibbled and sucked at the skin of his torso and then licked a trail from his belly button to the waistline of his jeans. With Cade's skilled mouth so close, Brett's cock swelled in his pants.

Cade lifted his head, a crooked grin spreading across his lips as he tracked his fingertips over the bulge in Brett's pants. Brett watched, hypnotized as Cade got to work on his belt, unbuckling it and leaving it hanging open. Then his face fell as Cade moved away from him to stand at the foot of the bed.

"Get up," Cade said as he started on his own belt buckle. "We need to get you out of those pants."

Brett thought his balls would explode as he moved to the end of the bed and kicked off his boots. Then he stood and shucked out his pants, letting out a groan of relief as his cock sprang free, jutting toward Cade.

"That's it," Cade said huskily, his eyes fixed on Brett's dick which bobbed between his legs. "Lie back again."

Brett got back onto the bed and lay back, once again rising

up on his elbows, eyes fixed on Cade. The man stripped down to a pair of black silk boxers and then climbed between Brett's open legs. His hot breath bathed Brett's cock and he couldn't tear his eyes away as Cade's tongue darted out and licked the swollen head. At the touch of Cade's tongue, Brett hissed out a breath through his teeth. Cade licked again, and then again, the movement of his tongue captivating Brett's gaze. Cade opened his mouth wide and swallowed the head. As he closed his lips tightly around the shaft, Brett clamped his jaw together and watched the length of his cock disappear into Cade's mouth.

He guessed it made sense a man would be so good at sucking cock. No woman could ever know the perfect amount of suction, the exact rhythm that made a blowjob incredible. Cade knew it all and worked Brett's cock with his whole mouth, using his lips, tongue and even teeth to tease the tight skin and sensitive glans. As Cade tongued the underside of Brett's cock, Brett lifted his hips, thrusting his cock further down Cade's throat. Cade accepted him eagerly, letting him slide over his tongue again and again until drops of come seeped from the broad head. Brett had to clench every muscle in his body to keep from coming as Cade dipped the tip of his tongue into the slit on the head of his cock. Then Cade released Brett's dick and lowered his head to his balls. He sucked one ball into his mouth, rolling it over his tongue before doing the same to the other. The scratch of day-old beard between Brett's thighs had to be the most erotic sensation he'd ever experienced and he clutched at the sheets on either side of him as he fought for self-control. He didn't want to come yet, not until Cade was—he swallowed hard as he realized what he craved—not until Cade was inside him.

Reaching down, he grabbed a fistful of Cade's shaggy hair. "Stop."

Cade lifted his head, his mouth red and swollen, his eyes glassy with desire. "Why?"

Brett shuddered out a breath as he let his gaze roam over what he could see. Moonlight danced into the room, casting Cade's upper body in a mixture of shadow and light. He could make out the roped muscles, the flat nipples and when Cade stood his mouth dried as he realized the black boxers had been discarded. He drank in the sight of the long, thick cock jutting out from a thatch of golden wiry curls. His own dick, wet with Cade's saliva, stretched up to his navel. He forced his gaze up from the powerful evidence of Cade's arousal to the man's eyes.

"I want you to—" He swallowed, his mouth suddenly sawdust. "Put it...put it—"

Though he didn't finish the sentence Cade seemed to understand. The fire in his eyes blazed as he climbed over Brett's body and covered his mouth again. Brett tasted himself on Cade's tongue and gave a low moan as their cocks rubbed together, pulsing heavily and hot as hell.

Cade's lips still pressed to his as he asked, "Do you have anything? Lube or something like that?"

Brett's thighs shook at what the question suggested. "I think," he said, trying to keep his voice steady. "Maybe there's some Vaseline in the locker."

Cade reached over him to pull open the locker door. After rummaging for a couple of seconds, his hand emerged with a pot of the stuff.

"Pretty old school," Cade said, the corner of his mouth quirking in a small smile, "but it'll do."

Brett expelled a shaky breath. "Good."

The smile faded from Cade's face as his eyes narrowed. "You sure about this, Brett? We don't need to rush it."

Brett nodded. As it was his cock was nearly leaping out of its skin each time it brushed Cade's erection. He wanted, no he *needed* to feel Cade inside him, and if it was going to happen it had to happen now. "I need this," he mumbled, gritting his teeth as his cock found Cade's again. "Please."

"Yeah," Cade muttered back, "as if you need to ask." He shifted his body to the side and stroked a hand over Brett's hard stomach. "Turn over."

As he rolled over on the bed and rose on his hands and knees, the night with Jessica flashed in his mind. He remembered being in this very position, waiting for her to drive a toy into his ass. Now he was getting the real thing and his body trembled with anticipation. He realized now he'd wanted this back then, that as he'd watched Cade jack off while the dildo penetrated him, he'd wanted Cade's cock pushing inside him, setting him on fire.

He bunched the sheets in his fists as Cade's fingers, sticky with Vaseline, rubbed between his buttocks, coating his entrance until he was well-prepared. His muscles went rigid as the hot tip of Cade's cock pushed between his ass cheeks and probed his hole. Sucking in a deep breath, he forced himself to relax.

"I'm gonna go real slow," Cade promised, his voice as shaky as Brett's limbs. "If you want me to stop, just say so."

Brett nodded, but he knew he wouldn't ask Cade to stop, not tonight. His eyelids flickered shut as Cade pushed forward, penetrating him with just the head of his dick. His whole body stiffened, his tight ring of muscles stretching around the width of Cade's cock. Cade entered another inch and pain flared from where the breadth of his dick rubbed against the nerve-endings that had almost never been played with. Sweat broke out across Brett's forehead as he fought through the pain. Cade propelled forward and this time slid a good three inches inside. The pain intensified, grew hotter, ripped through him until his eyes bulged. But then it melted, transformed into pleasure—a hot, stinging pleasure that made his stomach ripple and clench. A groan caught in his chest as Cade withdrew and then invaded again. With each easy thrust, Brett's muscles gradually relaxed and welcomed Cade's dick, clenching around him and sucking him deeper inside.

"Fuck," Cade growled in his ear as he slid in so far his pubic hair grazed Brett's buttocks. "You're so *fucking* tight."

Cade's harsh words turned Brett on even more and he growled back, the sound rumbling up out of his chest. Sweat poured down his back. The veins stood out along his neck from the exertion of taking Cade this way. The fierce pleasure burned in his ass and spread outward, heating his body. His cock jutted out, rock hard and begging for attention, but if he tried to support his body on one hand he knew he'd collapse.

As if sensing his dilemma, Cade stretched over his body and reached beneath him to grasp his cock. While he jerked his hand up and down Brett's skin, Cade's chest rubbed along his spine. Feeling Cade's heart pounding against his back had emotion clogging Brett's throat. The closeness, the intensity of the whole thing rocked Brett's insides, shook him up so hard he couldn't see past the color behind his eyes, couldn't hear anything except for the light slap as Cade's hips rolled against his ass. The strength of Cade's thrusts increased, his cock sinking deep inside Brett's ass, and Brett's balls drew up beneath him.

He let out a long moan as his stomach muscles clenched and his ass started to quake around Cade's dick. The sensations blazed through his body, pleasure reaching from his scalp to his toes and eventually tearing the climax from him. He howled with the force of his orgasm as his vision blurred and his mind spun in rapid, dizzying circles. His come spurted over Cade's fist in thick loads and his ass clenched hard around Cade's cock. He'd never come so hard in his life. Cade quickly followed him over the edge, his shout of release echoing in Brett's ears. Brett soared higher, head spinning so fast he thought he'd pass out. When his body finally stilled except for the occasional jerking of his hips, his arms and legs collapsed beneath him and he buried his face in the sheets. Cade's warm, sweat-slick body fell over him, as spent as he was. Brett fell asleep like that, feeling safer than he could remember as his eyes drifted shut.

When Cade awoke the following morning he was alone. Blinking to clear the haze from his eyes, he lifted his head. There was a dip in the sheets where Brett's body had lain and when he ran a hand over it, he found the sheet almost cold. He'd been alone for a while.

Gingerly, he moved his body to the edge of the bed and sat up. Rays of sunshine streamed through the window, flooding the bedroom with light. He reached a hand behind him to rub the top of his shoulder and glanced around the room. His clothes still lay strewn at the bottom of the bed but Brett's had been removed. Wondering how long the other man had been gone, Cade rose to his feet and started pulling on his clothes. He realized he needed a shower as he stepped out into the hallway. But he'd go home first.

The only sounds downstairs were a clock ticking and the gentle hum of the refrigerator. When Cade closed the screen door behind him and started down the steps to where his car was still parked, he saw the blue pickup was gone. A smirk twisted his lips as he pulled open the car door and slid inside. It figured. Brett had run away.

He couldn't blame the guy, he thought to himself as he shot down the driveway, clouds of dust billowing in his wake. The first time was always going to be a big deal, and coupled with the fact that Brett's state of mind hadn't been what anyone could call clear, Cade wouldn't be surprised if Brett was gone for good.

Guilt welled inside him as he took the turn for his house. Had he taken advantage of the situation last night? When he'd followed Brett inside his house all he'd wanted to do was make him feel better, to take the pain away. He hadn't intended on taking the man to bed. The thought hadn't even crossed his mind until Brett's mouth had slanted over his.

Remembering the jolt of electricity that had sparked between their lips, Cade tightened his hands on the wheel. A stronger man would have stopped it right there before things could get out of hand, but not Cade. The pressure of Brett's mouth on his had ripped away any honorable intentions he'd had before. He couldn't have held back, especially after Brett's request.

Come upstairs with me.

The breath hitched in Cade's throat as he heard Brett's deep voice in his mind. He'd never dared to dream that one day he'd get to touch Brett Miller, not even as a teenager when he'd watched Brett make out with his many girlfriends behind the stables. But last night it had happened. And the fierce intensity of the encounter had thrown all his previous sexual experiences into shadow.

He pulled up outside his house and turned the key in the ignition. He closed his eyes as the engine died and rested his face on the wheel. In his mind he saw Brett's face as it had been last night. Clenched jaw, parted lips, dark eyes desperate with need. There'd been no hesitation as Cade had touched his body, tasted the saltiness of his skin, sucked on the hard length of his pulsing cock. Brett had been so willing, a direct result of the pain he was suffering, Cade guessed. If Dixie hadn't passed away last night, they'd still be in limbo, Brett ignoring whatever he was feeling.

Maybe they were still in limbo, albeit a different kind. They'd crossed the line now. They couldn't go back. But would Brett want to continue? Cade hoped he did because the idea of never being that close to Brett again made his gut clench.

Slowly, he climbed out of the car and started up the steps to the porch. He stepped inside the house, already unbuttoning his shirt. Though his stomach growled with hunger, he headed straight for the shower and let the hot spray wash away all traces of Brett.

Brett drove all the way to El Paso that day and spent the afternoon wandering through the city. His mind worked overtime, sifting through what had happened the previous night. It had been brewing for weeks, he could see that now. Dixie's death had been the straw that broke the camel's back, the final nail in the coffin. He'd snapped, let his confused feelings for Cade take over.

For fuck's sake, what the hell did he do now?

It wouldn't happen again, he decided, keeping his head down as he wound his way along the bustling sidewalks. He didn't want it to happen again. It was too fucked up. It would throw the whole ranch into chaos. He and Cade could never work. It wasn't even a possibility.

But it felt so good, his mind reminded him, triggering an

onslaught of memories from the night before—Cade's hot mouth tugging on his nipple, his tongue swirling around his cock, the thick length of Cade's shaft invading his body. Brett's hands balled into fists at his sides as a shudder of desire passed down his spine. Gritting his teeth, he focused on blocking out the remembered sensations.

A leggy brunette caught his eye as they passed one another on the sidewalk. Her eyebrows lifted suggestively, her pink lips smiling a come-on. He looked away, wishing with all his might he could summon some level of interest, but right now the only body he longed for was Cade's.

He fought the urge to stop and slam his fist into the nearest wall, to let the physical pain chase away the emotion weighing him down. Instead, he joined a crowd of people waiting to cross the street and watched the numbers count down until the "go" sign flashed. He strode across the street and headed back to where he'd parked. He'd keep driving until he felt he could face Cade again. He'd drive all night if that's what it took.

"Oh my God," Jessica exclaimed down the phone as Cade shoveled a forkful of chili into his mouth on his way into the living room. "You fucked him, didn't you?"

Cade coughed, nearly choking on his food. "How the hell do you do that?" he demanded when he could speak.

Her amazed laugh tinkled down the line. "You sounded a little off and I took a shot in the dark."

He frowned and sank into the sofa opposite the TV. "Good shot," he said reluctantly.

"I can't believe it actually happened," she said breathlessly and he could imagine her eyes widening with wonder. Then her tone became sharp. "I can't believe I didn't get to see it!"

He let out a dry chuckle. "Guess I should have videotaped it for you."

"Yes, you should have." There was a pause before she asked, "So where is he now?"

"No fucking clue." He put down his bowl of chili and lifted his feet onto the coffee table. "He was gone when I woke up."

"So you spent the night together? Whose bed?"

"What does that matter?"

"Just answer the question."

He rolled his eyes. "His bed. Happy?"

She let out a breathy sigh. "You know what that means, don't you?" When he remained silent, she continued, "Every time he gets into bed he's going to think of you and what happened between you guys. That is so *hot*."

"Well, considering I haven't seen him since we fell asleep, I'm guessing he's going to do his darnedest to block it out."

"Don't let him," Jess said simply. "And believe me, forgetting you ain't easy. I know."

He grinned. "Thanks, Jess."

"You're welcome." Her voice lowered to a sultry whisper. "Now tell me everything."

He laughed, feeling the tension in his body lighten slightly. "Not a chance, sweetheart."

She gave a cry of protest. "That's not fair. If it hadn't been for me, the idea of fucking you probably never would have crossed his mind."

"Maybe." Rubbing his hand over his stubble-covered jaw, he expelled a long breath. "It was different, Jess. I never felt anything like that before."

"That's a good thing, honey," she said, her voice soft. "Don't let him run away from you."

"I don't think I have a choice."

Her frustrated groan made him smile again. "Get over yourself, Cade," she ordered, "and use every filthy trick in the book. Make him yours. Do it for me."

"For you?"

"Yeah, you have no idea how hot I get when I think of you guys together."

"I'll try my best," he promised, wondering if Brett would be home yet. "Thanks for checking up on me."

"No problems, babe. You just make sure you keep me updated."

He laughed as he rang off, feeling a million times better than he had before her call. He'd give Brett a little time to sort his head out, but Jess was right. If he wanted Brett, he had to go after him. And that's exactly what he intended to do.

Chapter Ten

As Cade rambled past Brett's house to the stables the following morning, Brett's truck was parked in the drive. Anticipation coiled low in his belly as he stepped into the stables and went straight to Marci's stall. He greeted their beautiful new mare, stroking a hand over her mahogany coat. She gave a snort of approval, pushing her muzzle into his hand. He smiled sadly, thinking of Dixie. There'd never be another one like her, but Marci's eyes reminded him of Dixie's in the way they sparkled with intelligence and vibrancy.

"Wait here, sweetheart," he said to the horse, backing out of the stall. "You and me are going for a ride." After fetching a saddle and bridle from the tack room—he wasn't riding her bareback again—he returned to her stall and saddled her up.

Her hooves clattered on the cobbled ground as he led her out of the stables and across the yard. They bumped into Jimmy when rounding the corner of the stables and upon seeing Marci the old man's wizened face lit up.

"Now there is a fine beast if I've ever seen one," Jimmy said, looking the horse up and down in admiration. "You picked a good one there, boy."

Cade nodded and then glanced past Jimmy to the paddocks. "Have you seen Brett this morning?" he asked casually, pulling on Marci's reins as she stomped her foot impatiently.

"Helping Paul and Danny with the cattle," Jimmy said, his face twisting in a grimace. "Those boys don't have two cents to rub together when it comes to branding."

Grinning, Cade shook his head. "I can't say it's my favorite job either." As Marci gave another tug, he started forward again. "I'll see you later, Jimmy."

He led the mare across the paddocks to where his favorite trail began. When he reached the dusty, juniper-lined path that declined down the mountain, he mounted the horse and dug his heels into her sides. She immediately launched into a full canter and they sped along the path. After thirty minutes or so, the path widened and then opened completely into the valley of Steeplecrest Ranch. He drank in the massive expanse of flat land that rolled on for miles and ended at the bottom of the next mountain over. Most of the land they used was hilly as the ranch sat nestled between the peaks of the Glass Mountains. Cade loved riding down into the valley between their mountain and the next and galloping across these grassy plains. At the moment the grass was browning in the heat and crackled beneath Marci's hooves. He breathed in a lungful of hot Texas air and made a mental note to talk to Brett about a new irrigation system down here.

While they cantered across the valley, he savored every second of familiarizing himself with Marci. He pushed her hard, riding her over the plains and tightening the reins each time she made a move to follow her own direction. She wasn't easy to tame but he thrived on the challenge. Later that afternoon, as he headed back up the mountain, taking a detour past the creek so Marci could take a drink of water, he realized he'd managed to push Brett out of his mind for a couple of hours.

But when he rode back around the paddocks Brett crashed

right back to the front of his mind. He watched Brett's biceps flex as he lugged the branding equipment toward the barn. He was bare-chested as he usually was at this time of day and sweat glistened all over his upper body. Cade's throat dried as he remembered how Brett had sweated the other night. Nothing to do with cattle equipment.

He jumped down from Marci and led her into the yard. The sound of her hooves on the ground caught Brett's attention and he turned. His whole body stiffened as he saw Cade approach.

"Hey there," Cade greeted, wishing he could see Brett's eyes but they were lost in the shadow of his Stetson. "Wondered if I'd see you today."

The man's mouth tightened as he stood stock-still in the middle of the yard. Then, without saying a word, he turned and continued into the barn.

Amusement triggered a smile from Cade's lips as he watched Brett's large frame disappear into the barn. He didn't think he'd ever seen anyone look so uncomfortable.

"Come on then," he said to Marci, pulling her toward the stables. "Let's get you cleaned up."

After washing down the horse and settling her back in her stall with something to munch on, he headed back into the yard and couldn't resist taking a peek into the barn. Brett was still there, shifting the equipment around the tiny space he'd allocated for it.

"Shit," he cursed as he caught his finger on something. Seeing the blood ooze from his finger, Cade stepped forward.

"You okay?"

Brett swung around, his finger in his mouth. He'd taken off the hat and his dark eyes stared accusingly into Cade's. "Fine." He turned his back pointedly and Cade grinned.

"So where were you yesterday?" he asked, leaning against a stack of bales. "Wondered if you'd decided to let me have the ranch all to myself."

Brett snorted but kept his focus on the equipment. "If that happened this whole place would fall apart."

Cade didn't argue. Instead, he waited, knowing the heavy silence would break Brett eventually.

He was right. After catching his finger again, Brett swore beneath his breath and lashed out at Cade. "What the hell are you hanging around for?" he demanded, throwing a glare in his direction.

Cade lifted a brow, knowing what he was about to say would really set the guy off. "You don't think we should talk?" He fought a smile as he stepped forward, holding Brett's defensive gaze. "You know, about the other night?"

The color drained from Brett's face and he backed up, knocking into the equipment he'd spent so much time organizing. "We ain't got nothing to talk about." His tone was fierce but the slight shake in his voice diluted the strength of his words.

"Sure we do," Cade said smoothly, taking another step forward. "It's not every day I fuck someone I work with."

Brett's sharp intake of breath was loud in the barn. "It was a mistake," he hissed through gritted teeth. "I didn't—I mean I wasn't thinking straight."

"No," Cade conceded, "you most definitely were not thinking straight." He grinned crookedly and moved even closer to Brett, so close he could feel the heat radiating from the man's body. "That was the fun."

As confusion and lust—a combination he was becoming familiar with—blazed in Brett's eyes, Cade reached out and ran a fingertip along the waistband of Brett's pants. Maybe he

167

should wait, give Brett the space he needed. But as Brett's eyes heated further, Cade couldn't help himself. He lowered his hands to Brett's groin and stroked the thickening bulge in his jeans.

Brett didn't appear to breathe as Cade touched him. His cock lengthened with each rub of Cade's hand and Cade's own dick reacted to Brett's arousal.

"I'm not gay," Brett blurted out as Cade increased the pressure of his hand on the man's cock. "I'm not—I mean, I like women." He gave a low groan and swiped his hand over his face. "I like tits, I like pussy."

Cade nodded. "And you like cock too." He leaned in, letting his lips brush Brett's earlobe as he inhaled the smell of fresh sweat. "It doesn't have to be one or the other," he whispered, cupping Brett's hard-on through the denim. "You can have both."

At his words, Brett's cock leaped in his pants. He didn't say anything as Cade got to work on his belt buckle, didn't make any sound of protest as Cade jerked down the zipper of his jeans.

Dropping to his knees, Cade pulled Brett's cock out of his pants and groaned at the sight of rock-hard, plum-colored flesh. He wrapped his hands around the thick base and brought his lips to the swollen head. Sucking Brett's dick the other night had made him harder than he'd ever been and he was desperate to experience the pleasure again. He opened his mouth wide and swallowed the ridged head, letting the heady taste of Brett's salty skin fill his mouth. Lowering his head, he took more of Brett's dick into his mouth and the thick shaft glided over his tongue, making his taste buds tingle and his mouth water. He bathed the tight skin with his tongue and groaned as the pulsing in Brett's cock increased.

As he sucked with an eagerness he'd never felt for any other man, he let his hands glide up over Brett's muscular thighs and around to his denim-covered buttocks. He kneaded Brett's ass and, when Brett's fingers weaved into his hair and gripped hard, Cade's cock jerked between his legs. Releasing Brett from his mouth, he dragged the tip of his tongue along the heavily veined underside as he looked up into Brett's glassy eyes.

"What if someone comes?" Brett asked huskily, hands still tangled in Cade's curls.

Cade smiled. "The only one who's gonna come is you," he mumbled against Brett's erection, knowing how his words would vibrate against the throbbing skin. "Jimmy and the guys are out on the pastures with the cattle. They ain't got any business coming in here."

This seemed to satisfy Brett as his hips started to pump. A growl of approval stuck in Cade's throat as Brett drove his cock across his tongue, increasing the pace with each steady thrust. He swallowed all of him, loving how Brett's hot skin burned his tongue. He gripped Brett's ass as tightly as Brett gripped his hair and waited for the man to lose control. It finally happened with a sudden double jerk of his hips and Brett's creamy release pooled on Cade's tongue. He swallowed it down greedily and licked Brett's cock until he'd caught every drop. Then, rising to his feet, dick still throbbing in his pants, he grinned at Brett's defeated expression.

"It doesn't have to be a bad thing," he said, cupping Brett's shadowed jaw in one hand and making him look at him. "No pressure, no big deal. Just fucking."

Brett's throat worked as he swallowed. "It's not just fucking when it's with another guy."

Cade's heart clenched in the face of Brett's vulnerability.

Damn, this man made him feel and he didn't know whether to go with the strong emotions or run the hell away from them. Losing himself in the dark depths of Brett's eyes, he decided he needed to go with the emotion. Easing Brett's fear would be hard enough without worrying about his own.

Wanting nothing more than to turn Brett around and bend him over the stacked equipment, he backed up toward the barn doors. Enough for today. If he rushed things too fast there was a bigger chance he'd lose Brett altogether. And he wouldn't risk that, not even to ease the ache between his legs.

"I'll see you later," he said, walking out of the barn. He kept going, heading in the direction of his house. He waited until he was hidden by trees before he stopped and unbuttoned his pants. He jacked off there at the side of the road.

He thought of Brett when he exploded in his fist.

The next day, after leading the horses out to one of the paddocks, Cade spotted Brett's frame approaching in the distance. Raising an eyebrow in surprise, Cade lifted his hand to his hat and tugged the brim down over his eyes to take away the sun's glare. Yep, that was Brett alright, and there wasn't a chance the guy hadn't seen him.

A grin started to spread across Cade's face. He'd expected Brett to spend the day ignoring him as he had after all their other encounters. But there he was, long legs carrying him forward, though Cade did have to admit he still looked a little uncomfortable.

"Mornin'," he greeted when Brett closed in on the paddock. "You seen Jimmy yet?"

Brett shook his head. "He's on a day off."

"About time too." The old man worked himself to the bone. He was going to keel over if he didn't let up.

Stopping at the fence and propping one booted foot on the bottom rail, Brett jerked his head to the horses. "Marci looks good."

Cade glanced behind him and grinned as the mahogany mare gave a derisive snort when one of the others bumped against her. "Yeah, she's a fine specimen," he agreed, looking back into Brett's shadowy eyes. "Still looks a little empty without Dixie around though."

Brett gave a curt nod. "Sure does." He cleared his throat as if to say something, then hesitated.

"You want something?" Cade asked, studying the man's expression for a clue. He was difficult to read with that damn Stetson on his head.

Brett paused again and then took a step back. "No, I'll leave you to it." He turned on his heel and started back toward the yard. He'd crossed about ten yards before he turned back. "You want to come over for the game tonight?"

Cade blinked. Had he heard the guy right? From Brett's awkward stance, he guessed he had. "Uh, sure," he blurted out and wished he hadn't sounded so surprised. "I'll be there around seven?"

"Yeah." Brett hesitated another second and then turned again and set off into the distance.

Cade turned back to the horses and pulled his hat from his head. "Did you hear that?" he asked Marci, shaking out his hair. "I'm gonna watch the game with Brett tonight."

Her large chocolate gaze stared into his and he could have sworn she rolled her eyes.

When seven o'clock rolled around that evening, Cade

climbed the steps up onto Brett's veranda and walked straight through the open door.

"Brett?" he called, making a beeline for the kitchen that was releasing the enticing aroma of fried chicken. "You in here?"

He stepped inside, found the kitchen empty, and then started as the back door swung open and Brett entered from the backyard.

"Sorry for barging in," Cade said, his body reacting immediately to the jeans that clung lovingly to Brett's strong thighs. "Door was open."

"I know." He strode past Cade to the frying pan and flipped the chicken pieces. "You hungry?"

Cade's gaze swept the length of Brett's body, resting for a second on the tight ass. He swallowed thickly. "Starved."

As if he'd picked up on Cade's double meaning, Brett tensed his shoulders but kept his focus on the food. "There's beer in the fridge."

"Thanks." Cade grabbed two beers from the refrigerator and set one down on the kitchen table before uncapping the other. As he let the cold liquid trickle down his throat, his mind flashed back to the first time he'd been in this kitchen after the funeral. Remembering the tension between them, the hostility that had oozed from Brett in truckloads, Cade grinned. Back then he'd never for a second believed he'd one day get to fuck the guy, though he had fantasized about it while sitting at this very kitchen table. Things changed fast around here.

"What's so funny?" Brett asked as he grabbed two plates from one of the cupboards.

Not sure Brett was ready to hear how long Cade had been lusting after him, he just shrugged. "Heard you were teaching the two boys how to brand cattle yesterday."

Brett let loose a sound that was half-groan, half-laugh. "It was a fucking nightmare," he said, sliding fried chicken onto the plates. He carried them over to the table and took the seat opposite Cade. "Didn't think we were going to get it done."

"At least now they know," Cade said, lifting a piece of the crispy chicken to his lips.

Brett snorted. "I wouldn't trust those two with a hot iron if my life depended on it."

"Well, Paul's taking off for college next year," Cade said after swallowing a tender bite of chicken. "Danny seems to have a bit more sense. We can keep him and take on someone else."

"Yeah, I was thinking that. But who is there to take on? Most of the kids don't want to work all the way out here, especially when their folks are throwing money at them to keep them in school."

"Not the way we were raised."

Brett shook his head. "Not even close."

They ate in silence after that and Cade found himself lost in thoughts of their shared childhood. Brett's dad had been tough, but his dad had been tougher, especially when he'd had a few too many drinks down at Billy's. When he'd been sober he'd been a decent man with strict morals and a big heart. Cade just wished he could have been sober more often.

"You okay?"

Cade looked up from his food and felt his stomach clench at the tenderness in Brett's eyes. It disappeared half a second later but the memory of it made Cade's heart ache. This wasn't just sex. Not for him and not for Brett either.

"You can turn on the TV if you want," Brett said, getting to his feet and carrying the empty plates to the sink.

Cade lifted a brow. So they really were going to watch TV

after all. He headed out into the hall and stepped into the living room. Brett joined him a couple of minutes later with another round of beers and they sat on the sofa to watch the game.

With Brett in such close proximity, Cade couldn't keep track of the score, couldn't even be sure what players were on the field at any given time. His eyes kept slanting in Brett's direction, watching him gulp down some beer or stretch his leg out on the coffee table. To hide his growing erection, Cade crossed one leg over the other, resting the side of his shin on his knee to give his lap plenty of breathing space. When the game finally ended, Cade didn't have a clue who'd won.

Brett slid his foot off the coffee table and leaned forward to set his beer down on the glass. "Good game," he said, leaving the TV on as the commentary began.

Cade nodded. "Sure."

They drifted into silence again and Cade became aware of the tension in Brett's body. He was still leaning forward, elbows resting on his knees, eyes focused on the screen, but his breathing was far from even. He was waiting for something to happen.

Uncrossing his legs, Cade shifted to the edge of the sofa cushion and turned his head to Brett. "Why don't we turn this off?"

He heard Brett's breath catch as the man aimed the remote control at the TV and clicked the off button. He dropped the remote, still looking at the black screen.

Cade reached out and touched his arm. Brett's gaze, dark with desire, shot to his.

"Sit back," Cade told him, increasing the pressure on Brett's arm. The man held his eyes as he shifted back on the sofa and settled fully into the seat. Cade glanced down, feeling a tug on his dick as he noticed the bulge at the front of Brett's pants. *For Christ's sake, how long's that been there for?*

He swallowed and then lifted his body to swing one leg over Brett's lap. "I didn't think that game was ever gonna end," he muttered, looking straight into Brett's flashing eyes and feeling the man's cock jerk beneath his body. He leaned in, feeling Brett's sharp breaths caress his lips. "You trying to kill me, Miller?"

Brett's lips parted wordlessly and, unable to help himself, Cade swooped down and claimed his mouth. Heat burst inside him as he worked his mouth over Brett's, running the tip of his tongue along the firm lips before thrusting it inside. Like before, Brett remained still, keeping his arms at his sides and letting Cade explore his mouth. His cock pushed into Cade's groin with every sweep of Cade's tongue and Cade rubbed up against him, feeling the delicious friction burn between them.

He could kiss this guy forever, he realized as he tangled his hands in Brett's thick hair and deepened the kiss. From the abrasive texture of his tongue, to the velvety cavern of his mouth and his taste of pure sin. He sucked lightly on the tip of Brett's tongue and then pulled back to nip at the man's luscious bottom lip. A low moan fell from Brett's mouth as he shifted beneath Cade's body and curled his hands around Cade's hips, pulling him closer.

"Easy," Cade warned as the throbbing in his cock intensified dangerously. "You want this to last, right?"

Brett didn't answer, just dipped his head and caught Cade's lips with his. Blood surged straight to Cade's cock as he felt the need in Brett's body increase tenfold. The man tangled his tongue with Cade's and the velvety surfaces rubbed together as Brett's fingers dug into Cade's hips.

Groaning into the back of Brett's throat, Cade reached between their bodies and got to work on Brett's zipper. The rasp of metal on metal reached his ears and hot, burning cock leaped into his hands. He wrapped his fingers around Brett's staff and began to pump his hand up and down. Brett's mouth hardened on his and a growl rumbled up out of his chest. He ripped his lips from Cade and gasped for air, his eyes darting to where Cade's hands stroked his dick.

"I wanted this," he said on a heavy rush of breath. His gaze came back to Cade's and their faces were so close Cade could distinguish every eyelash circling Brett's eyes. "All through the game," he continued, his lips almost brushing Cade's, "I wanted this."

"Well you should have fucking said so," Cade growled, swiping his thumb over the head of Brett's cock. "We could have done this hours ago."

Brett nodded, his face tight with oncoming climax. "Stop," he rasped, his hips jerking upward. "I'm going to come."

Wanting to make this last as long as possible, Cade eased his grip and moved down onto the sofa. The plum head of Brett's dick bobbed between the guy's legs as he drew in deep breaths to calm himself.

"Take your clothes off," Cade ordered after a few moments, getting to work on the buttons of his own shirt. He watched Brett tug the black T-shirt over his head and lift his hips to shuck off his pants. Feeling a bolt of desire surge through his veins, Cade drank in the lines of Brett's body—the strong arms, the smooth, muscled torso, the long hair-dusted thighs that cradled his magnificent cock. He unzipped his own pants and felt his balls react to Brett's low moan of approval. Looking from his engorged dick to Brett's lust-filled gaze, Cade gritted his teeth and rose on his knees.

"Lie back," he ordered, staring down at Brett. "And open your legs."

The man hesitated briefly and then arranged his body so his head rested on the sofa's armrest and his legs spread on either side of Cade's body.

Cade caught Brett's calves and pushed, forcing Brett to draw up his knees. Sitting back for a second, Cade admired the new angle. His eyes roamed from the tip of Brett's erection down to his sac and along the ridged extension of his penis to the small bud of his ass. Cade leaned down and sucked each ball into his mouth, rolling them over his tongue. Moving down, he licked his way along the sensitive ridged flesh before circling Brett's hole with the tip of his tongue. Brett lifted his hips and his choked moan made Cade's cock lurch.

Raising his head, he dug into his front pocket where he'd shoved some lube on the way out the door.

"No Vaseline this time?" Brett croaked out, humor glinting in his eyes as Cade warmed the lube between his hands.

Grinning, Cade shook his head and reached between Brett's legs to smooth the substance over his ass. Then he squeezed out another blob from the tube and coated his dick with the stuff.

"Pull your legs up higher," he told Brett and felt his mouth dry when he saw how ready the guy was.

He positioned his cock against Brett's lubed-up hole and pushed forward, feeling the ring of muscles give way a lot quicker than they had the first time. He entered him slowly, one hand gripping the side of the sofa, the other resting on Brett's knee.

He's smooth as silk, Cade realized as his cock slid deeper inside Brett's ass, *and tight as hell*. He shifted his gaze upward to Brett's face and felt his cock leap inside the man's passage. With his jaw clenched and his brows drawn together in concentration, torture and pleasure were written plain across

Brett's face.

"You okay?" Cade whispered, withdrawing slowly from Brett's body and then propelling forward again.

"Yeah," Brett said hoarsely, squeezing his eyes shut as Cade sank even deeper. "That feels—you feel good."

Cade let loose a pained chuckle as Brett's passage tensed around him and sucked him in further. "So do you," he ground out, his thighs starting to tremble. He'd never been so close to coming so fast. "Touch yourself," he ordered, watching a drop of pearly liquid appear on the head of Brett's cock and aching to lick it off. As he continued to rock his hips against Brett's ass, he watched the man's large hand grasp his cock and start to pump up and down.

"That's it," he urged, upping the pace of his thrusts and groaning when Brett's ass clenched around him again. "Does that feel good?"

Brett's bloodshot eyes came to his and, as come spurted out of his cock, the creamy liquid shimmering on Brett's plum-red skin, it was all the answer Cade needed. He shouted at the ceiling as Brett's ass squeezed his cock, milking it until he exploded, spilling inside Brett's body. His body shook and jerked until his balls were empty. Then he fell forward between Brett's knees and buried his face in the man's sweat-covered chest. As he fought for breath, Brett's chest started to vibrate with husky laughter. Raising his head, Cade looked at his lover in surprise.

"What's so funny?"

Brett shook his head, eyes half-closed. "Can't believe I'm fucking guys now."

Unsure how to respond to that, Cade blinked. Then he started to laugh too.

Chapter Eleven

"This is getting a hell of a lot easier," Brett admitted later on, lounging against the sofa as Cade buttoned his shirt.

"What's getting easier?" Cade asked, humor glinting in his blue eyes. "Having a cock shoved up your ass or watching me get dressed?"

A wry grin spread across Brett's lips as he propped his hands behind his head. "Both."

Cade's laugh warmed his insides. "Good," the man said, standing over him. "We're making progress." The humor faded from his face as his gaze swept over Brett's body, naked except for a pair of boxers. "You are so damn sexy," he muttered almost to himself.

Sharp bolts of lust tripped down Brett's spine. He didn't know if he'd ever get used to being with a guy, to hearing a man's baritone tell him he was sexy, but he sure did like the rush it gave him. As a matter of fact, the whole situation was giving him a rush. Sitting here, watching Cade gather himself, Brett felt like a goddamn kid who'd just lost his virginity. Excitement coursed through his veins, his palms sweated, nerves fluttered in his stomach, he wanted to do it all over again. In a way, he guessed he had just lost his virginity. Being with a guy was a completely different experience to being with a girl.

"How long were you waiting for this?" he asked, drawing Cade's attention to his mouth.

The man frowned and took a seat on the coffee table. "You really want to know the answer to that?"

Brett shrugged. "It can't hurt now."

"No, I guess not." Cade made a face and then said, "Since we were teenagers."

A bark of laughter rose in Brett's throat. "You're shitting me."

He shook his head. "Wish I was."

"But you had girlfriends all the time," Brett said, remembering the long line of chicks who used to follow Cade around the stables until Jimmy told them to get lost.

"Sure I did. I still do." Cade seemed to zone out, lost in thought. "I didn't try guys until I'd left my old man behind."

Brett nodded, remembering how heavy handed Ken Armstrong had been with his son. A flashback of the day he'd walked into the barn and caught Ken lashing his belt across Cade's bare back entered his mind and he winced. Cade had only been about twelve or thirteen at the time, but even though the leather had sliced into his skin not a sound had escaped his lips. When he'd straightened and faced Brett there hadn't been a single tear on his face. After that day, nobody on Steeplecrest Ranch had been able to ignore Ken's problem. He'd entered rehab a week later and returned home a different man. From the pained expression on Cade's face, Brett supposed he hadn't ever gotten over it and, feeling a surge of anger toward Cade's dad shoot through him, he could understand why.

"I'm sorry," he said when the anger faded enough for him to speak. "I'm sorry it happened."

Surprise flashed in Cade's eyes and a small smile quirked

the corner of his mouth. "Forget it, it's in the past."

Brett let the subject rest. One day they'd talk about it properly. He didn't know whether it was the fact they'd grown up together or that they'd lost their folks at the same time, but he had a feeling sharing things with Cade would be a whole lot easier than sharing with anyone else.

In front of him, Cade rose to his feet and moved toward the door. "I'm going to take off," he said, setting his hat on his head. "Early start and all."

Brett nodded, sitting forward on the sofa. A large part of him ached for Cade to stay, to spend the night with him and make it last. The offer formed in his throat and the words were ready to trip off his tongue but he held them back. Much as he wanted Cade here with him, trepidation still lined his stomach. He needed time to get his head around this and he appreciated Cade not pushing him into anything.

"I'll see you tomorrow," Cade called from the hall and the sound of the front door opening nearly made Brett jump up and run after him. But half a second later the door slammed shut and he sat back on the sofa. There was always tomorrow.

That night he dreamt of Cade—the hard contours of his body, the pleasure he wielded with his cock. When Brett awoke his dick was throbbing heavily between his legs. Beneath his morning shower, he soothed the ache with his hand.

Sultry Texas air greeted him when he stepped outside later that morning, and for the first time in a while he appreciated the beauty of the ranch. The land spread out before him, rolling hills, tree-studded ridges, grassland plains. The potent smells of dried grass and manure wrapped around him and he breathed it all in.

"Now I don't believe what I'm seeing," a male voice drawled

from the yard. "Is that a smile on Brett Miller's face? It can't be, not at this time of the morning."

Grinning, Brett glanced to his left to where Cade stood in the middle of the yard, an ironic smile lifting his lips.

"Nah," Brett said, walking along the veranda. He braced his hands on the railing and let himself feel the desire that curled in his chest. The Cade from his dreams was no match for the reality of that crooked grin and lean, ropey muscle. "I'm not smilin'. It's just a twitch."

Cade's grin widened. "Figures." He strolled forward and reached his hands up to grasp the veranda railing, his palms resting on either side of Brett's. "You gonna stand up there all day like the king of the goddamn castle, or are you going to do some work?"

Brett laughed and booted his way down the steps. "Don't get your panties in a twist, Armstrong. I'm right here."

"Then let's go." Cade brought his hand down on Brett's shoulder, steering him toward the stables. The warmth of his palm heated Brett's skin through the thin material of his T-shirt and the sudden feeling of being out of control hit him.

Relax, he told himself, reining in the rush of panic. Though right now he wanted nothing more than to pull Cade into one of the empty stalls and rub up against him, he knew he could control himself. If they were working together, he'd have to.

Surprisingly enough, working with Cade wasn't the torturous experience he'd expected it to be. It could have been that they were completely caught up in driving a herd of over a hundred cattle to a fresh pasture or the fact that Jimmy's presence was bound to dampen any kind of sexual intentions. Regardless, they spent the day focused on the work at hand and had a few laughs in between. The relaxed, friendly atmosphere put Brett's mind at ease. Getting into whatever the hell he was getting into with Cade wouldn't be the ranch's downfall. They both cared about it too much.

Cade came over for dinner again that night, and then every other night that week. It always started out the same way—Brett cooked and they ate before going into the living room to watch TV. They never got around to actually watching the TV. Instead, Cade went down on Brett or filled his ass with his cock. He always took control, showing Brett how good they could be together. After a few hours of playing around on the sofa, Cade would bid farewell for the night. Brett felt himself easing into the new setup quickly and spent the sundrenched days looking forward to the evenings. He still wasn't sure what the hell had happened to him over the past few weeks. But he wouldn't worry about it. Not yet.

Chapter Twelve

"Here you go, honey, have some more sweet potatoes."

Three weeks after Dixie's death and three weeks since his first time with Cade, Brett was sitting at the Dawes' dining table surrounded by food. He'd received many invitations to dinner from Tommy's mom since the funeral and he'd turned down every one of them. He knew Mrs. Dawes would fuss over him like he was her own child, feeding him and spoiling him until he passed out on her sofa. And much as he appreciated the woman's kind heart, he hadn't been able to summon the courage to face her warmth which reminded him so much of his own mother. At least not until tonight.

It was Cade's doing, he realized as he dug into the plate of ham before him. Since he'd given in to where his feelings for the guy were leading, he'd been a lot more relaxed. Part energetic sex, part figuring out what had been bothering him about the man. It made sense now why he'd been so hostile towards Cade when he'd first returned to town. Hiding from his feelings. What kind of pussy was scared of his own damn self?

"Catch the game Friday night?" Tommy asked from across the table.

With his mouth full, Brett pulled a face. "Wish I hadn't," he said when he'd swallowed.

"I'm with you on that." Tommy nudged his father. "The old

man here nearly had a coronary."

Mr. Dawes snorted and then wiped his mouth with a napkin. "Can you believe this kid?" he asked, looking at Brett while he jerked his thumb toward Tommy. "Thinks he's a smart-ass."

Brett grinned, watching father and son throw jibes at one another. His relationship with his dad had been like that, always riling each other up from dawn to dusk. It was something he'd really missed these past couple of months.

Mrs. Dawes seemed to pick up on his feelings and rose to her feet, giving the back of Tommy's head a light smack. "Enough of that, you two. We've got company, remember?" She shook her head as she pottered out to the kitchen. "Tell Brett about what happened last week at the shop."

"We're trying to keep that quiet, Mom," Tommy called back to her, making Brett chuckle. Great as she was, Mrs. Dawes liked to gossip.

"Oh, Brett can keep his mouth shut," she argued as she brought a peach cobbler to the table. "Can't you, sweetie?"

Brett glanced at Tommy and grinned. "Won't say a word."

Tommy rolled his eyes. "It was nothing really. Some kid tried to break into the shop."

Brett frowned. "No kidding. Did he get anything?"

"Nah. Mitch was leaving Barney's at the time. Saw him trying to break the window."

"It was Joan Harbor's boy," Mrs. Dawes cut in, her tone hushed as if there were people listening in. "Knew there was trouble in that house."

"That's enough, Carrie," Mr. Dawes said, putting an end to the conversation. "The boy's been punished, let's leave it at that."

While Mrs. Dawes liked to throw stones on occasion, her husband was endlessly fair. A good trait to have in a town sheriff.

Brett dug into his cobbler and had inhaled it within a minute. Before he'd put his fork down, Mrs. Dawes served him another portion and he focused on that, cherishing each bite of homemade pie.

"So how's Cade coming along?" Mr. Dawes asked, nearly causing Brett to choke with the sudden question.

He looked up from his dessert and swallowed. "Uh, he's doing okay." He coughed to clear his throat. "We're both busy on the ranch."

"I'll bet you are." The older man nodded thoughtfully to himself. "Always found Cade to be a good kid, even as a boy."

Brett shrugged, feeling heat crawl across his skin. "He does his bit." What would he do if the Dawes found out about his relationship with Cade? They'd never look at him the same way again.

A sudden cloud of claustrophobia smothered him and he jumped to his feet. "You know I really should get going."

Mrs. Dawes looked up at him in surprise. "Oh, all right," she said, getting to her feet. "It was so good to see you."

He forced a smile. "You too." He nodded to Mr. Dawes before he made a beeline for the door, feeling that if he stuck around too long somehow they'd *know*. "Thanks for dinner."

He stepped outside and then turned to find Tommy on his heels.

"You okay, man?" Tommy asked, patting him on the shoulder.

He nodded, feeling like a goddamn drama queen. "It was just a little hot in there, that's all."

They started to walk toward Brett's truck and, feeling bad about rushing out, Brett glanced at Tommy. "Sorry I didn't stick around longer."

"No worries. Mom was just glad you came by."

Brett pulled open the door of his truck and stepped up into the cab. "You on for Barney's this Friday?" he asked, feeling a need to do something "normal".

"Well, Mitch called me just before you came round. He's having a pool party on Friday night. You should come."

A pool party sounded normal enough. "Thanks," Brett said, "I'll do that."

"Sure." Tommy stepped away and looked up. "What about Cade? You want him to come?"

Brett's head snapped up from where he'd been inserting the keys in the ignition. "Cade?" A rush of defensiveness surged within him. "Why're you asking me?" he said stiffly.

Tommy shrugged. "I know you had some problems with the guy at the start, that's all."

Brett studied Tommy's expression for a trace of tension, anything to suggest he knew about him and Cade. He let out a breath after finding nothing. "No, me and Cade are good now," he said casually as the engine roared to life. "When I see him tomorrow I'll ask him."

"Great." Tommy patted the hood of the truck and waved. "See you Friday."

Brett thought about the evening the whole way home, and with every inch of ground that disappeared beneath the Chevrolet's wheels, the muscles in his back and shoulders tightened further until he wanted to ram his fists into the dashboard. He was being paranoid, freaking out over nothing. Tommy and his folks didn't suspect a thing. The idea that Brett was sleeping with Cade wouldn't even enter their heads, not even for a second.

Then why the hell was he wound up tighter than a minister's wife?

He scrubbed his hand over his face and focused on the road ahead. He needed to chill out, stop thinking so damn much. Or else he'd be driving himself to the loony bin.

When he reached the junction to turn off for Cade's house he slowed down the truck. Was Cade really worth all this paranoia? He could drive down there now and settle this whole thing. He could end it. Then he'd never have to freak himself out like this again.

But damn it, he didn't want to end it. Not even close.

He pressed his foot on the accelerator and headed uphill toward his own place. He pulled up outside the house and jumped down from the driver's seat. The fresh country air calmed him in a way the Chevrolet's air con hadn't managed to do. He breathed deeply and then blew it out slowly. He'd take tonight for himself, get a good sleep. Maybe the morning would bring the clarity he needed.

He went inside, switched the foyer light on and headed straight upstairs. He took his time taking his clothes off. Paranoia had made him sleepy as hell. When he was naked he padded out of the bedroom and into the bathroom. He turned on the shower, stepped under the water and waited for the hot spray to ease his muscle ache.

He must have been in there five minutes when he sensed movement behind him. He twisted to the side, but two large hands caught him by the shoulders and held him in place.

"Easy there, big guy," Cade muttered through the steam. "It's just me."

Brett stiffened at the deep sound of Cade's voice, fists clenching at his sides as Cade's hands rubbed his shoulders. He wanted to pull away, to resist what was about to happen. But Cade's masterful touch had Brett leaning forward. He rested his forehead on the damp tiled wall and closed his eyes as Cade's fingertips dug into his shoulders, erasing the stress from his muscles. Ironic how Cade could make the tension disappear when he'd created it in the first place. But that was Cade. He was everything—a colleague, a friend, a joker, a lover. He made Brett's head spin, and when the head of Cade's swollen cock brushed the seam of his ass he couldn't bring himself to say no.

He straightened and turned slowly to face the other man. Cade's blue eyes studied him, desire flaring in the black pupils. Brett's cock rose between his legs, hardening the longer Cade watched him. As Cade moved in and brought his lips down on Brett's, the heat of the contact drove thoughts of anything outside the shower stall to the back of Brett's mind.

"Know I should have called," Cade mumbled against Brett's lips. He reached down and wrapped his fingers around Brett's shaft. "Couldn't help myself."

Cade squeezed his cock and Brett groaned into the man's open mouth, the sound disappearing down his throat. Cade pushed forward, backing Brett up to the wall. When Brett's back was flat against the tiles, Cade's tongue drove between Brett's lips, conquering his mouth in long, harsh sweeps. As need flared deep within him, Brett dug his hand into Cade's wet curls and pulled the man closer, deepening the kiss. Their mouths melded together, their sharp breaths mingling while their erections rubbed together in a friction that had Brett on the brink.

He pulled his head away and drew in a deep breath. Cade moved in again and nipped at the base of Brett's neck, then sucked and bit his way along Brett's shoulder. Leaning his head back, Brett let Cade's mouth torment his skin, his nipples, the indent of his belly button. But instead of continuing the descent and enveloping Brett's cock in his mouth, Cade straightened and reached for the shower gel.

"Let's get you nice and clean, huh?"

Through half-lidded eyes, Brett watched as Cade soaped up his hands and started to run them over Brett's body. It felt so good, so right to be here with Cade, to see the man's cock leap as he stroked his hands over Brett's torso. They worked. In bed, out of bed. Why the hell had he been worried?

"Turn around."

At Cade's order, Brett faced the wall again. Cade glided his hands down his back to his buttocks. He worked the flesh with his hands and Brett's cock speared against the tiles, straining so hard he thought his cock would break through the wall. Cade moved closer and sucked at the crook of Brett's shoulder. The heat of his mouth sent sharp, electric sensations shooting down Brett's spine and he pressed his ass into Cade's hands.

"What is it?" Cade muttered in his ear, his voice dark with sex. "Want me to fuck you? Is that it?"

Unable to speak, Brett could only growl. Cade's deep chuckle echoed in his ears as the man slid his hands between Brett's buttocks. His balls tightened as Cade slicked up his hole with soap, making him nice and slippery, ready for Cade's cock.

When the guy settled the plum head of his dick at his entrance, Brett dipped his head and squeezed his eyes shut. Cade entered him smoothly, stretching his passage until his cock was rubbing against all the ridges. Brett clenched his jaw, his breath coming in harsh pants as he waited for Cade to withdraw. He needed it fast tonight. Hard and fast.

As if reading his mind, Cade pulled out and then drove right back in. He penetrated Brett in short, quick strokes, groaning in Brett's ear on the in-stroke. Reaching around, he grasped Brett's cock and started to pump up and down. Intense pleasure burned through Brett's body and his hands slid along the slippery wall as he tried to hold himself together. But he couldn't last. With a howl that caught in his throat, his hips jerked forward and he came all over the white tiles. Cade drove into his clenching ass one last time before joining him in white-hot pleasure. As he shuddered his release, Brett finally slackened against the wall. For long minutes, Cade lay against him, water still streaming down their bodies. When Cade straightened, Brett did too and they rinsed off in silence before shutting off the water.

"The soap was okay, right?" Cade asked as he dried off with a towel.

Brett looked at him, his mouth watering at the sight of smooth muscled torso. "Uh, what do you mean?"

"The soap was enough to make you ready?"

"Oh sure, yeah." He nodded, grabbing a pair of boxers from the hook on the back of the door.

"Good." There was a pause before Cade spoke again. "Everything okay, Brett?"

He glanced at Cade again to find the guy wearing a pair of sweats. "Yeah." He hesitated and then shook his head. "Listen, you should have called first."

Cade gave a small smile. "Knew you were going to say that." He walked past Brett out of the bathroom.

"You did?" Brett followed him to the top of the stairs.

"Sure." Cade shrugged. "I know this isn't easy for you. It's just when I saw your lights on tonight..." He trailed off. "Won't happen again, I promise."

Brett stared at Cade in confusion. He'd expected the guy to be mad, insulted that he had to call before coming over. But instead he was being reasonable, more than reasonable. It instantly put Brett at ease and he couldn't help but smile.

"You wanted me that bad, huh?"

Cade grinned back. "Get over yourself." He started down the staircase. "I'll see you in the morning."

Brett watched him disappear through the front door and then headed for the bedroom. He could breathe again.

As Cade twisted the key in his car's ignition and pressed down on the accelerator, his mind was still in Brett's bathroom. The sex had been hot—shower sex always was—but Cade was more concerned with the tension he'd sensed within Brett when he'd first stepped into the shower, and the resistance he'd felt before the other man had finally given in. It was the first time Brett had tried to hold off since the day in the barn and Cade knew in his soul that it wasn't a good sign.

Pulling up outside his house, he cut the engine and blew out a long breath. Maybe dinner with Tommy's folks hadn't gone so well. Or maybe Brett just hadn't been in the mood when Cade had first stepped into the shower. Slamming a palm on the steering wheel, Cade swore loudly. He shouldn't have surprised Brett like that. Though they'd been screwing for almost a month now, Brett was obviously still getting his head around it. Cade knew from past experience that when guys first accepted that they could like other guys, the fear of being outed stayed with them for a long time.

He got out of the car and went into the house. After he'd locked up he headed upstairs and pulled his cell out of his pocket. Jess wouldn't mind a late-night phone call if Brett was involved.

"I don't know what to do about it," he told her after he'd explained what had happened. "Do I keep my distance for a while?"

"I don't see why," Jessica replied. "I think you're overanalyzing."

He smirked. "I thought it was only girls who did that."

"Jerk." She yawned down the line. "You're telling me that he hesitated when you surprised him in the shower. That sounds pretty normal to me. He probably thought you were an intruder."

He shook his head despite the fact that Jess couldn't see him. "Even after he knew it was me he was still tense."

"So what? I get tense all the time. Work, friends, the weather. You said he had dinner at a friend's house, right?"

"Right?"

"Well, they were probably talking about his folks. His *dead* folks. That would make anyone tense."

Remembering the way Mrs. Dawes had held Brett at the funeral, Cade saw Jessica's point. "You might be right."

"I'm always right," she corrected.

He smiled, lowering down onto his bed. Then, remembering Brett's silence after they'd finished fucking, he frowned. "I still think he's having doubts though."

"He probably is. You're the first guy he's been with. I'd be having doubts too."

"And you don't think I should be worried about that?"

"Not yet. He's still screwing you, right?"

Feeling a hell of a lot better, he lay down on his back. "Anyway, enough of me. How's everything there?"

"Good," she told him. "My boss has me working like a dog but I'm used to that."

"Sorry for calling so late."

"Anytime, honey," she said with a smile in her voice. "It's not like I'm sleeping. I've got a presentation tomorrow and I'm shitting myself."

"Bullshit." Jess never stressed about anything. "You go get some shuteye and I'll talk to you soon."

"Okay." She yawned again. "Say hi to Brett for me."

"Will do." He grinned. "'Night."

"'Night."

He dropped the phone on his bedside table and propped his hands behind his head. Jess was right. No point worrying about Brett until it came down to it. For now he'd just enjoy the ride.

Chapter Thirteen

"Damn, I'm beat," Cade said on Thursday afternoon as they doused themselves with water from one of the outside faucets.

"Me too." Brett shook out his hair, sending droplets of water flying in all directions. "Can't wait to get into a hot shower."

Cade slanted a glance in his direction. "A shower, huh?"

Remembering how it felt to slide up against Cade, both of them covered in soapy water, steam rising around them, Brett felt heat crawl up his neck. He'd returned to normal since dinner at the Dawes' house. Every time he thought back to that night, he couldn't figure what had gotten him so weirded out in the first place. Not that he'd had much time for thinking about it. They'd been flat out on the ranch this week, working fifteen-hour days. And when they weren't working, he and Cade were fucking. Life was good.

He was about to suggest that he and Cade try out the shower scene again, but before he could make any kind of offer Jimmy appeared around the barn and strolled toward them.

"Hey, boss, I want you to take a look at one of the troughs," he called in his gravelly voice. "I think there's a leak."

Brett wiped his wet hands on the front of his jeans. "Sure, I'll be right there." He started to follow Jimmy, glancing back at Cade with regret. "Guess that shower will have to wait."

Cade shrugged. "Guess so." He backed up toward the drive and then stopped. "You want to come over for dinner tonight?"

Dinner at Cade's? He hadn't been at the guy's place since the night with Jess. If he wasn't ready to go back now, he'd never be. "Why?" he asked, holding out his arms. "Is there a game on I don't know about?"

Cade flashed him a grin, the dimple in his cheek deepening. "You never know. I'll see you around six. You can shower first."

Laughing as the other man ambled off into the distance, Brett turned to follow their wrangler. It was long after six when he knocked on Cade's front door, clean-shaven and fresh-smelling.

"Come on in," Cade said when he pulled the door open.

Brett stepped inside and brushed past the other man's body, feeling a tingle of electricity buzz down his spine. "So where's the food?" he asked, eying the kitchen door. "I'm starving."

"Actually, bad news about that."

Turning back, Brett couldn't help but grin at the sheepish expression on Cade's face. "What?"

"I figured out about ten minutes ago that I don't have two slices of bread to rub together."

"And there was I thinking you were a smart guy."

Cade shrugged. "I have other qualities."

Damn right. And as Brett stepped forward, backing Cade up against the wall, it was an entirely different hunger zipping through his veins. "So what now?" he asked, eyes focused on Cade's firm lips.

"Well, I thought we'd get dinner at Delia's," Cade said, the words caressing Brett's mouth. "My treat."

Brett straightened. "Delia's?" The wheels of his mind spun into overdrive. Delia's was a public place. People would see them, they'd think—

"Hey," Cade said lightly, bringing him back down to earth. "We'll just eat like any other two guys who work together."

The reason behind Cade's words permeated Brett's mind and he released a breath. "Sure." Then realizing he might have offended the other man, he continued, "It's not that I—"

One long finger covered his lips, silencing him. "It's okay," Cade soothed, his blue eyes holding Brett's. "I don't want people talking either."

Warm relief washed over Brett and he nodded. "Thanks."

"No problem." The words were barely out of Cade's mouth when his lips found Brett's, moving over his mouth until Brett opened for him. Bracing his hands on either side of Cade's body, Brett leaned into the kiss and thrust his tongue along Cade's. The rolling lust in his stomach tightened and then fanned outward, curling around his cock and tugging on his balls. He aligned his whole body with Cade's, loving the hardness of the man's chest and thighs. He'd never have to worry about pushing Cade too far, of breaking him. Men weren't delicate. It was a definite perk of screwing a guy, he noted. He'd have to start a list.

Abruptly, Cade ended the kiss, tearing his lips away and sucking in a deep breath. "Not yet," he said, placing his hands on Brett's shoulders and pushing him backwards. "You'll go longer with food in your belly."

Though his body screamed at him to pull Cade back into his arms, he gave a shrug of defeat. "Fine. But we're eating fast."

"You got it." Cade headed for the stairs and turned on the first step. "Wait here. I just need to get my wallet."

Brett wandered through the hallway while he waited, scanning the space for what remained of June Armstrong's trinkets. Cade had cleared most of them away but the antique clock Brett's mom had given June as a Christmas present one year still hung beside the phone, and along the walls a few framed photographs broke up the sheet of floral wallpaper.

Brett's gaze caught on a photo of June with her arms wrapped around her pre-teen son. Brett and his mom had been close but he'd never seen a mother-son bond as strong as the one shared between Cade and June. It probably had a lot to do with Ken's abusive past—they'd taken care of one another when the man of the house wasn't in a fit state to look after his wife and kid. Again, anger twisted inside Brett as he thought of all the pain Ken had caused his son.

Focusing in on June's smiling face, he felt the anger retreat. She was always a sweet lady, never yelling or slapping his hand away from her freshly baked desserts. In a way she'd become almost a second mother to him after Cade had taken off for college. Brokenhearted without her son around, she'd thrown her soul into the ranch, helping the men with whatever was needed and fussing after Brett like a mother hen.

He smiled sadly at the memory and then another thought entered Brett's head. Had June known about Cade's loose sexual preferences? Had it ever occurred to her that her son might end up with a man instead of a woman? Brett's brows drew together in a frown as he studied the photo more closely. He could almost hear her now, chattering on and on about Cade's college girlfriends while they sat around the dinner table. *"He'll meet his perfect woman soon,"* she'd always said with a knowing glint in her eyes, *"and he'll settle down faster than Brett here can eat a steak."*

His gut clenched with guilt and he took a long step back from June's sparkling eyes. What would she think about his newfound relationship with Cade or about what would inevitably happen between them tonight, probably right under her roof?

Cade's footsteps on the staircase jarred him from his thoughts. He looked up as Cade jogged down the stairs.

"Ready to go?" Cade asked as he stuffed his wallet into his pocket.

Brett stretched his lips into a smile. "Yeah."

He couldn't get June's face out of his head all through dinner. It left him distracted and without an appetite.

"You sick or something?" Cade asked, halfway through the meal.

"Nah, I'm okay." He looked down at his plate and force-fed himself some steak. He tasted nothing.

While they were waiting for the check, Brett saw Mitch drive by in his car.

"Forgot to tell you," he said as he pulled out his wallet, "Mitch is having a pool party tomorrow. Want to come?"

"Yeah, sounds good." Cade tapped his wallet on the table. "Put your money away, I'm paying."

"No way." He planted a fifty on the table. "Let me get this."

"No. This whole thing was my idea." He pushed the fifty back to Brett. "It's on me."

Brett opened his mouth to argue and then started to laugh instead.

"What's so funny?" Cade asked, grinning as Brett tried to silence himself.

He shook his head, unable to put it into words. Two guys out on a date fighting over the bill. He didn't know why but it was just damn funny.

"How about this?" Brett said when he could speak. "We split the bill."

Cade hesitated and then huffed. "Fair enough."

Brett nodded and started to laugh again.

"You should be at home, old man," Cade declared the following evening when he found Jimmy in the tack shed. "It's almost eight. You work too damn hard."

Jimmy's wrinkled face broke into a smile. "Hate to tell you this, kid, but you can't talk. You and Brett are going to work yourself into the ground, you hear me?"

Cade laughed and fell into step with the older man as they headed into the yard. "You'd be surprised, Jimmy. We won't be working tonight, that's for sure."

"Ah, one of those parties." Jimmy tutted beneath his breath. "You boys have all the luck. In my day there wasn't no such thing as a bikini."

"You were deprived, old man."

"Lord, you better believe it." Jimmy pulled his hat lower over his eyes and turned to look at Cade. "You're a good worker, kid. It's a good thing you're here."

Taken aback by the sudden change of subject, Cade didn't know what to say for a minute. Then he smiled and slapped the old man's shoulder. "Thanks."

He watched Jimmy head for his dusty Ford and then took a moment to observe the yard. It was a good thing he was here— good for himself at least. No amount of money could tempt him back to New York, not now anyway.

"Daydreaming again, Armstrong?" a deep voice drawled

from behind him.

He turned to find Brett on the other side of the yard coming toward him. "Always been a dreamer," he said with a shrug. "What time do we need to be at Mitch's for?"

"Whenever we get there."

"Okay, well I'll go change into something clean." He looked down at his dirt-encrusted jeans. "I'll do the driving. I know how much you like your beer."

Brett snorted. "Forget about it. I think it's your turn to get wasted."

Half an hour later, they were in Brett's truck on the way to Mitch's place.

"He doesn't live in town?" Cade asked when Brett ignored the turn for Steeplecrest.

"No, he built himself a house on the other side of the creek."

"Good for him."

They were quiet for the remainder of the ride and Cade started to wonder if his presence at the party was a good idea. Brett seemed tense about something and Cade would wager a bet that it had a lot to do with the fact that they were going to be surrounded by Brett's oldest friends. Reminded of the night in the shower, he stiffened in his seat. The last thing he wanted was to give Brett any reason to worry.

"Listen," he said, "we don't have to do this."

Brett glanced his way. "Do what?"

"I don't have to go in."

Brett shook his head. "It's okay, really. I'm not worried about it."

Not believing him but unwilling to argue about it, Cade let the subject drop. He'd give Brett some breathing room when they got inside. Hopefully that would help the guy relax.

"Brett Miller. I heard you were here."

Brett groaned inwardly at the instantly recognizable squeak of Mary Ellen's voice and forced himself to turn around from the bar. Dressed in a skimpy bikini that consisted of three triangles of red, she was staring up at him, a pout on her lips.

"Hey, Mary Ellen," he said, doing a quick scan for anyone who could help him. "How are you?"

"Not so good." She stepped closer, so close her tits pressed into his chest. "Last time I saw you, you skipped out on me."

Remembering the night Dixie died, he frowned. "Right, I forgot about that. There was an emergency on the ranch."

She stroked a fingertip along his bare forearm. "Now that's just not good enough," she said sweetly. "All work and no play makes Brett a very dull boy."

"Uh huh." He stepped back and almost knocked a six pack of beer to the ground. "Look it's been great catching up but—" he caught Mitch's eye over her shoulder and waved, "—I need to go talk to Mitch. I'll see you later."

He sidestepped her before she could argue and made a beeline for his friend.

"Hey, man," Mitch greeted when he'd made his escape. "You still jerking Mary Ellen around?"

"I'm not jerking anybody around. She just won't take the hint." Brett dragged his hand through his hair and glanced at the other side of the pool. When he spotted Cade locked inside a circle of half-naked girls, he grinned. "Do you even know those broads?" he asked Mitch, pointing across the pool.

Mitch shrugged. "They're over eighteen. That's all I care about."

They sat by the pool for a while, shooting the breeze. By the time Cade and Tommy came over to join them, Brett had eaten two hot dogs and a hamburger. Between the food and the warm night, he was completely at ease, even when Cade took a seat beside him.

"You looked like you were having fun," he noted, gesturing to the gaggle of babes standing by the pool.

"Ah, you know me." Cade flashed a grin. "Can't hold 'em off."

"So you guys are doing okay now," Mitch said after he'd downed his fifth beer in an hour. "Saw you through the window of Delia's last night. Looked pretty cozy to me."

Brett froze at the insinuation but Cade laughed it off.

"Easy, Mitch. We're trying to play it cool here."

Mitch snickered and punched Brett in the arm. "See? He ain't so bad, is he?"

Brett tried to relax but a knot of tension was growing in his stomach. Brett kept his eyes on the pool as Cade rose to his feet.

"I'm going to find some food," Cade said. "Maybe some beer to go with it."

"And some women too," Mitch shouted after him. As the guys hooted and hollered at Cade, Brett lifted his head. If there was one thing Cade could do, it was play straight.

"Hey, guys," Mitch said, drawing everyone's attention. He got to his feet and nodded his head toward the man who was headed their way. "This is my cousin Rick." He hooked his arm around Rick's shoulder and went through the introductions. "Rick's folks moved out of town twenty years back."

Brett shook the guy's hand as he took the seat Cade had vacated.

"Your family runs Steeplecrest Ranch," Rick said as he set his beer bottle between his feet. "I worked up there for a couple of summers."

"Really?" Brett narrowed his eyes, searching his mind for a Rick. "Can't say I remember you."

"Well, your grandfather took on a few of us kids every summer."

Brett nodded, thinking of Old Man Miller. "Did you know him well?"

"Well enough to know he didn't care what anyone thought of him."

Brett laughed. Though he'd always been very fond of his grandfather growing up, the man's views on the world had always been extreme and he hadn't conformed to one bit of political correctness, laughing it off as horseshit. He'd been a stickler for religion, for old-fashioned morals. Brett could still hear him ranting about his pet hates—working women, alcoholics and faggots.

The breath caught in his throat as his grandfather's words ran through his mind. He could just imagine what the old man would have to say about him and Cade. Lord knows he would have rather seen his grandson fall off a horse and break his neck than cross a line like the one he was crossing with Cade.

But it doesn't matter what he thinks, a voice at the back of Brett's mind told him as he struggled to get his grandfather's face out of his head. The man had been dead a good fifteen years. His opinion wasn't worth dust anymore.

"Knew your dad too," Rick continued. "He was a good man. Always made sure we got paid well."

Brett nodded wordlessly. Unlike his old man's, Henry Miller's nature had always been easygoing. He'd never been one to throw stones and had raised Brett to be open-minded. But Brett knew in his gut that if he'd ever brought a guy home he'd have been lucky to see Steeplecrest Ranch again.

As his stomach twisted nastily, Brett got up. "I'm gonna get another drink," he muttered. He headed inside the house, fast as his legs could carry him. The kitchen was covered in trash but at least it was empty. He held onto the worktop and tried to stop thinking.

The sound of the door opening had his body tensing further. He straightened and then stiffened again when Cade's voice filled the room.

"Thought I saw you come in here." His footsteps on the tiled floor echoed as he approached. "Having a good time?"

Brett felt every muscle in his body lock together as Cade stepped even closer. The heat of the man's body crowded Brett and a claustrophobic sensation constricted his throat. He needed air. He needed to get out.

"Who was the guy you were talking to out there?" Cade asked.

Brett shook his head, afraid to turn around and look into Cade's eyes. His dad would never have let himself get caught up in something like this.

"Hey." Cade put a hand on Brett's shoulder. "You okay?"

He shuddered and forced himself to turn around. When he looked at Cade the guy's eyes filled with concern.

"Jesus, you look bad, Brett," he said, putting his free hand on Brett's other shoulder.

That's how Rick found them when he walked into the kitchen. Cade dropped his hands straight away but the damage had been done.

Rick's brows lifted in surprise. "Sorry, guys," he said, backing out of the kitchen. The door closed behind him and Brett felt his insides clench. He looked Cade square in the eyes, feeling raw anger hurtle through his veins. He could barely sort his thoughts from his emotions but he was damn sure of one thing. The buck stopped with Cade. If Cade hadn't hung around after the funeral and weaseled his way underneath his skin, Brett would still be fucking Mary-goddamn-Ellen or some other chick who wouldn't tie him down. What the fuck had they started? *How* had it started?

The worry in Cade's blue eyes sickened him further. Needing to get the hell out, he pushed past Cade and strode to the front door. In the yard, he sucked in a breath of cool air and shuddered. He felt hot and cold at the same time, clammy as if he'd just thrown his lungs up. Rick knew. Mitch's cousin. Before the end of the night they'd all know. They'd all fucking know.

He heard Cade's boots thudding down the porch steps behind him and spun around to face him.

"It was Dixie," he spat out, realization slicing through him. He tugged his Stetson from his head and pointed it accusingly at Cade. "You waited until something shit happened and then you—" He cut off, not knowing how to even finish that sentence without keeling over.

Cade approached slowly and then stopped and raised his hands when Brett backed up to the car. "I know you're mad, Brett, but just because Rick saw us like that doesn't mean—"

"Shut up," Brett barked, putting up his hand. "Just shut the hell up." He scrubbed a hand over his face, wishing he could break into a run and chase away the anger crawling up inside him. But he had to stay and end this now. "I don't know what your game is, but it stops here."

Cade folded his arms over his chest. "What the fuck are you talking about, Brett?" he bit out, concern becoming frustration. "If you want to say something then out with it."

"I want you gone." The words left his mouth on one simple breath. He watched Cade's face which went slack with shock. "I want you off the ranch and as far away from me as you can get."

There was a long pause as Cade stared dully at him. Then, shaking his blond head, he strode forward, his long legs carrying him faster than Brett had anticipated. He didn't have the chance to pull away before Cade grabbed his arm.

"You're confused and you're freaked out. Rick walked in at a bad time," Cade said, voice strained with emotion as Brett tried to shove him away. Cade's grip was resolute. "I get that. But I know this is what you want. It's what we both want."

"No." Brett dropped his gaze to where Cade's hand gripped his forearm and then looked up into the guy's desperate eyes. "I don't want this," he bit out, still fighting against Cade's unyielding grasp. "I never did."

Long moments dragged out as they stared at one another. Brett held his breath, anger and pain flaring inside him on a constant burn. He just wanted to go.

As if picking up on his thoughts, Cade's expression changed, dulled. Abruptly, his hand went limp and he released Brett's arm. When Cade stepped back, Brett could breathe again. Brett turned and stalked away on unsteady legs.

He didn't look back.

Chapter Fourteen

"So you'll be back here Monday morning then? I can tell Susie to set up your desk?"

Cade rolled his eyes and resisted the urge to snap his cell phone shut. How many times did he have to repeat himself? "Yeah, Mike," he said down the line, reining in his irritation. "Bright and early Monday morning. Just like I said."

"Glad to hear it, Armstrong. Sullivan & Robson hasn't been the same without you."

Cade tried to force a smile but quit halfway. No point when the guy couldn't see him. "Thanks, Mike," he said, mustering up a shred of enthusiasm and working it into his voice. "I'll see you next week."

As soon as he hung up, he threw the cell onto the sofa and stormed out into the hallway. He almost tripped over one of the boxes lining the walls and let out a string of curses. "Goddamn shit," he muttered under his breath, shoving the box out of the way with his foot.

The shrill sound of the kitchen phone rang through the house and he winced. He'd ignore it. He still had the whole upper floor to pack up and he was leaving in two days. The last thing he felt like doing was answering the phone.

The phone rang until the machine picked up. As Jessica's soft voice filtered into the hallway, he straightened from the boxes and walked into the kitchen.

"Just wanted to see how the packing is coming along," she said lightly. "I'll pick you up at JFK when your flight comes in. I've got the times all written down."

He smiled at that, knowing she probably had yellow Post-its stuck to every available surface in her apartment. If it wasn't a fashion show or an appointment with her manicurist, it would sail right out of her pretty little head.

"I've made reservations at Chow's," she said, referring to their favorite restaurant at the corner of his apartment building. "My treat."

Softening to her efforts to cheer him up, he crossed the kitchen and was ready to lift the receiver before her following words wiped the smile from his face.

"I know you don't want to hear this," she continued, her tone becoming tentative, "but honey, I think you're making a big mistake."

He closed his eyes, annoyance simmering inside him. She was right, he didn't want to hear this and she damn well knew it. He turned from the blinking machine and strode out onto the deck. He looked out across the backyard, past the trees and up toward the pastures. Slowly, the tension eased in his shoulders and he let out a groan.

He didn't know why Jess kept pushing the issue. The last time she'd called he'd told her flat-out to shut the hell up about it but still she continued to press on. She didn't seem to get that each time she brought it up, every time she mentioned his name, the pain deepened. Gripping the railing with his outstretched hands, he bent at the waist and stared into the wooden slabs between his feet.

Two weeks had passed since Brett had walked away, two long, painful weeks. About as long as their brief relationship had actually lasted, Cade noted. He'd expected Brett to freak out at some point. He just hadn't expected it so soon.

Remembering the rage and disgust that had spilled from Brett's dark eyes that night, Cade felt his face contort in pain. As he'd stood there, facing Brett's anger, he'd known he'd lost. There was nothing he could say or do to dispel that kind of resentment, that kind of hatred. When Brett said he was done, he was done and Cade couldn't summon the strength to fight any more.

Over the last two weeks he'd realized this was the first time he'd felt this kind of hurt. He'd never really done serious relationships. There'd never been anyone who'd held his interest long enough. But Brett—sure he'd always felt stirrings of lust toward the guy, but he hadn't realized his feelings went much deeper than that. He could see it now, he could *feel* it now. He loved Brett Miller, plain and simple. And he couldn't stay here when he felt like this, not when he had to face Brett every day while he tried to do his work.

His throat tightened and he swallowed thickly. For a second there he'd believed they had a chance. When Brett had surrendered the way he had Cade's heart had taken a giant leap. He'd been sure for so long that Brett was a no-go, off-limits when it came to sex. In one night Brett had dispelled that belief as he'd allowed Cade to undress him and make love to him the way no woman could. And then a couple of weeks later Brett had ripped the hope away, taking it with him as he'd disappeared into the dark.

"Bastard," Cade thought to himself, squeezing the wooden railing with his hands and feeling a splinter pierce his skin. *Son of a goddamn bitch.*

Along with the pain had come a boatload of rage that bubbled to the surface at various intervals throughout the days.

He kept a tight leash on it. It wouldn't be fair to Jimmy or the two boys to let his anger spill over into his work. And it wasn't like he could let loose at Brett. In the two weeks that had trundled by not a word had passed between them. As a matter of fact, they'd barely seen each other. Cade couldn't blame the distance on Brett. Before, it had been Brett who'd done the avoiding. Now not only was Brett avoiding Cade, but Cade was avoiding Brett right back. The thought of facing him made Cade sick to his stomach. He couldn't do it. He didn't have the energy.

As soon as he got back to New York he'd have his lawyers draw up the papers to sell his half of the ranch. If he wasn't here, he wasn't keeping it. There was no point in hanging onto something he couldn't have.

A coyote howled in the distance and he lifted his head. A sudden desperation to get out of the house flooded him and he turned to head back into the kitchen. He'd take a drive around Steeplecrest, say goodbye to the old spots he hadn't taken the chance to re-explore since getting back.

Grabbing the keys from the hall table, he jogged down to the car and pulled open the door. Three months in town and he was still driving a rental. He grimaced as he turned the key in the ignition. He hadn't wanted to tempt fate by buying a car. Now he could see that it sure as hell wouldn't have made a difference.

Rick hadn't said anything to anyone. It had taken two weeks for Brett to believe that, but now he could finally breathe again. The guys were all acting the same as ever around him and from what Mitch had told him that morning, Rick had left town on Monday. He was safe. No one would ever know. He could go back to normal. So could Cade. They'd be able to work with each other again. Just work. Sex would only complicate things and Brett couldn't bring himself to go there again.

As he brushed down one of the horses he realized he felt like himself again. He wasn't fully there. He sure as hell wasn't happy. But he felt like Brett Miller and that's all that mattered.

He was walking the horse back into her stall when Jimmy's voice reached his ears. He was spouting curses beneath his breath as he stamped into the stables.

"What's this about Cade?" he demanded, scowling at Brett.

Brett stepped out of the stall and closed the door. "What about him?"

"What about him?" Jimmy said as if Brett should know the answer. "He's going back to New York tomorrow. Not coming back. That's 'what about him'."

"Tomorrow?" Brett repeated the word out loud and then said it twice more in his mind. Cade was leaving tomorrow, jetting off to New York with no plan to come back. Giving his head a quick shake, Brett waited, but it refused to sink in.

He turned from the stall and looked at Jimmy. "You sure about that?" he asked, narrowing his eyes. There had to be some kind of mistake. Cade's stubborn ass wouldn't give up this easily. He wouldn't hand over the ranch without putting up a fight.

But the old man was nodding as he leaned against the stable door. "He told me himself." Holding his hat to his head, Jimmy frowned. "He didn't say anything to you?"

Brett stiffened and for a moment he couldn't speak. "Uh, no," he grunted eventually, striding past Jimmy into the yard.

"I gotta say I'm surprised," Jimmy continued and Brett grimaced as he realized the old man wasn't about to let the subject drop. "He's always been a decent kid. Didn't think he had it in him to leave us in a rut like this."

The urge to defend Cade swept through Brett and he gritted his teeth. He didn't owe the guy shit, not after what he'd pulled him into. "We managed before," he said instead, keeping his tone neutral. "We can do it again."

"Yeah, we managed. But the horses are in love with that kid, every goddamn one of 'em." Jimmy heaved a sigh, his anger replaced with disappointment. "I don't want to let Paul anywhere near Marci. He's weak enough with the horses as it is, but with Marci he'd wet his pants."

"We'll figure something out."

"We better."

Brett waited for Jimmy to walk away before crossing the yard. He stared out at the pastures, watched the cattle nudge one another and munch on the grass. He waited for the relief to wash through him, to ease the ache in his shoulders. It didn't. If anything, the tension increased.

Cade was leaving. The news should have filled him with respite, the sense of being free. Instead, his stomach rolled and his fists clenched.

Regret? Was that what he was feeling? He had a hard time getting his head around the fact that the situation had come to this. Maybe if he'd handled things better, handled *himself* better, he and Cade would still be able to work together, throwing banter back and forth like two regular guys instead of bitter ex-lovers.

Ex-lovers. He winced at the term and felt even sicker when he realized the route their relationship had taken. It was wrong, should never have happened. He didn't want Cade that way and he couldn't figure out what had possessed him to think he did.

"Grief plays tricks on people," he remembered his father

213

telling him after Jimmy's wife had died all those years ago and the man had hit the bottle hard. *"It screws with your head."*

With the sun beating down on his back, Brett wiped the back of his arm over his forehead and turned back toward the yard. A sudden longing for a swim struck him and he changed his direction, ambling toward the garage. He'd take the four-wheeler up to the creek and spend a couple of hours in the water. Maybe a shock of cold current would pull him out of this funk.

Later that afternoon, after a long swim, Brett climbed out of the water and dragged his fingers through his hair, squeezing out the wetness. The sun's rays would dry it quickly enough, he thought as he pulled on his jeans. He glanced at one of the boulders by the bank and, as a wave of exhaustion rolled over him, he decided to lie out for a while and enjoy the heat before heading back.

He was standing over the rock when he heard the clattering of hooves approaching. He looked up, every muscle in his body going rigid as Marci's mahogany coat galloped into sight, the rich color shimmering beneath the sun. Swallowing hard, he lifted his gaze a notch and faced Cade. The man's eyes were shaded beneath the brim of his hat but Brett felt his gaze piercing into his skin, sharp as a knife. A heated chill shuddered through him as droplets of water trickled down his bare chest. He wished he'd pulled on his shirt so he wouldn't feel so exposed.

A good ten feet away, Cade tugged on Marci's reins and his heels dug into her sides. Brett cursed himself for noticing the strength in the man's thighs as they clamped around the mare's large body, forcing her to halt.

When Marci came to a stop, her brown eyes which were so

like Dixie's glared at him almost accusingly. Did she know? Brett wondered, meeting her stare. Did she know he was the reason her new master was taking off?

As the silence dragged on, Brett forced his gaze back up to Cade and cleared his throat. "Hear you're leaving," he said flatly, folding his arms over his chest.

Cade paused before his mouth twisted in a bitter smile. "First thing in the morning," he said, his tone clear but low. "Guess you can start counting down the hours."

The acidic words cut through Brett and his gut clenched painfully. "What about the ranch?" he forced out.

Cade's mouth hardened. "I'm selling." His legs tightened around Marci as she tried to move again. "It's yours if you want it."

"Just like that?"

Cocking his head to the side, Cade nodded. "Yeah, just like that."

The bitterness in his tone had faded to resignation and Brett's throat burned as he watched Cade back up the horse. Despite the anger he still felt toward him, Brett hadn't intended on hurting the guy. But he clearly had. The raw pain that emanated from Cade curled around Brett and nearly brought him to his knees.

He wanted to comfort him, to tell him he was sorry. Instead, he stood with his feet rooted to the ground and watched in silence as Cade and the horse disappeared into the trees. Deep down he knew he wouldn't see Cade again before he left. The knowledge that should have brought truckloads of relief made him sick to his stomach.

Slowly, he pulled on his shirt, leaving it unbuttoned as he climbed onto the four-wheeler and started back toward the ranch. He didn't say anything to Jimmy or the two boys before heading into the house for the night. He didn't eat, just went straight to bed.

He was still awake in the early hours of dawn. He heard the purr of Cade's car in the distance as it drove away.

Chapter Fifteen

At the window table of an exclusive Fifth Avenue restaurant, Jessica tapped her pen against her notepad and watched the stream of shoppers pass her by. She stole a quick glance at her watch as a waiter refilled her glass with mineral water. Ugh, she'd been alone for over thirty minutes and if Cade didn't show up soon she'd have to walk out, looking like the stupid broad who'd been stood up by a date. If Cade humiliated her like that in one of her favorite lunchtime spots, she'd kick him all the way back to Texas.

Finally, he appeared at the maître d's side and his sheepish grin softened her slightly. She relaxed into her seat and casually lifted one leg over the other, admiring his designer suit and loose-limbed walk. He didn't look like a cowboy anymore and a twinge of regret stung her. Delicious as he appeared in Armani, his cowboy hat and faded jeans were what really made her melt.

"You're late," she said as he sat opposite her and took a menu from the maître d's hand. "He'll order now," she told the waiter, still glaring at Cade.

He raised an amused eyebrow at her clipped tones and then ordered his usual. When the maitre d' whisked off toward the kitchens, Cade looked at her.

"I'm sorry," he said, sounding genuine as he reached for

her hand. "Work is kicking my ass."

She harrumphed, maintaining the façade of irritation when underneath it all Cade's tired face and quiet voice unnerved her. She couldn't even remember the last time his dimple had made an appearance. "I suppose I should be grateful to see you at all," she added drily, noting how quickly his gaze dropped from hers.

Studying the tablecloth as if it were the most intricate piece of art he'd ever laid eyes on, he asked, "Why's that?"

"You've been back in town for almost a month and I've hardly seen you," she reminded him, leaning forward in her chair. "And when we do see each other, you're so distant. I'm worried about you."

His gaze flickered to hers and then returned to the table. "I'm fine, Jess. Getting back into the swing of things ain't easy."

She squeezed the hand that held hers. "I know that. Of course it's not easy. But..." She trailed off, not certain she wanted to finish the sentence. If she did they'd get into another fight. She had a feeling that was why he was avoiding her. He didn't want to talk about what he needed to talk about—Brett. "I think you came back too soon," she said eventually and sighed as he tugged his hand from hers.

"Don't start this again, Jess," he said, tone ragged with exhaustion. He looked up at her and the dullness that shaded his usually bright eyes broke her heart. "This is where I belong, I know it."

She shook her head. "No, honey, you belong on that ranch. This city is all wrong for you, I see that now." At his continued silence she changed her angle and gestured to the clothes he wore. "Look me in the eye and tell me you don't hate that suit. Go on, I dare you."

Annoyance clouded over his defeated eyes and she felt a

little better at the sign of life.

"I'm not going back," he said clearly. "And you need to drop it. This shit is getting old."

She hesitated. Then, straightening, she hooked her arm over the back of her chair and tipped her head to the side. "Okay, I'll drop it. But you need to do something for me first."

He lifted a hand for her to continue. "What?"

"Tell me you don't think about him," she said simply, hoping the challenge in her tone would knock some sense into him. "Tell me you don't spend every minute of the day wondering what he's doing, wondering if he's thinking about you."

The moment the words left her mouth she ached to grab them back and stuff them down her throat. She stiffened in her chair, watching Cade's face contort in pain. Why she had to be so forward on things like this, she didn't know. Her harsh say-it-like-it-is attitude stood by her in the workplace, but this was one moment when she wished she'd spent more of her childhood developing her sensitive side.

"Cade," she whispered, reaching across the table for his arm. He jerked away from her touch and the agony that flared in the depths of his blue eyes had tears burning in her throat. "Don't leave," she pleaded as he pushed his chair back, the legs squealing across the wooden flooring. "I'm sorry, I promise I won't—"

Anger battled the pain in his eyes as he glared down at her, face still twisted. "Leave it, Jess," he snarled, grabbing his jacket from the back of the chair. "I'll see you around."

She watched him stride out of the restaurant, feeling about as helpful in this situation as a damn goldfish. The maitre d' arrived at the table with Cade's iced tea. The man glanced from her to the empty seat.

"Please cancel his order," she said politely, wishing the waiter didn't regard her with those pity-filled eyes. "It's just me today."

As he nodded and backed away, she propped her elbow on the table and rested her chin in her hand. She had to do something about Cade. She cared too much about him to leave him alone.

A thought formed in her mind over lunch, growing bigger and more powerful with each bite of her creamy risotto. Glancing at her cell that rested beside her plate, she wondered what her boss would say when she asked for another couple of days off. She'd make up an event, an important family occasion or something along those lines. She definitely wouldn't tell him what part of the country she was flying to. If he knew she was heading back to Texas for the third time in as many months, he'd probably tell her to move there.

Less than a week later, Jessica was following the dusty road that wound a path from the ranch to the town of Steeplecrest. The old man up at the stables had told her she'd find Brett at the local bar. She took the turnoff for the town and drove slowly along the main street, peering at the store fronts in search of a bar. She found Billy's at the end of the street and pulled up in the lot outside.

"Well, here goes nothing," she muttered under her breath, leaving the red Beemer behind—the same car she'd rented last time.

A low wolf whistle drew her attention to a group of beefy guys who looked like they belonged in the NFL. She smiled and shrugged lightly as she brushed past them into the bar.

Another time, another place. Tonight she was here for one man only.

When she stepped inside the bar she nearly choked as a combination of cigar smoke, body heat and cheap perfume rushed up her nostrils. Clearing her throat, she worked a path through the crowd and finally reached the bar that was covered in scratches and water rings.

"Hey there, darlin'," the bartender greeted her, shouting over the country music which blared from the stereo system. "What can I get you?"

"Rum and coke," she said, smiling up at his handsome face. She watched him fix her drink as she fished in her purse for some change. "Do you know Brett Miller?" she asked when he set her glass in front of her.

"Sure I do."

"Is he here tonight?"

He jerked his head to the right and she glanced down the bar. About three people down Brett sat on one of the stools nursing a brandy. He looked miserable as hell.

She turned back to the bartender and winked. "Thanks, honey," she said, sidling along the bar.

"Anytime."

Forcing her way to Brett proved more difficult than getting to the bar had been and she soon figured out where the problem lay. Two chesty microskirt-wearing blondes stood on either side of Brett, thrusting their boobs in his face and begging for his attention. Noting the non-interest in Brett's dull eyes, she couldn't help but grin. These girls needed to take a hint.

"Excuse me," she said loudly, pushed her way past one of the blondes. Brett didn't even look up from his drink. She studied his face as she waited for him to notice her. He looked tired, worn-out. There were dark circles under his eyes and blue-black stubble shadowed his jaw. Sexy as hell of course— the kind of sexy that made a woman want to put her arms around a man and kiss the pain away. If it were possible, he looked even more depressed than Cade had last week.

She sashayed closer to him, close enough to inhale the burned cinnamon flavor of his cologne. Moisture pooled between her thighs as she stroked her fingertips along his hair-dusted forearm. His gaze moved to her red fingernails and then slowly shifted upward until his dark, haunted eyes met hers.

"Hey there, cowboy," she said softly, feeling her heart clench at the sight of his pain. "Missed me?"

It took a couple of minutes for Brett to believe what he was seeing. He stared at Jessica's angelic face, a face that contrasted drastically with the mischievous twinkle in her eyes. Angelic be damned, she was the devil in disguise.

"What do you want?" he asked flatly, curling his fingers around his brandy glass. "Are you lost?"

Her eyes widened and she smiled. "Not at all," she said, leaning in so her body brushed his. "I've just found exactly what I'm looking for."

A short, humorless laugh fell from his lips. "You flatter me, Jess."

"I'm not trying to flatter you. I'm serious." She tipped her head to the side, a knowing glint entering her eyes. "Who else would I be here for, Brett?"

His throat constricted as he thought of Cade. Nope, she wasn't in town to see him. He didn't live here anymore. "I'm not in the mood for your games," he told Jessica tightly, lifting his glass to his lips. He downed the last few drops of the amber liquid and then nodded to the bartender for another one.

"No games," she said, her eyes intent on him. "I just want to talk, that's all."

"Talk?" *Yeah right.* "About what?"

"About why you look like hell."

He smirked. "Thanks."

Edging between him and the bar, she rested her elbows on the wooden surface and tilted her head back. "I mean it," she said, looking up at him, "what's got you looking so rough?"

His eyes narrowed. She was a clever little thing but he wouldn't say what she wanted him to say. "Maybe I've been missing you, darlin'," he suggested coldly, meeting her gaze head-on. "Maybe my bed's cold without you."

"I never slept in your bed."

He shrugged. "You know what I mean."

One perfect eyebrow arched as she pressed her hips to his. "If you miss me so much how about we get out of here?"

The intention behind her words left him cold. He wasn't in the mood to fuck, he hadn't been in a while, but telling her that would be as good as admitting defeat. So taking her by the arm, he started to lead her toward the exit. Outside, he headed straight for his pickup. He pulled open the passenger door and helped her up. Then he moved around to the driver's side.

"Where do you want to go?" he asked when he was in the truck.

Her hand snaked over his thigh and squeezed. He glanced up at her and watched her slide across the bench seat.

"I think I'd like to stay right here," she whispered, stroking her hand over the front of his jeans. Inside his pants, his cock twitched mercifully. He didn't want to imagine the consequences if he couldn't get hard.

"Then that's what we'll do," he said evenly, letting her crawl into his lap. She wrapped her arms around his neck and rolled her hips against his.

"So that's why you were ignoring those girls back there?" she asked, grazing his lips with her open mouth. "Because of me?"

As her tongue tracked a line down his neck, another flash of Cade entered his mind and he could almost feel the man's mouth on his skin. "Yeah," he said, his cock hardening beneath her body. "All because of you."

Her laugh vibrated against his skin. "That's really hot, sweetie," she murmured, lifting her head and moving her hands to the zipper of his jeans. "I just wish I could believe it."

Eyes closing as she released his cock from his pants, Brett asked, "Why can't you believe it?"

She didn't answer, instead focusing her attention on his dick. Her small hand wrapped around him, her fingers not meeting around his thickness. Remembering how Cade's large palm had encased his shaft so easily, he jerked in Jessica's hand.

Her blonde hair fell in a curtain in front of her face as she worked her hand up and down his length. "You haven't fucked recently, have you?"

He grimaced. "I've been busy."

"Too busy for sex?" She drew her grip upward and swiped her thumb over the head of his cock. "Nobody's ever too busy for sex."

Ignoring the way she was testing him, Brett concentrated on the sensations she was eliciting from his body. With each stroke of her hand, he swelled further. It was a nice change to the non-existent sex drive he'd been suffering with these past few weeks.

"I gotta say," Jessica continued, dragging her long nails along the underside of his dick, "you're not the only one who's been out of the game for a while."

He stiffened, begging her silently not to take that train of thought any further. If she said Cade's name he'd turn limp as spaghetti.

Thankfully, she didn't continue and, as she raised her body over his and bundled her dress around her hips, he relaxed slightly at the sight of smooth-shaven pussy. Yes, he could handle this part.

She sank down onto his cock, her warm, wet cunt enveloping his length greedily and squeezing around him. He gave a small groan at the familiar sensation and ran his hands up her thighs.

"Mmm, you feel good," she murmured as she started to ride him slowly. "I forgot how big you are."

Her compliment barely registered as he lifted his hips to meet hers, thrusting up inside her hot passage. She tugged down the straps of her dress, revealing her small breasts. He leaned forward dutifully and sucked one pink nipple into his mouth. He was still rolling the little bud over his tongue when she asked the question he'd been dreading.

"Why did you let him leave, Brett?" she whispered, holding his head to her breast. "If it's hurting you so much, why are you doing this to yourself?"

He bit her nipple, drawing a cry of pleasure from her mouth. "Quit talking," he ground out against her soft flesh. "This is about you and me. Leave him out of it."

"Oh, come on," she said harshly, weaving her fingers into his hair and tugging his head away from her breast. "This is all about Cade and you know it."

At the mention of Cade's name, he didn't go limp as he'd

225

expected. Instead, he hardened further inside Jessica's body and she laughed breathlessly.

"I knew that night when we were all together," she said, slamming her pussy down on his cock. "I knew you wanted him more than you even wanted me. The way you looked at him—"

"Shut up," Brett spat out, driving his dick upward with all the strength he could summon. "You were fucking with my head. So was he. It wasn't real."

She laughed again. "Then why do you look like death?" she asked, cupping his face in her hands and forcing him to look at her. "You boys need each other. He needs you. I can't bear seeing the pain in his eyes every time we meet."

He twisted his head out of her hands, a burning sensation flaring inside him. "Stop it, just leave it alone."

Her eyes softened as she shook her head. "I can't do that, honey. I've known Cade for God knows how long and I've never seen him hurt like this. And now that I'm here, I can see how much you're hurting too. It's unnecessary."

He squeezed his eyes shut. Yes, the pain was unbearable but he'd get over it eventually. He had to. Being with Cade was impossible. It could never work.

"Listen to me," Jessica begged, her hips stilling over his. "I know you see things a certain way. All I want you to do is open your eyes. You're throwing away something really great."

"No, I'm throwing away something I don't want." Even as he forced out the words, his stomach clenched.

"That's a lie, honey. You need to get over yourself and fast. Cade wants you more than he's ever wanted anyone but eventually he'll move on." Her voice lowered, became more urgent as she asked, "Do you want that, Brett? Do you want him to move on?"

"Yes," he choked out, grabbing her hips and urging her on. He thrust upward, spearing her pussy with his cock. "I want this to be over."

"It's not that simple, you and Cade—" She let out a cry as he pressed his thumb to the swollen bud of her clit. Her pussy convulsed around him, squeezing his dick as she orgasmed. Her climax seemed to last forever but he wasn't even close to the edge. In fact, he didn't think he was going to come at all.

His stomach gave a sickening lurch as Jessica's body stilled and her eyes found his. She knew he hadn't come and she knew why. It was Cade he needed, not her.

"Brett," she whispered, stroking the side of his face tenderly. "Honey, please come back with me. I know we can—"

"No." Shaking his head, he lifted her body off him and swung her onto the passenger seat. "Get out," he ordered, jerking his zipper over his still-throbbing erection. "Go home to New York and don't come back."

"But—"

"Enough." This time he yelled, glaring at her in the darkened cab. "I don't want you and I sure as hell don't want Cade."

There was a heavy pause during which a tear trickled down Jessica's cheek. She swiped it away, holding his gaze as she opened the passenger door. "Okay," she said quietly, "I'm going. But don't think for a second that this ends here because even when I'm on the plane back to New York, the pain isn't going to leave you. You're not going to feel better until you get a grip and face up to what you need." She jumped to the ground and pulled up the shoulder straps of her dress, covering her breasts. "I just hope by the time you get your act together it won't be too late. I know Cade. The longer you let him suffer the less likely he'll be able to forgive you." And then she slammed the door shut and strode across the parking lot on her four-inch heels.

Long after Jessica's red BMW had disappeared from the lot, Brett was still sitting at the wheel, staring out into the night. Her parting words resounded in his head and he waited impatiently for the numbness he'd been feeling these past few weeks to drown out the pain. But the numbness didn't come and the pain deepened, spreading from the pit of his stomach through his body until he felt like his limbs were on fire.

He'd done a lot of thinking since Cade had left the ranch. His initial assumption that his grief had confused his feelings for the other man didn't sit right. He'd figured that with Cade out of the picture he'd be able to move on, but it wasn't happening. He couldn't sleep. He didn't eat. He lived like a robot, moving through the day mechanically, barely aware of what was going on around him. Every so often he caught Jimmy watching him with worried eyes and he snapped at the old man. Then guilt would bite at him and he'd feel even worse than before.

Exhaling heavily, he turned the key in the ignition and the engine roared to life. He drove home, glad he knew the twists and turns of the road like the back of his hand so he didn't have to pay too much attention. As he rolled through the gates of the ranch and accelerated for the incline up to his house, he glanced to his left, noting the dark mass that had been the Armstrong household for so long. Each time he set his eyes on that house these days, his whole stomach turned over. Maybe once the papers had been signed and the building belonged to him he'd have it knocked down. What use was a second house to him anyway?

When he pulled up in his front yard, he couldn't bring

himself to go inside the house. He stepped down from the truck and slammed the door shut behind him.

"What would it be like to go home to Cade instead of an empty house?" he wondered, staring into the darkened windows. Longing coiled inside him and he closed his eyes against the sharp bolt of need. Instead of climbing the steps up to the veranda he turned on his heel and headed across the yard in the direction of the stables.

The stables were silent with sleeping horses, but he knew even before he reached Marci's stall that she'd be wide awake.

"Hey there, girl," he said softly as the beautiful horse moved toward him. She pushed her muzzle into his hand, greeting him with an affection that had begun after Cade had left. It was almost as if the guy's departure had forged a bond between them. They both missed him. They both needed him. "What am I going to do, Marci?" Brett asked, stroking his hand over the mare's nose. "Is Jess right? Am I screwing things up here?"

Marci stared dolefully at him and he gave a small smile. "Don't know why I'm asking you. Of course you want him back."

The smile dropped from his lips as he considered what would happen if Cade came back. It wasn't like they could have an open relationship. His reaction when Rick had walked in on them had proved that. He could just imagine what Jimmy would say and the talk it would start in the town. But maybe it was worth it. Maybe the connection he had with Cade would get him through it.

A lump formed in Brett's throat as he remembered how easy it had been to lean on Cade, how certain he'd felt that he could trust the other man. It was as if everything had come together when they'd lain side by side. After Dixie's death he hadn't overanalyzed what he was feeling for Cade. He'd just allowed it to happen. He'd discovered something he never would have discovered otherwise. Even now he knew that he and Cade could have something great—friendship, sex and trust all in one. He wanted it, wanted it so much his bones ached. Yet still he was resisting. What was he so afraid of?

"What if it doesn't last?" he whispered, looking to Marci for answers. "What if I screw it up?"

She continued to stare at him, an almost haughty look entering her eyes.

He gave a short laugh. "I know. I guess I've already screwed it up, right?" Dropping his hand from Marci's coat, he took a step back. "Think I can fix it?"

There was a long silence before he nodded and tipped his hat to the horse. "Guess I'll have to try."

Chapter Sixteen

On a Wednesday afternoon, Cade sat behind his desk in his glass-fronted office throwing a mini stress ball up into the air and then catching it in his palm. A stack of paperwork sat on the floor beside him and he had over sixty emails to get through before the end of the day, but his focus centered solely on the little ball as it hurtled through the air and then back down again.

His intercom buzzed and he let the ball drop to the floor as Sandy's voice filled the office. "Your three-thirty is here, Mr. Armstrong," she simpered and he gave an exasperated smile. Sandy, his new secretary, had been more than accommodating since he'd started back at Sullivan & Robson Properties and had made it perfectly clear she was at his disposal for his every waking need. She made him wish they'd hired a middle-aged housewife to answer his calls instead.

Pressing his finger on the button, he spoke into the intercom. "Send them in, Sandy."

Less than a minute later Sandy, wearing a tight-fitting black skirt and a low-cut blouse, sailed into the room, closely followed by one of his longtime clients.

"Richard," Cade greeted, getting to his feet and stretching out a hand. "It's good to see you. Please take a seat."

He barely heard a word the man said through the twenty-minute meeting, and he had to wonder as he said goodbye to one of the firm's most prestigious clients, how long would it be before his bosses noticed how off his game he'd truly become.

Sitting behind his desk again, he swiveled in his chair to stare out the windows. He'd treasured this office before he'd taken a break from the company. The view from up here was gold—the city of New York was spread out before him, skyscrapers and Central Park and crowds of people bustling along the yellow-taxied streets. The vast majority of his colleagues had turned green with envy when he'd been offered this office. But now, when he thought back to the canyons and the valleys and the peaks of Steeplecrest, the view of the city left him cold.

Behind him, the intercom buzzed again and he let out a groan of frustration. *What now?* As far as he was aware his appointments were done for the day.

"Mr. Armstrong, you have a visitor," Sandy sang into the line.

Clamping his lips together, he scrubbed a hand over his face. He leaned forward to press the button on the intercom. "Who is it?" he asked tersely.

There was a pause before Sandy replied, "A Brett Miller to see you, sir."

He froze in his chair. *Brett Miller?* He had to have misheard. Surely there'd been some kind of mistake. He swallowed, his finger shaking as he held down the button. "Send him in."

Once again, the door swung open and Sandy entered the room. This time it wasn't a businessman who followed her inside. Instead, a very uncomfortable-looking cowboy stepped inside, his hands shoved in the pockets of his jeans, an item of clothing that rarely saw the interior of this building. As Cade drank in the familiar lines of Brett's body, the chiseled jaw, the thick black hair, he felt himself weakening and thought for one god-awful second he was about to break down. But after a few moments, he managed to pull himself together and rise to his feet.

"Thanks, Sandy," he said, dismissing her as he kept his eyes trained on Brett. Once the door closed behind the girl he circled the desk and leaned back against it, crossing his arms over his chest. Jesus Christ, what did he say? After a few seconds he cleared his throat and asked simply, "What are you doing here?"

The question—basic as it was—seemed to throw Brett off his game and he shifted his weight from one foot to the other as his gaze darted around the office. "This is a nice setup you've got here."

"Yeah, it is." He watched Brett peruse the space and, as he crossed over to the floor-to-ceiling windows to stare out at the city, Cade couldn't help but admire the tight curve of his ass. Ignoring the bolt of lust, he focused on getting an honest answer. "What are you doing here?" he repeated, watching Brett's reflection in the glass.

Brett's shoulders seemed to droop forward as he expelled a long breath. "I don't know," he admitted, keeping his back to Cade. "I guess I—" He turned abruptly and the urgency in his expression caught Cade off-guard. "Jess came to see me," he said, "did she tell you?"

Cade blinked as the information sank in. "She went to Texas?" A sinking feeling weighted down his stomach. Was this why Brett had come? To tell him and Jess to back the hell off?

"I didn't know," he said stiffly. "If that bugged you so much take it up with her. It ain't got nothing to do with me."

Brett's expression became confused and then angry. "You want me to leave then? Is that it?"

No, he didn't want him to leave. All he wanted to do was pull him close and feel those firm lips on his again, but his pride wouldn't let him do that. And hell, Brett would punch him in the stomach if he even tried.

"Just tell me why you're here, Miller," he said eventually, wiping his sweaty palms on the front of his pants. Enough was enough. He'd left the ranch and moved back here just as Brett had requested. What else did the guy want?

Brett didn't answer immediately and a tense silence filled the room as they stared each other down. Then Brett tore his gaze away and started to pace along the windowed wall. He dragged one hand through his already ruffled hair, the other hand still stuffed in his pockets. Finally, he swiveled on his heel to face Cade, and for the first time Cade noticed the lines of exhaustion around his eyes. It bugged him that he cared.

"I don't know why I'm here," Brett said quietly, standing with his feet apart in front of the window. "I don't—I mean, I guess—" He blew out a frustrated breath. "She said that you were hurting," he said, throwing his hands out. "She said that you..." his voice lowered, softened as he continued, "...she said you missed me."

Cade stared blankly at him, unable to breathe as he registered Brett's words. He was going to throttle Jess when he got his hands on her and as for Brett...

A sudden surge of anger shot through his veins and he strode forward until only inches separated them. "What of it?" he demanded, glaring at the other man. "You think it makes me feel better to have you here? What the hell do you want? You told me to leave and that's what I did. Why can't we just—"

The rest of the sentence was silenced by Brett's mouth on his. Cade's whole body stiffened, his mind not daring to believe this was happening and for long seconds he forgot to breathe.

As he struggled against Brett and tried to end the kiss that was ripping him to shreds from the inside out, the man clamped his hands around his face, holding him still as the tip of his tongue probed the seam of Cade's mouth.

Unable to help himself, Cade opened for him and—*sweet mercy*—he groaned into the back of Brett's throat as their tongues tangled, the surfaces rubbing together as their bodies fused. Barely aware of anything except the firm pressure of Brett's lips, Cade let himself be backed up until the edge of his desk bit into the backs of his thighs. Between his legs, his cock thrust upward, a reaction he hadn't felt since leaving Steeplecrest.

Too soon, Brett ended the kiss and his sharp breaths rasped against Cade's skin. "I miss you," he said, calloused hands still holding Cade's face. "I don't know how we can make it work but—I need you."

The shaky admission tore at Cade's heart and he let out a low groan. He didn't know how long he'd been waiting to hear those words and the reality of them sliced through his soul.

"I know I fucked up," Brett continued, his breath caressing Cade's lips. "I wasn't ready."

Leaning back, Cade searched the depths of Brett's pained eyes. "You sure you're ready now?"

"Yeah, I'm ready." The muscles of Brett's throat worked as he swallowed and Cade's cock leaped as he felt the man's hands at the front of his slacks. Slowly, Brett unbuttoned the pants, his eyes staying on Cade's as he said, "Let me show you."

Cade gripped the edge of his desk as Brett lowered to his knees in front of him. He pulled down Cade's pants and cool air wrapped around his swollen shaft. Transfixed by the sight of Brett's face so close to his cock, Cade stared, hardly believing what he was seeing. But as the wet tip of Brett's tongue darted out and licked the broad head of Cade's dick, the intense sensation drove home the fact that this was really happening.

"Brett Miller is sucking my dick!" his teenage self screamed in his mind as the tentative strokes of Brett's tongue gradually gained authority as he hit his groove. When his mouth wrapped around Cade's breadth and swallowed him right to the back of his throat, Cade reached down and grabbed a fistful of silky black hair. Brett may have been a virgin at sucking cock, but like any other man, he knew what made a damn good blow-job. He moved his head up and down in a steady rhythm, his tongue gliding over Cade's throbbing skin, and when Cade tugged on his hair, he gave a small groan that vibrated against Cade's dick.

Between the fact that he'd had no release for the past few weeks and that Brett was the one sucking his cock, Cade neared the brink quicker than he usually did during oral sex. As his balls tightened dangerously beneath his body, he tried to pull Brett's head away, but the guy ignored him, increasing his suction until Cade spurted into his mouth. Shaking with the force of his release, Cade watched through blurry eyes as Brett sat back and licked his lips.

"Was that good for you?" he asked throatily, lifting a brow.

Cade held his breath, drinking in the sight of Brett's swollen mouth, then started to grin. "Not bad for a first-timer." He watched Brett get to his feet and said nothing as they stared at each other.

"What?" Brett asked, his tone soft as he braced his hands on the desk behind Cade.

"Just waiting for you to freak out." Though he said the words lightly, he meant them and from the tightening in Brett's face, he knew it.

"I'm still here, right?"

"Yeah. But for how long?"

The challenge hung in the air between them and Cade wondered if Brett would snap and walk out the door. He didn't want to push him away but he didn't want to risk a repeat of what had happened a few weeks ago. He could still remember the way Brett had looked at him before he'd stormed away. Hell, the memory had haunted every one of his dreams since his return to New York. Much as he wanted Brett with him, he had to protect himself from that kind of pain.

Cade's heart froze when Brett took a step back and he was sure the man was about to walk out. But Brett simply glanced at the desk piled high with contracts and messages and then looked back at Cade. "Think you could leave early?" he asked. "Maybe we could go somewhere and talk."

Thank God for that. "Uh, sure," Cade stammered as the dread melted away. "Give me a minute. I'll just shut everything down."

Ten minutes later, after muttering excuses to Sandy, Cade and Brett sat in a cab headed for Cade's Upper East Side apartment. Throughout the ride, Cade was achingly aware of Brett's closeness and the urge to reach out and touch him nearly did him in. Fortunately, traffic wasn't so bad and soon they pulled up outside Cade's apartment block.

Brett let out a low whistle as he stared up at the fifty-six-floor building. "Nice digs, Armstrong," he said as they headed toward the entrance.

Cade grinned and then thanked the doorman as he held the door open. "It does the job," he admitted as he led the way to the elevator. "It's nothing compared to the ranch, though."

An elderly couple joined them in the elevator for the ride up so they couldn't say or *do* anything. The elevator halted at the fortieth floor and Cade and Brett stepped out. Sticking the key in his lock, Cade turned it and pushed the door open.

"You want something to eat?" he asked, crossing the open-plan living space to the kitchen. "A drink maybe?"

"I'll take a beer if you've got any," Brett replied as he ambled through the apartment, taking everything in.

Cade watched him as he grabbed two beers from the refrigerator. What did he think of the modern, clean-edged apartment he'd furnished with only the bare essentials? Did Brett see what he did? A cold, impersonal apartment that could have belonged to anyone.

"Here," he said, handing Brett a beer. As they drank, he absorbed the sight of Brett standing in his home. He swallowed a mouthful of beer and then laughed.

Brett's eyebrows drew together. "What's so funny?"

Sitting on the armrest of one leather sofa, Cade shook his head. "Never thought I'd see you in here, that's all."

Brett smiled. "Never thought I'd be here, to be honest."

"What do you think of the Big Apple?"

"It's loud."

"Yeah." Cade set down his beer on the coffee table and clasped his hands between his knees. "So what made you come out here?"

"Jess can be pretty darn persuasive," Brett said wryly. "But even if she hadn't paid me a visit, I would have come eventually." His gaze dropped from Cade's as he walked over to the window. "It's not the same without you," he admitted after a while. "Now it's not just Mom and Dad who aren't around. You're gone too."

Cade felt something shift deep inside him as he stared at Brett's squared shoulders. The guy came off tough as nails, but underneath it all he was in a lot of pain.

"You want me to come home?" he asked, watching for Brett's reaction.

Brett turned and offered a small smile. "Yeah, I want you to come home."

Cade's heart lurched but he forced himself to remain calm. "You're sure this isn't about the accident? Maybe you want me around because we've been through the same shit. When the grief is gone, you might—"

"No. I thought after Dixie died that might be the case, but I was wrong." Brett's eyes were intent on his as he crossed the room and stood over Cade. "The grief made me more open to you, to what I was feeling, but even if the accident had never happened, even if Dixie was still alive, I would still want you. What I feel for you—" He broke off and shook his head. "I ain't ever felt anything like this before." He brought his hands down on Cade's shoulders, holding him. "I'm sorry I hurt you that night," he said huskily, pain clouding his eyes. "I wanted to push you away. I couldn't figure out what I was feeling. It took me a while to get it together." He swallowed thickly and brushed the pad of his thumb over Cade's bottom lip. "I want to make this work."

Warm relief filtered through Cade as he stood and aligned his body with Brett's. Their lips met again, moving urgently together as their tongues entwined. Through the double barrier of their pants, Cade felt the heat of Brett's erection and a desperate need to feel the pulsing skin in his hand ripped through him. He tore open the guy's belt and tugged on the zipper, growling into Brett's mouth as the damn thing jammed. He pulled on it until it loosened and came all the way down. Then, pushing his hand inside the opening, he grasped Brett's burning cock.

Brett ripped his lips away and laughed breathlessly against

Cade's cheek. "Ever heard of a thing called patience, Armstrong?" he asked as his hands roamed over Cade's ass.

Squeezing Brett's cock lightly, Cade grinned as the man shuddered. "Screw that," he muttered, biting at Brett's stubble-covered jaw. "Want to come to bed?"

"Hell, yes."

Their mouths fused again as Cade backed up toward the bedroom. He stumbled through the door and moved away from Brett as he started to unbutton his shirt. For a second, Brett watched him undress, his plum-red cock jerking out of his jeans. Then he got to work on his own clothes, making Cade's mouth water with each patch of skin he revealed. When they stood bare-ass naked in front of one another, drinking each other in, Cade's throat dried at the effect he had on the other man's body. If he hadn't believed Brett before when he'd said that his feelings were all about Cade, he sure as hell believed him now. He'd never seen him so aroused, so obviously desperate for release.

He was about to tell the man to get on the bed and turn around, but Brett got there first. His body heat surrounded Cade as he strode forward, cock jutting out from a cushion of black curls. The head of his cock pressed into Cade's stomach as he walked him backwards, trapping him against the bed.

"Lie down," Brett ordered, his tone harsh as he pushed Cade's shoulders back.

Sliding up over the sheets until the pillows were right behind him, Cade rested back on his elbows and watched Brett climb between his legs. A tremble worked its way through his limbs as he absorbed this change of roles. When they'd been together before he'd always played the aggressor—he'd licked and sucked Brett's skin, he'd been on top, he'd penetrated the man's body. Locked beneath Brett's muscled body was nothing short of intimidating...and extremely arousing. Brett's cock brushed the inside of his thigh as the man settled over his body, bracing his hands either side of Cade's head.

"You look scared," Brett noted, the corner of his mouth lifting in a devilish smile. "What are you afraid of?"

Cade shook his head silently and then held his breath as Brett's head descended to his chest. He breathed over Cade's nipple and then licked the flat disc. Brett's hot tongue on his skin sent little shocks down Cade's spine, sensitizing his skin until he burned all over.

"Remember when you did this to me?" Brett mumbled against his skin. Still bathing Cade's skin with his tongue, he looked up to meet Cade's gaze. "I swear to God, nothing's ever felt so good."

Cade stroked a strand of dark hair out of his glassy eyes and then dug his hand into the man's hair as Brett resumed his mission, licking and sucking a trail down to Cade's dick. As his skilled mouth once again swallowed him whole, he let out a low groan. Brett's rough hands splayed across his thighs and ran down to his knees. When he lifted his head, his lips were swollen as he said, "Turn around."

Cade swallowed, his dick lurching toward Brett. He turned over slowly, feeling more vulnerable than he ever had with any other man as he lifted his ass in the air.

Brett's hands roamed over his buttocks, kneading the fleshy cheeks as the tip of his cock grazed the seam. Lifting a hand, Cade pointed to the bedside table. "There's lube in the top drawer," he said and watched Brett lean over and retrieve the tube.

"Hey," Brett said, stroking his palm down Cade's back soothingly. "Easy. It's just me."

Heat unfurled in his stomach as he nodded. It was just

Brett and he was about to feel what he'd been dreaming about since he was a teenager. As Brett pushed his lube-covered fingers between his buttocks and slicked up his entrance, Cade sucked in a breath. He waited, tension straining across his back as Brett positioned his cock at Cade's hole. And then he was pushing forward slowly, stretching Cade open with the thickness of his cock.

A sharp pain flared from where Brett entered him, but it soon melted into hot pleasure as Brett's cock rubbed along the nerve endings of his passage. Cade didn't think he'd ever had a cock this big inside him, throbbing so fiercely deep inside his body. He felt as if he were already coming apart. Dizziness swept through his head and a sweat broke out across his forehead. He'd imagined this so many times before, imagined being trapped beneath Brett's large body and being filled with his dick. He'd never dreamed it could feel this good, this intense.

As Brett withdrew and then propelled forward again, Cade's fingers curled into the sheets. His cock felt as if it were about to explode from its skin as it reached up to his stomach. Brett's hands gripped his hips and the heat of his touch spread outward, right up Cade's back and down to his feet. A moan choked in his throat as Brett entered him again, harder this time. It was all Cade could do to focus on his breathing, to stay as Brett filled him in an aching rhythm.

When his ass rippled around Brett's cock a growl rumbled up out of the man's chest and his hips snapped against Cade's. "Fuck, you feel good," he snarled, his chest rubbing along Cade's back in a friction that awakened all the nerve endings along his spine. "You're tight as hell."

Cade's mouth curved in a brief grin and then faltered as Brett's hand reached beneath him and grasped his cock. Damn, he caught on fast. Beads of sweat rolled down his neck as

Brett's grip worked his cock and the strength of the man's thrusts increased. Fire broke out low in Cade's belly and the flames flickered upward until his whole body was on fire. He groaned, barely hearing the sound through the thunder of blood in his ears. Turning his head to the side, he rubbed his face against Brett's coarse jaw and let out a roar as the pressure that had been building inside him released suddenly, tearing the climax from his body. He bunched the sheets in his hand and squeezed his eyes shut as his orgasm crashed through him. Come spilled from his cock and onto Brett's hand as his ass clenched around the man's cock. Then Brett was coming too, his shout of release echoing in Cade's ears as his hips jerked against Cade's buttocks. He felt the spike of heat in his passage as Brett spurted inside him and then he fell forward and felt Brett's shuddering weight collapse over him.

Brett's heart pounded so hard Cade could feel it against his back. With his head buried in the pillow, he stretched out his hand to where Brett's palm lay beside him and knotted their fingers together. Gradually their breathing evened out and Cade savored every second of lying there with the man he loved.

"You okay?" Brett asked, voice husky as he rolled off Cade's body.

"Uh huh." Glancing to the side and meeting Brett's dark eyes, Cade felt his heart clench. "I'm glad you came."

Brett grinned. "Me too," he said, stroking a hand over Cade's hip. Raising an eyebrow, he added, "Though I gotta say, I didn't think it'd be so easy to get you into bed."

Cade punched him in the arm and earned a rich chuckle that warmed his soul. "So what happens now?" he asked when Brett's laughter eased.

"Now?" Brett sat up in the bed and leaned back against the headboard. His eyes turned somber as he stared at Cade.

"Come home with me."

The quiet request made Cade's throat burn. He cleared his throat and asked, "You sure?"

"Yeah." Brett gave a small smile and nodded. "Never been more sure of anything."

Thick emotion welled within Cade as he drank in the tenderness in Brett's eyes. After the months of grief and loss, something good had come out of it all. He was going home to the one man he needed in this world. It didn't get any better than that.

About the Author

To learn more about Ava Rose Johnson, please visit www.avarosejohnson.com. Send an email to Ava at ava@avarosejohnson.com or join her Yahoo! group to join in the fun with other readers as well as Ava. http://groups.yahoo.com/group/avarosejohnsongroup

How far would you dare to go…to win it all?

Str8te Boys
© *2009 Evangeline Anderson*

Maverick Holms and Duke Warren share almost everything—a college soccer team, an apartment and the same extremely competitive nature. Thanks to that never-back-down spirit, they're about to share more than they bargained for.

The game is "gay chicken". The rule: get as close as possible without kissing, and the one that pulls away first is the loser. The problem: neither of them likes to lose. It isn't long before the game becomes an excuse to touch and kiss in every possible forbidden way. And after they pose for a gay website to earn extra money, things really heat up.

Suddenly Duke is talking lifetime commitment, and Mav is backpedaling as hard as he can, not sure if he's ready to accept all his best friend is offering him. Or the truth about what he is.

Warning: Hot M/M sex inside. Do not open this book if you don't like the idea of two deliciously muscular best friends becoming lovers.

Available now in ebook from Samhain Publishing.

Love can be found among the pieces of a broken heart.

Seeing You
© *2009 Dakota Flint*

The night his brother, Simon, was killed in an accident, Dylan took on a double load of guilt. Guilt for walking away unscathed...and for secretly loving Simon's partner, Wade. Unable to bear the pain, Dylan left the Lazy G ranch to rebuild his life elsewhere.

A year later he reluctantly responds to his sister's plea to come home, where he finds the Lazy G falling apart. And so is Wade. Wade has stopped caring about the ranch, about everything that should matter most to him.

Though there's more ranch work than one man can possibly handle, Dylan throws himself into the task. Wondering how he's going to find the strength to pull Wade out of the fog of grief when his own is still as raw as a fresh wound. Wondering when Wade will finally see that his second chance for happiness is standing right in front of him.

Warning: Contains explicit, emotionally charged m/m sex. Extra box of tissues required. You could use your sleeve, of course, but we don't recommend it.

Available now in ebook from Samhain Publishing.

YUCK
2/17

LaVergne, TN USA
29 November 2010
206674LV00005B/17/P

9 781605 049243